HOMESPUN FATE

HOMESPUN FATE
MARMALADE AND MAGIC™ BOOK 3

MICHAEL ANDERLE

This book is a work of fiction. All of the characters, organizations, and events portrayed in this novel are either products of the author's imagination or are used fictitiously. Sometimes both.

Copyright © 2022 LMBPN Publishing
Cover by Fantasy Book Design
Cover copyright © LMBPN Publishing
A Michael Anderle Production

LMBPN Publishing supports the right to free expression and the value of copyright. The purpose of copyright is to encourage writers and artists to produce the creative works that enrich our culture.

The distribution of this book without permission is a theft of the author's intellectual property. If you would like permission to use material from the book (other than for review purposes), please contact support@lmbpn.com. Thank you for your support of the author's rights.

LMBPN Publishing
PMB 196, 2540 South Maryland Pkwy
Las Vegas, NV 89109

Version 1.01, July 2022
ebook ISBN: 979-8-88541-667-2
Print ISBN: 979-8-88541-668-9

THE HOMESPUN FATE TEAM

Thanks to our JIT Readers

Christopher Gilliard
Jackey Hankard-Brodie
Diane L. Smith
Dorothy Lloyd
Angel LaVey

Editor

Lynne Stiegler

CHAPTER ONE

Jemma Nox couldn't believe her ears. Had her father just said...
My mother is a witch. Just like me. A fucking witch.

Delilah Anne Nox, the woman who had left her husband and daughter for a so-called better life over three years ago was...
Like me.

Jemma's mind reeled.
No, it's not true. It just isn't. I imagined him saying that. I'm tired. So fucking tired.

She had been awake all night, traipsing across a haunted mountain. After dealing with a dark spirit, her energy was spent. She didn't know how she was still awake.

No matter how much she wanted to deny what her father had said, she couldn't. What Tad Nox had told her was the truth. She knew it deep in her bones. She knew it as well as she knew she was still alive. Delilah had kept more secrets than Jemma had ever imagined.

The silence in the kitchen was tense. It was like a dagger suspended over Jemma's head, ready to drop at any moment. Painful memories rose to the surface. She wanted to banish the image of her mother from her mind. Didn't want to remember the despair on her father's face the day they knew it was over.

Tad looked grim and detached as he sat across from her. His mind was far away, revisiting the same memories that were plaguing Jemma's mind. He dragged a hand through his hair and sighed.

Jemma felt like a fish caught on a hook, thrashing to get away before being reeled in. For the past three years, she had defined her life by being different than her mother. Unlike Delilah, she had studied subjects in school that would allow her to have a stable future, and she had sacrificed time and energy for her father's wellbeing.

She had even abandoned favorite childhood movies, books, and activities that she and her mother used to enjoy together. As far as Jemma knew, she and her mother only shared two things now: their blood and the middle name "Anne," which was used by all the women in their family. Delilah Nox was her mother by blood, but that was it as far as Jemma was concerned.

Her heart sank as the truth seeped in. She had just found out that they shared more than just a name—so much more. Jemma struggled to find words to talk to her father. All she could get out were half-formed sounds. Tad looked at her with worry filling his face. He seemed as though he didn't have a good handle on the revelation either, despite having known it for…

"How long?" Jemma choked out at last. She clenched her fists, not out of anger but because it seemed like the only way to hold herself together.

Tad swallowed hard. "A long time, Jem. I've known for…" He ran a hand through his hair again. "Well, since before you were born."

Jemma wasn't sure if that made her feel worse. For her whole life, both parents had kept this secret from her. For her whole life, she had felt close to her father and had never believed they would keep secrets from one another. "Looks like I was wrong."

Jemma had meant to keep the thought in her mind, but it strayed out of her mouth.

Tad couldn't think of what to say. He knew he had hurt his daughter by keeping this from her, but she had also kept secrets from him. This whole time, each had thought the other wouldn't understand. Jemma wondered if things would have been better if they had both been honest from the beginning.

Jemma's mind churned. Had Mama B also sensed the truth and chosen not to tell her? The old holler witch, who had been in Solomon's Cross long before Tad had been born, always seemed to know things that others didn't. She could sense more and see more. Ever since she'd begun her holler witch training with Mama B, Jemma had wondered if one day she would attain the same kind of discernment. Right now, the discernment and clarity she needed seemed far out of her reach.

She also needed to get some sleep. Once again, she spoke her thoughts out loud. "Maybe I'm dreaming all this."

Tad confirmed she wasn't. "I'm sorry, Jem. It's not a dream." He did sound regretful.

Jemma wasn't the only one struggling. After dropping the bomb, Tad had paced in their dimly lit kitchen. It was early in the morning. Neither was paying attention to the position of the sun in the sky. Neither had slept all night. Tad sank into the chair on the opposite side of the table from his daughter.

The longer he waited for her to gather her thoughts, the more on edge he became. He knew they would have to hash things out. Jemma's silence unnerved him. He sighed deeply. "Look, Jemma, I wanted to tell you, but Annie..." He stopped, shook his head, and corrected himself. "*Delilah* didn't think it was best."

Since when do we care what she thought was best? Jemma thought with indignation.

Tad's words had faltered because he was thinking about his wife more than he wished to. When they were married, Tad had called her by her middle name. Delilah had called him Tad instead of Thaddeus. Since the divorce, Tad and Jemma had called Delilah by her first name, making any mention of her seem stiff and formal.

Sometimes, however, "Annie" slipped out of Tad's mouth. Jemma couldn't blame him. He had been married to her for over sixteen years before their divorce. Tad had been deeply in love with the woman, and the transition had been difficult for him. It still gave him no right to have kept secrets from Jemma.

Her anger bloomed. It might have been okay when she was little, but not after all they had been through together.

Jemma never could hide what she was feeling. Tad read the rising anger in her face and attempted to quell it. "To be frank, Jem, Annie kept her propensity for the Art from me for quite some time." He didn't correct "Annie" to "Delilah" this time. His mind was lodged in the past, in a time when the woman he loved wasn't trying to run away from him any chance she got.

"I didn't know about the witchery when we met and wasn't told before we married either. I only found out later when I caught Annie using some herbal remedy magic to help with being pregnant." A weak smile formed on his lips. "With you, of course."

He sighed, leaning back in his seat. "I freaked out, of course. At first, it just seemed like medicine, and then I thought she might have developed some kind of drug problem. But over time, I knew it was something more. When Annie finally confessed that it was magic—of all things in the world—I didn't quite take it well."

Jemma stiffened. Her father had never been prejudiced. He was one of the most understanding and accepting people she had ever met. He continued, "I wasn't freaking out so much at the magical aspect but because something so major had been kept from me for so long—and by my own wife."

"Yeah, tell me about it," Jemma replied dryly before she could stop herself. Her lingering indignation was audible.

Tad looked earnest. "I never forbade her from doing anything with magic, not that it would have done anything, but we were about to have a baby, and I just wasn't sure what it would mean for our family. Honestly, Jemma, I almost gave up." Tad paused for a moment. "I almost walked away. I hate myself every day for even thinking of it. For even *thinking* of leaving you before you were born." His voice conveyed his agony.

His hands fell from his head to the table. Jemma couldn't speak. She could only take in what her father told her. "Annie was desperate to keep our relationship together," he continued.

That was surprising since it was Annie who had ditched them three years ago for one of the flimsiest reasons possible. "She threw herself into being normal," Tad explained, "and hid that other part of her life even more. The result was that Annie got so used to keeping secrets from me and everybody else about the Art, she decided to have other secrets as well—other lovers and the like. To her, it was simple—just another lie in the name of keeping our family together." He shook his head. "I still don't understand it."

Jemma could tell that going back to these memories was taxing for her father. It was for her as well, but she had to know more. Before she could ask a question, Tad went on.

"Your mother swore she thought you would possess no connection to the Art, especially if she didn't teach you anything about it. She figured it would be a waste of time to talk about something that you might never be able to do anything with. Annie even figured it could hurt you if you grew up, couldn't do anything with magic, and then became resentful about it."

But having magic wouldn't be so bad, Jemma thought as she remembered dealing with the nest of haints just a couple of hours before. The ordeal had made her realize just how much she needed the power. Mama B wouldn't have been able to do it on her own. It had been Jemma, with the help of her friends, who had saved Solomon's Cross from further torment.

In a way, she was glad her mother had never told her. She had become her own person by being away from the frivolous, care-free, selfish lifestyle her mother had led. She was glad it was Mama B who had shown her the way instead.

"Over time, Annie began to blame and resent me for not being able to use magic," Tad recalled, drawing Jemma out of her thoughts. He put up his hands defensively. "But honest to God, I never discouraged her from the Art. I just never understood it."

Annie hadn't felt supported, so she had hidden. Jemma could understand that. She had done the same thing to her father. She had felt bad about lying and going behind his back before, and even more so now. She didn't want to be anything like the woman who had left her.

Her mother's face filled her mind. Annie had a charming smile and dazzling eyes. No one who met her disliked her. Well, except her family, who had to rely on her and trust her and could not.

"Truth is," Tad added, "I didn't bother trying to understand the whole time we were married. I can see how Annie would have blamed me for some of what she felt. It wasn't until after she left us that I learned more. I read books. Tons of books. Studied all kinds of things." Conflicting emotions showed in his eyes.

Jemma could tell he wanted to say more, but something was holding him back. She gave him a look that said, "Out with it."

"I never told you this, Jem, and I'm sorry about it, but…" He wouldn't look at her. He stared at his hands folded on the table. "I went after her about a year after she left us."

For a moment, Jemma couldn't breathe. It was like all the air had gone out of the room. "You…you went after her? Like, tried to get her back?" She choked on her words.

He confirmed, "Once I learned about the world she had come from and understood some of what she had been through, I wanted to see if things could be made better. I was a fool to think that. Witch or not, Annie didn't want me anymore. When I went after her, it turned out she hadn't gone too far."

Jemma understood. "She stayed right in town."

Tad nodded. "And later, as I learned more on my own, I figured out why."

Despite her anger toward her father for keeping this from her for so long, her interest was piqued. "Why?"

"She wanted to stay in that town because there was magic in the land that responded well to her." Tad sighed. "Though I don't think there was too much of it. Less than there is here, I believe. Anyway, I learned quickly that not only was she a witch, but she was also a very accomplished one." He swallowed a lump in his throat. "She had begun messing around on the darker edge of things."

A spike of fear went through Jemma's chest. She remembered Vesna Soucek, Mama B's old friend and holler witch sister. The woman had gone mad after losing her children. She had tampered with darker magic that had led her down a dangerous road. She had never been the same since. *Is my mother going down the same road?* Jemma wondered. Although she didn't give a shit about where her mother was in life, this struck a chord. If Delilah could reach for the dark side of the Art, then...

So could I. The thought made Jemma shudder.

Tad saw her concern, and his voice softened as he continued. There was more, always more. How deep did the secrets run? When would Jemma reach the bottom of the well? "I feared Annie had become someone else. Some*thing* else. I had met a couple of people who knew a lot more about magic than I did, and they told me that the age when girls' witchery would begin to emerge was puberty. You were thirteen at the time, almost fourteen. I didn't want your mother around in case it happened. I feared what she would try."

Jemma struggled to find words. "So, coming to Solomon's Cross wasn't just your way of escaping depression." She voiced her realization, and her father nodded.

What he said next sounded like a confession. "I came here to get you away from your mother in case she changed her mind and tried to take you away. I couldn't risk you getting hurt, and, well..." Tad rubbed his eyes. "I couldn't risk getting hurt either."

His weary, emotion-filled eyes met Jemma's. "I couldn't risk losing another person I loved, especially my own kid." He gave her a weak smile. "You might have your mother's gift for magic, but you're my flesh and blood too. That has to count for something."

Jemma wanted to squeeze her father's hand and assure him that it did count. It counted a hell of a lot more than anything connected with her mother. But, for some reason, she couldn't. He had kept all this from her. And after all that talk about trust, too.

Jemma wondered if her father understood what a witch could become by delving into the darker nature of the Art. Even she did not fully understand it. Mama B had hinted at how bad witches could become, and Jemma had gotten a glimpse of what untethered power could do when she had encountered the boo hag a few months ago.

Her thoughts became more disjointed and scattered the longer she sat there. Did Mama B know something about the bloodline Jemma was a part of? Had Tad guessed Mama B was a witch? She decided she would be shocked if the old woman hadn't at least sensed it. At some point, she needed to talk to her about it.

"Right now, I'm so fucking tired." She didn't realize she had voiced the thought aloud until her father's eyes met hers.

He nodded. "I know. You should get some sleep, but..." His voice wavered. He was still upset with her for lying and sneaking. Jemma felt the same way about him. They were at a standstill, and she didn't know if she could stand another lecture or any kind of punishment from her father after all he had just told her.

Jemma felt betrayed. Tad's mouth opened, but she wouldn't let him say anything. She needed sleep and time to think everything over. She stood. "I'm done talking about this right now."

"Where are you going?" Tad tried to be firm, but there was pleading in his voice. He was torn. Jemma was too. She felt empathy for her father, but her anger overrode it.

Jemma started to walk out of the kitchen. She hadn't intended to answer him, but she turned back. "I need to sleep, Dad. I'm trying to understand why you did what you did but I need time." She didn't let him answer. She left the kitchen, climbed up to her loft, and tumbled into bed.

With a troubled mind and heart, she fell asleep.

CHAPTER TWO

Jemma slept for a long time.

When she awoke, her room, which was a loft in the house she and her father had moved into, was darker. The curtains were pulled over the window, but Jemma could still tell that the sun had gone over to the western side of the house by this hour.

She sat up and stared around her room for a long time. All of a sudden, she felt like she had when she first moved here—like she had entered a whole new life she was not prepared for. The room still looked strange despite Jemma having slept in it for the past seven months. It contained many of her personal belongings. Across from her was a shelf she and her father had built together a couple of months ago. Piled on it were all her old Nancy Drew and Hardy Boys books, along with stones and other items she had collected outside as a child. The shelf reflected the twelve-year-old version of herself. The rest of the room showed an older Jemma.

Sixteen-year-old Jemma could be seen in the pile of schoolbooks on the desk beneath the window and the stickers of her favorite bands on her laptop. Jemma sighed. She felt like she had grown up a lot since moving here. As she sat there, leaning against her pillows and looking about the room, she considered all that had occurred here in Solomon's Cross since they arrived.

The small town within Kalhoun County, Tennessee had seemed odd to her at first. The people had been stand-offish, but once they got used to Jemma and Tad, they were the warmest, kindest people she had ever encountered. Still, they had their peculiarities and prejudices. Jemma knew a good number of them were wary of Mama B, AKA Eloise Brickellwood, who owned the bed and breakfast called Gran's Rest at the top of one of the town's mountains. The town was closed in by the two mountains: Gran's Rest and Kalhoun's Crest. Jemma didn't count herself lucky to have visited both.

More events took hold of her mind. She remembered the grounds of a so-called haunted mansion, a fenced-in facility and guards chasing them, and a dark cave swarming with magic that made Jemma nauseous just recalling it.

She thought back to the people of Solomon's Cross and how they considered Mama B. Many of them called her a witch, but they had no idea what they were talking about. The old woman was a witch, yes, but not a broomstick-flying, cauldron-stirring, pointed-hat-wearing, child-eating crone. She was a kind, sometimes cross, ancient woman with an online shopping addiction who made the best bread and jam anyone in Kalhoun County ever tasted.

A small smile crept across Jemma's lips as she thought about the old woman who had taught her all she knew about the Art. What would the people of Solomon's Cross think of Jemma if they discovered she was a holler witch too?

She considered how much she had come to love the town she lived in. She loved her friends Mama B and the McCarthy siblings Easter and Val. Others in town were much less pleasant, but the friendships Jemma had formed more than made up for any unpleasant encounters she might have with others.

Still, Jemma wasn't sure she could call this place her home.

She didn't want her life in Hendricks, Indiana back. Knowing what she knew now, though, she wasn't sure about her future here either.

Jemma got out of bed. *I need to go for a walk and clear my head.* She told herself she needed to do that so she could think more clearly, but really, she just didn't want to have to see or talk to her father yet. She pulled on a sweatshirt and boots before slipping out of the house through the side door in the kitchen. On her way to the door, she did not see her father. His bedroom door was closed, so she assumed he was still asleep. He had been up all night, after all.

The thought made Jemma stiffen as she closed the side door behind her. Tad had been with Linnea Strang the entire night until he had received a call from the police saying his daughter had been brought into the station for trespassing. Jemma doubted the two had slept. She shook her head, not wanting to consider the implications. Linnea Strang was a pleasant woman and one of Jemma's favorite residents in town. In the end, her father had kept something else from her, and the bitter sting of betrayal lingered within her.

She rounded the house to the front driveway before heading to the road and turning left so she could go up the mountain toward Gran's Rest. She did not intend to go to her place of employment, not yet. She needed to be alone a while longer.

It was nearing dusk by the time she made it to the edge of the forest and slipped past the first line of trees. Here, not much of the sun leaked through since it was beginning its descent over the mountain. She didn't mind being in the woods in the dark. She had done it the night before, and it was safer here. At least, she hoped it was. She pulled a flashlight out of the pocket of her sweatshirt just in case.

Jemma found the narrow path which wound through the forest up the mountain. It took her twenty minutes or so to reach a large clearing. Here, the last snow of the winter was beginning to melt. Small wildflowers along the base of trees and moss had begun to grow. Spring encroached and with it a wild, warm thrumming of magic beneath the earth. Here, Jemma had been trained by Mama B in all she knew about the Art. Here she had practiced laying traps of nettle and hives. She had practiced binding and sealing. What she had spent most of her time doing, however, was just standing with her eyes closed and feeling the power thrumming in all the living things around her.

As she walked, Jemma touched the trunks of trees with the tips of her fingers. The life in this forest responded. It liked the power stirring within her. It gave her power life, and her power helped this place remain whole and untamed.

The only sounds reaching Jemma now were the soft wind blowing through the trees and the snapping of twigs beneath her boots as she continued her upward climb. Thoughts invaded Jemma's mind, and try as she might to banish them, they persisted. Had her mother had similar training? How had Delilah learned about magic? Who had trained her? How long had it taken for her to come into her full power? Jemma also wondered what her mother's power had been like when Jemma was born compared to what it was like now.

She stopped short at another thought and shuddered. The thought of her mother dabbling in the dark aspects of the Art made her stomach knot. Jemma shook it off and tried not to think about it anymore.

Eventually, Jemma came to a fallen tree a little way outside of the clearing where Mama B had trained her. Exhausted from her walk and still needing more sleep, she sank onto it. Still, her mother's face lingered in her mind, and Jemma wondered if there was some kind of tonic Mama B could give her to make unwanted memories and questions go away.

Was her mother a witch of some kind but not a holler witch? Delilah had lived in a city, and Tad didn't seem to have a concept of such a thing. Otherwise, why would he allow and even encourage Jemma to work with Mama B?

As Jemma sat there, her mind reeling, she began to slide into a trance. Her exhaustion made the hills around her seem to be rippling. That wasn't just her seeing things, she knew. It was the magic within the land around her coming to the surface so only she could see it. Jemma realized that she had sensed something more here ever since she and her father first arrived.

She laughed roughly. "He tried to keep me from the witching world but then brought me to a place soaked in it." Hearing her own voice with the wind around her felt strange to Jemma. She continued anyway. "Bringing me here guaranteed I'd find my way to it." It was funny how life worked. Mama B had often used the words "destiny" and "calling" around Jemma in reference to her propensity for the Art. Jemma still wasn't sure how she felt about all of it, but…

"If I do have a destiny or calling or whatever, it certainly followed me here."

In a way, Jemma was glad Mama B had found her as quickly as she did and, as a result, kept her from having her connection to the Art disrupted or coopted. Jemma's thoughts continued until she sensed someone approaching. She slid out of her trance. She sensed more than heard the oncoming person even though the person wasn't trying to be quiet.

She could tell the person approaching her had a pale aura, which meant they were drained. The person was bone-tired, like Jemma, and had come here for a reason. Turning, Jemma saw Easter McCarthy climbing up the path to the fallen tree. Jemma felt Easter reaching out to her with the Art. She doubted the other girl knew she was doing it. It came easily for her. Easter didn't have the kind of raw, coursing connection as Jemma, but her connection was deep.

Jemma considered how well that explained some things. The boo hag who had tormented Easter for months, making her sick, hadn't been able to kill her. It was also the reason the foul spirit had tormented its victim for so long.

By this point in her training and experience, Jemma could throw herself into her magic because, as Mama B would put it, her "connection ran wide." It was how she was able to do so much magic on the fly, but it rarely lasted very long.

Easter, however, would be able to use magic for much longer if she learned how to tap into it. Jemma held these realizations in as her friend approached. Part of her didn't want to reveal such things because she didn't want to scare her friend. Another part of her envied Easter for her steady, unflagging personality, which had become more obvious with her recovery. The longer Easter recovered, the stronger both her body and magic would become.

I'll need her constancy, Jemma realized. In order to take proper holler guardianship over the mountain, Jemma would need a steadiness in her life. Out of anyone she wanted to work with, it was Easter McCarthy.

At last, Easter made her way to the log and, sharing a weak smile with her friend, she sat down. "Sleep much?" Her voice was quiet and gentle.

Jemma nodded. "Yeah, but not enough."

Easter waited, having sensed Jemma was in a rough spot mentally.

"You?" Jemma asked after a long moment of silence.

"Not much," Easter answered. "My parents came home, and we had to give them the fake story. They took it without many questions but…well, let's just say we're lucky not to be grounded. We're lucky we need the money and that Val and I have to work. Otherwise, we'd be shut up in our rooms for weeks." Easter paused for a moment, and when Jemma couldn't come up with an answer, she added, "It's all right, though. We did what needed to be done. Well, you and Mama B did."

The barest smile formed on Jemma's lips. She and Mama B had dealt with the nest of haints, yes, but Easter and Val had played a valuable role in getting control over the mountain. She remembered Val with an enchanted bat and Easter holding her family's hunting rifle. She didn't want to consider how sideways their task would have gone without the McCarthys' aid.

"What about you?" Easter asked. Worry filled her expression. "What did your dad say?"

Jemma blew out a long breath. "The better thing to ask would be what did he *not* say." Where to even start? "Hey, just found out my mom who left me is also a witch and might be the bad kind." Jemma was damned tired of thinking, but she had to tell Easter. She knew that she would feel better once it was all out, so she began.

Jemma started with how she had told her father everything—the real reason Easter had been sick months ago, how her recovery had come about, and their reason for going up to Kalhoun's Crest and what they had really done there. Jemma imagined that, by now, her father understood why the three teenagers and the old woman had lied to the police. Easter listened in silence, nodding along as Jemma spoke.

Jemma sighed as she approached the big revelation. "Then my father dropped a bomb on me. He told me my mother is a witch too."

Easter's eyes went wide, but she didn't say a word as Jemma struggled to explain. She repeated the story her father had told her. Easter knew very well her struggles regarding her mother. Although Jemma had refused on many occasions to give Delilah a thought or word, she had told Easter just enough for her friend to know how hurt Jemma had been by her mother leaving.

Easter had never pushed Jemma to tell her more. Being a sensitive, empathic person, she didn't need to know the full story to tell how much the painful memories weighed on Jemma.

"So, your father has known since before you were born?" Easter asked once Jemma had finished. She shook her head in disbelief. "And he hid it from you this whole time? I can't imagine holding a secret like that for so long."

Jemma pulled her knees to her chest and hugged them tightly. It was growing colder now that the sun was nearly gone. She nodded. "And I thought I was being the secretive one." She still felt guilty about all she had hidden from her father, but a lot less now that she knew what he had hidden from her. Was there more? How deep did her parents' secrets go?

Easter sighed and placed a comforting hand on Jemma's shoulder. "Everybody has secrets, especially grown-ups who have been around a lot longer than us." She motioned at their surroundings. "Everybody in this town has a secret or two. Some are simple and stupid, and some are dark and have been around for a long, long time. Be glad your father kept a secret because he wanted to protect you."

Easter had a point, but Jemma didn't want to acknowledge it just yet. She wanted to brood for a while longer. She didn't reply, and Easter let her sit in silence for a long time. They sat side by side, and gradually, Jemma took comfort in just having her friend with her. The wind howled. The darkness crept in. They would need to leave this fallen log and the forest before it became too uncomfortable to stay here.

At last, as they could see the moon through the trees, Easter squeezed Jemma's shoulder once more. "I'm with you for the long haul, Jemma Nox." Jemma turned and found Easter wearing a kind, warm smile. "But you'll need your father too. When you're ready, I think you should go make peace."

CHAPTER THREE

It wasn't until Jemma noticed how dark it was getting that she realized Easter had walked all the way from the road to where they sat together on the fallen log. Jemma rose to her feet. "How did you get here?"

Easter didn't drive yet. The cost of a car and driver's ed was too high. Jemma wasn't even sure Val had a license.

"Val and I went to your house, but when we knocked, no one answered the door. Your dad's truck was there, but he didn't answer." Easter shrugged. "We figured you might have gone to Gran's Rest. We went up there, and Mama B said she hadn't seen you, but she winked and told us we might find you here." Easter gestured at the clearing where Jemma had her training. Until now, only Mama B and Jemma had come here.

"Where's Val?" Jemma asked.

The smile on Easter's face faded. She looked solemn. "He's at Gran's Rest. We both figured it would be better if I came to you alone in case it hadn't gone well with your dad." Easter gave a nervous laugh. "I didn't expect to hear the story you just told me."

Jemma offered Easter her hand and pulled her up from the log. "I didn't either." They decided to be on their way since it was getting dark and it was a hike to Gran's Rest. Jemma glanced at her phone to see if Val or her father had tried to contact her, but she had no signal.

Jemma turned to Easter. "I'd like to keep this between you and me until I've had the chance to tell Mama B, so please don't tell anyone else. Not even Val."

Easter almost spoke but decided just to nod. They continued up the road, and Jemma pulled out her flashlight. Once they reached the top, they could see the cheery glow spilling out of the windows of Mama B's bed and breakfast. Jemma switched off her light. It was early evening, and from up here, they could see the very last rays of red light on the horizon.

Jemma looked around. Val's truck was nowhere in sight. "Where did he go?" She was still sleep-deprived, and her mind was reeling from the events of the past twenty-four hours, so she couldn't help but feel worried. Easter heard it in her voice.

Easter looked at her phone just as it dinged with a text from her brother. "Val says he went home to check on the kids. He'll be back later whenever I'm ready to go." She smiled. "The kids are doing much better. Val is very grateful to you for everything you've done, and I'm sure he'll tell you when he sees you next."

Jemma forced a smile. Seven of the children in the McCarthy's neighborhood of Cider Creek—the poorest part of the county, had become the latest victims of the Kalhoun' Crest's haint. Now that the haint had been dealt with and the children had been treated with Mama B's special brew, they were well on their way to full recovery. Jemma didn't like thinking about how many of the children had been hooked up to ventilators since the dark spirit had made it so they couldn't breathe on their own.

Jemma just hoped they wouldn't have to deal with anything like that again for a long time. She had enough new shit on her plate now. She was relieved that Val wasn't here. She wanted to tell Mama B about her father's revelation before Val found out.

Getting Mama B alone, however, did not seem like it was going to happen very soon.

Gran's Rest was abuzz with evening activity. Every other Saturday night, the cook, who normally just worked in the morning, stayed and made a special dinner for any weekend guests. The girls stepped inside to find the dining room and parlor occupied by many of Gran's Rest's guests. Now that it was warming up in Kalhoun County, many sought a vacation in the eastern Tennessee mountains. A few months ago, Solomon's Cross wasn't even on any maps. Now, with help from Jemma, Tad, and others, Mama B's bed and breakfast was hopping with business. It was one of the only businesses in Solomon's Cross that had done much better without the help of the ETRAA.

Jemma smiled as she entered the parlor and saw how many guests were eating, laughing, and enjoying piano playing by the fire. Here, almost everything going wrong in her life could fade away for a moment. She didn't have to think about being a witch, her family history, or how tired she was. Mama B moved about, sharing smiles, conversation, and her homemade marmalade and bread with her guests. Everyone was drinking coffee. Dinner had just ended. In one corner, two older men played a game of checkers. Two children played with their toys on the floor as their parents looked on.

Mama B didn't look like she had been in a police station a little over twelve hours ago. She had slipped back into her routine, acting as though nothing had changed. *But everything has changed,* Jemma thought. The warmth and merriment she had felt left her. She had to talk to Mama B as soon as she could get her alone.

Jemma and Easter lingered on the threshold between the front hall and the parlor until Mama B sensed they had arrived. The old woman looked up and, clucking like a mother hen, directed the girls to help her in the kitchen. They made their way to the kitchen, where they found the cook cleaning up. "We'll finish up here for you," Easter told the older woman. "Take the rest of the night off." The cook gave Easter a relieved smile and accepted her offer.

Jemma helped Easter wash and dry the remaining dishes, pour out the grounds from the coffee maker, and take out the trash. When they were putting the dishes back into the cupboards, Mama B finally appeared. "I didn't expect you girls to come today. You both must be tired still."

Jemma and Easter shared a look.

"What about you, Mama B?" Easter asked, laughing. "Did you get any sleep after coming home?"

Mama B waved a dismissive hand. "Oh, don't worry about me, my dear. This is a business. I had things to do." There was a twinkle in her eye and cheer in her voice, but Jemma could tell the old woman was bone-tired beneath the surface.

"You need to rest," Jemma insisted. "Gran's Rest won't run like a well-oiled machine without you."

Mama B waved her hand again. "Like I said, dear, don't worry about me. I'm always prepared." She reached for a cup of tea from the counter. It had gone cold, but she didn't seem to mind as she sipped it from a chair in the breakfast nook section of the old kitchen. All around them were counters full of jars of herbs, sauces, jams, and remedies. The whole bed and breakfast was cluttered in a pleasant, welcoming way.

Mama B finished her tea and watched the two girls. Both Jemma and Easter didn't know what to say. Easter was waiting for Jemma to say something, and Jemma couldn't figure out what words she wanted to use. Finally, after noting how hesitant her employees had become, Mama B set down her teacup and gave them each a stern look. "Now, don't be keepin' secrets from me, girls. After all, we've been through, don't act like rabbits scared of gettin' run over."

Jemma sighed, set aside the towel she had been using to dry dishes, and sat across from Mama B. There was less commotion in the next room. Many of the guests had gone up to bed. Still, she kept her voice low as she told Mama B the same story she had told Easter in the forest an hour earlier.

Unlike Easter, Mama B's eyes did not go wide. She listened with quiet interest as Easter had, but the longer Jemma spoke, the more the old woman's brows drew together. Her eyes narrowed, and her hands tightened around her empty teacup. When Jemma finished, she felt like everything had been poured out of her.

Mama B was silent. She looked at Jemma and then Easter and then into her empty cup. Then she nodded and murmured something to herself that Jemma could not make out.

"Please," she begged. "Say something." No reply. "Did you know? Did you ever sense it?"

Mama B looked up. "I expected as much, my dear, but I did not know for sure. It is common for those of us who have a propensity for the Art to come by it through our blood. That is, by the women in our family who have come before us." She gave Jemma a weak smile. "Your mother being like you does not surprise me, though I can see it has come as a great shock to you."

"Was your mother a witch?" It was Easter who spoke this time.

Mama B skirted the question. "What we have to be concerned about now is how long your mother was dabbling in the dark aspects of the Art."

Jemma straightened. She hadn't thought about that.

"We can only hope she was not doing such a thing while she was pregnant with you," Mama B added. A solemn look came into her eyes, but it left a moment later when the old woman's tired smile returned. "I am thankful you came to me when you did, my dear, so you could learn your way around the Art with me and not with someone who has messed around with the dark stuff." Her expression hardened. "I wouldn't worry about it now, my dear. Your mother is far away, and I am sure your father regrets waiting so long to tell you."

She reached across the table for Jemma's hand. The old woman's warm touch brought the girl the comfort she needed. "Make peace with him when you can," Mama B told her. "When you are ready."

Jemma stiffened, wondering if her father deserved her forgiveness. But she didn't feel like arguing, so she just nodded. She stood. "I think we should get home now." Jemma didn't want to go home. She didn't want to see her father again, but she was also dead tired despite having slept most of the day.

Mama B could see the reservation in Jemma's eyes. "You girls can stay here for the night in the spare guest bedroom. No need for you to return home this late."

Easter chuckled. "I'll tell Val. He'll be upset he's not in on the sleepover, but I'll tell him it's a girl thing."

Jemma fidgeted with the strings on her hoodie and looked at the floor. "I will call your father, dear," Mama B told her. "You don't have to worry about it." Jemma was relieved.

She and Easter made their way to the guest bedroom on the second floor, where they shared a large, four-poster bed that was much older than both of them. The mattress itself was comfortable enough, and since both were exhausted, they tumbled right into bed.

A candle flickered on the end table beside Jemma's side of the bed. She had just turned on her side away from Easter when her friend spoke in a small voice. "It's going to be okay, Jem. I just know it. It might get harder first, but we're going to be okay. At least we have each other." Jemma didn't know how emotional she was until she heard Easter's words. Tears rolled down her face. Quickly, she wiped them away before Easter would see them.

She leaned over and blew out the candle. "Thanks, E. That means a lot." Soon enough, Jemma heard Easter breathing peacefully in her sleep. She wondered how her father had responded when Mama B called to say his daughter would be spending the night at Gran's Rest, but she was too tired to care.

Jemma awoke in the darkened room by having her shoulders shaken and a quiet but anxious voice speaking to her. "Jemma, wake up." After a few seconds of having her eyes opened, Jemma could make out the outline of Easter's face above her. She sat up.

"What's wrong?" She felt groggy and stiff. She just wanted to go back to sleep. She couldn't have been asleep for more than a couple of hours.

"Shh," Easter placed a finger to Jemma's lips. "Do you hear that?"

It took Jemma a moment to understand what Easter was talking about. Then, gradually, she began to hear low voices from the floor below. One of the voices sounded angry. Jemma glanced at her phone. It was one in the morning. Who the hell was awake and talking downstairs in the middle of the night?

Easter crept out of bed, determined to find out what was going on. After feeling apprehensive for weeks now, Jemma followed. The girls snuck out into the hall, careful not to let the bedroom door squeak too loud on its old hinges. They crept to the landing of the stairs and peered down. The front hall was dimly lit by a light switched on by the door.

The girls saw Mama B standing behind the welcome desk, conversing with someone. The other person was tall and large but familiar to both girls. "RJ," Easter murmured. What was he doing here at this hour?

Or early, Jemma thought, since it was now Sunday morning.

The town's hardware store owner leaned over the counter with a furious expression on his face. A growl escaped his lips. Jemma's heart pounded. Why was he acting like this? Why was he here? She could not tell what he was saying to Mama B.

The old woman, on the other hand, was still, calm, and as resolute as ever. Jemma and Easter looked on in shock. The huge man, who looked like he could flatten Mama B with one finger, had never acted like this before. Until now, he had been the gentle giant of Solomon's Cross.

Jemma and Easter crept down one of the stairs, careful not to make the floorboards creak or to be seen by either of the people they were eavesdropping on. RJ wagged a finger at Mama B. "My son has had a hard life, and yes, he gets himself into plenty of trouble, but it wasn't until you started involvin' yerself in this town again that he got himself into *illegal* matters. I saw you at the police station. I know you were on that mountain with those kids!"

Many people in Solomon's Cross were suspicious of Mama B because she was so old and had kept to herself for so many years. Any time the town had a chance to create a spooky story out of nothing to sate their boredom, they did. Until now, RJ had not been one of those people. Was he really accusing Mama B of being responsible for his son's wild behavior? If anything, Mama B was the reason AJ wasn't worse. If the boo hag had continued to torment AJ...

Just the thought made her shudder. RJ continued, giving Mama B no time to respond. "AJ can't remember a thing! Now, I find it hard to believe that's just because he hit his head. Us Kilmers have been a part of Solomon's Cross for generations, and I've never much believed in the witchy stuff folks have said about you, but I'm suspicious now."

Mama B objected. "Your son is a troubled young man, but I assure you it has nothing to do with me reopening my business." She spoke calmly but firmly, not allowing the large man to intimidate her. If it weren't for her advantage in years, experience, and magic, RJ could have flattened the old woman in a second.

If he made one wrong move, Jemma would spring to her defense. Easter took out her phone, finger poised over the number nine in case she had to summon law enforcement. RJ waved off Mama B's words. "Nothing you can tell me is going to help. I'm starting to think AJ hangin' around here and with those kids who work with you has made him act like a dick for so long."

At these words, Jemma stiffened. Her hands formed into fists. AJ hadn't been "hangin' around here." He'd been spending time at an old fishing shack a mile or two down the road. RJ had asked Jemma, Easter, and Val to spend time with his son. *And we tried!* she wanted to shout at him. *But it didn't work out too well, did it? And how is that our fault?*

RJ lifted his cap and ran his large fingers through his greasy hair. The stress caused by his son's disappearance Friday night seemed to be getting to him even though AJ had returned. *With no memory of what happened,* Jemma reminded herself.

Val had told the police that AJ had hit his head in the cave when, in reality, Jemma had given the young man a tonic to make him forget all that had happened. She had done it in his best interest. As much as she didn't like AJ Kilmer, she didn't think he deserved to be tormented by a dark spirit. Wiping his memory of the experience was the best she could do to reverse the horrid event.

At least, that was what she hoped. Even now, she still wondered if she had done the right thing. Trifling with magic, not knowing the whole effect it would have, wasn't wise under any circumstances. This was the first lesson Mama B had taught her young pupil.

Giving him the tonic had caused other problems, of course. AJ couldn't remember a thing, and now his father was here, trying to get answers out of Mama B. In the process of helping AJ, Jemma had seen into his memories. Doing so made her feel like she had invaded his mind. She knew she shouldn't have been there, shouldn't have seen what she did. It was too late now, and what was she supposed to do? Apologize to AJ? It would be better, she thought, if he never found out.

It was obvious that RJ Kilmer was scared. She couldn't blame him despite his ill-treatment of Mama B.

The old woman shrugged. "I don't know what to tell you, Mr. Kilmer, but I do know you're doing no good coming here. Go home and be with your son."

RJ huffed with fury. He turned toward the door anyway and wrenched it open. Jemma was surprised it didn't come off the hinges. Before leaving, RJ glared at Mama B over his massive shoulder. "You and your little cult stay away from my son, or there will be consequences." He closed the door and was gone.

A long moment of tense silence passed. Jemma and Easter shared a look as if to say, "What the hell just happened?"

Finally, without turning, Mama B called out, "It's okay, girls. You can come out now." Hesitating only a moment, both Jemma and Easter climbed down the rest of the stairs and met the old woman in the front hall.

Mama B's expression was woeful and solemn. She looked Jemma in the eye. "What exactly did you do to AJ in that cave?"

Jemma fidgeted with the zipper on her hoodie and avoided Mama B's eyes. At last, she confessed she had used a tonic to help AJ forget all that had happened to him. "I thought I was doing the right thing. I really did. I—"

Mama B waved her hand to silence Jemma. "You should never have done such a thing without knowing what effect it would have on the young man. Have I taught you about those tonics yet?"

Jemma shook her head. She had learned about it from Vesna's journal, which held many details on remedies, brews, tonics, and spells.

Mama B sighed. "I need to think on things for a bit. In the meantime, I think it best for all of us to lay low. With Mr. Kilmer so angry, no doubt the whole town will hear about it tomorrow. Best we avoid AJ too. For the time being, at least."

Jemma's heart sank. She had only meant to keep the town safe from a dark magical threat. How was she ever going to explain this? Mama B shuffled up the stairs, sighing. "It's high time I get to bed. You too, girls. Back to bed with ya."

Jemma and Easter obeyed, but they stayed awake for a long time, lying side by side and saying nothing. Each turned RJ's encounter with Mama B over in her mind and dreaded what might come next.

CHAPTER FOUR

Jemma spent as much time as possible at Gran's Rest for the next few days. She even took her laptop and schoolwork there. Mama B, Easter, and now Val as well, knew she was doing it to avoid seeing her father. None of them said a word. Each gave her the space she needed, knowing she would act when she was ready.

The morning after Jemma and Easter's overnight stay at Gran's Rest, Easter told her brother about what Jemma had learned from her father. Val was just as shocked as the rest of them. On her way home that evening, Jemma received a text from him.

On your side, Jem. I'll do anything to help.

Jemma smiled down at her phone. She was touched but wasn't sure how her friends being on her side could change her past or make her feel better about her future.

It was late when she got. She grabbed something from the kitchen and went to her loft. After long, hard days of work on the mountain, she found sleep easily. Jemma didn't go anywhere but home and Gran's Rest for the next four days. Easter and Val only went to school and work. None of them wanted to risk running into RJ in town, not for a couple of days at least. Each of them followed Mama B's advice to keep a low profile. In those four days, RJ did not come back to Gran's Rest.

The trio decided to forgo their usual fun Friday evening at Harv's Diner so they wouldn't have to run into RJ. When Friday rolled around, Jemma went home alone to an evening of video games and reading. When she arrived home, she found the driveway empty. Her father wasn't there. She spent the evening making dinner, playing a game or two, and trying to read. All of this she did in a distracted state. Where was her father? The only thing she could think of was that he was out with Linnea Strang again. Jemma just hoped they wouldn't be coming back here together.

Over the past four days, Tad had attempted to talk to his daughter. It started with cheery calls of "Good morning!" and "Going to work today?" Each time, Jemma pretended not to hear him or found an excuse to be distracted. She got lucky a couple of times when Easter called her just as her father attempted conversation.

When the clock read 11:05 p.m., Jemma heard her dad's truck crunching over the drive. When he came in, she peeked over the edge of the loft. He entered with a soft smile on his lips. He was happy about something. Jemma's heart sank. So, he had been with Linnea again.

Of all the women in Solomon's Cross for Tad Nox to date, Linnea was the one Jemma most approved of. But since she and Tad were at odds right now, the whole situation was awkward for her. She pulled back before her father looked up. Humming to himself, Tad went into his bedroom at the back of the house.

Jemma sat back in her bed and sighed. Suddenly, she felt foolish about the distance between her and her father. She knew she couldn't avoid him forever, and if she wanted to know about her father's life—dating and all—she needed to start by making peace.

"I'll do it in the morning," she murmured. Then realizing that waiting would give her a chance to chicken out, she sighed again and climbed down the ladder.

Tad opened his bedroom door with a look of surprise on his face after Jemma knocked. "I thought you'd be asleep."

Jemma didn't speak. She looked at her bare feet on the hardwood floor. Finally, she raised her head. "I'm sorry." Another long pause. "I'm sorry for sneaking around and lying to you." She figured she should leave it there.

Tad didn't respond for a long time. When Jemma dared to look at him again, he pushed his hand through his hair. "It's all right, kid." He spoke in the same tone he'd used when she was little and caught doing something like drawing on walls. "I'm sorry too—"

Jemma cut him off with a shake of her head. "I'm done being mad, Dad, but that doesn't mean I'm going to have an easy time with…you know." She didn't want to mention what he had shared with her, even in vague terms. She let out a long, shuddering sigh. "I don't want to talk about my mother or what is going on with Mama B. Not right now."

Tad nodded. "I understand."

Jemma hadn't expected that. She hadn't expected him to accept what she wanted without argument. Before she could turn and go back to her room, Tad closed the distance between them. He pulled her to his chest, giving her a tight hug.

Jemma tried to hold in her emotion. *I really don't want to cry right now.*

The following day, Jemma found out from Easter that her father was more concerned than he was letting on. "I heard Mama B talking on the phone with him just this morning." It was Saturday afternoon, and the girls were repainting an old shed on the grounds. On Saturdays, both Easter and Val spent almost the whole day at Gran's Rest.

"Who called who?" Jemma asked.

"It sounded like Mama B reached out to him," Easter

answered. She proceeded to tell Jemma that Mama B had ensured Tad that his daughter was doing well and enjoying work. Mama B had urged Tad to give his daughter space until she was ready.

Jemma wasn't sure how she felt about Mama B and her father talking about her, but nothing harmful had been said. It would keep her father off her back for a little bit, so she made no objection. There were many things to deal with around Gran's Rest anyway.

There was still cleaning and many repairs to do. She set to work organizing the books in Mama B's office and dusting the furniture. A second coat of paint had to be put on the shed, and the walls in the cellar had to be power-washed. After spending her mornings working, Jemma went into the forest with Mama B for more training. Much of what Jemma needed now, her teacher deemed, was "practical learnin.'" There was less use of straight magic, and Jemma was once more taught about herbs and mixing the right ingredients for different tonics and brews. "What we're doing now comes with time," Mama B told her.

"I want to learn more of what you can do," Jemma replied. "I want to be able to sense things like you can before you actually even know it."

Mama B gave her a knowing smile. "That, my dear, will also come with time. Once you're able to do it, it will take very little effort on your end. It will just come to you."

Jemma also wondered how the old woman could make things appear out of thin air. Mama B would often be standing beside her and then, suddenly, have a cup of tea or bread with jam in her hand.

When Jemma inquired about this, Mama B frowned. "I don't just wave a wand around and make things appear!" She shook her head, disappointed that such an assumption could be made.

"Well then," Jemma pushed, feeling exasperated, "how do you do it?"

"It's not that I'm pulling things out of thin air," Mama B explained. "It's that you don't notice as well as you should."

Jemma's brow rose. "So, you're just saying it's me not looking hard enough?"

Mama B smiled. "Precisely."

Jemma still had the notion that there was more to it. Was Mama B keeping something from her, or was she just so old and so used to how magic worked that she forgot what it was like to have very little or none of it at all?

Jemma thought over these things one day as she and Val applied the second coat of paint to the shed. This time, Easter was not with them. Val had a lot to update Jemma on. "The kids at Cider Creek are all pretty much recovered." He smiled, and Jemma was happy for him. "And I don't think they'll be put in danger again anytime soon." He explained that the ETRAA, which had been digging holes into Kalhoun's Crest and thus drawing out the darkness stirring beneath its surface, had quietly but completely withdrawn.

"Of course, many people in town are pissed off," Val told Jemma.

"Because they were lied to or because their business deals were ended?" Jemma asked.

"Both." Jemma wondered if her father had become disappointed when he learned he would no longer have a job with the Eastern Tennessee Rural Advancement Association. She put this thought aside as Val continued. "RJ Kilmer was dismayed. Closed shop for a couple days to recover."

Jemma paused with her paintbrush in midair. The smell of fresh paint mixed with the early spring wind and freshly cut grass all around them. It was a warm day on the mountain, and they were thankful for the shining sun since it would help dry the paint faster. She turned to Val. "Did Easter tell you what we overheard?"

Val nodded. "It's weird as shit to be in town ever since."

"What do you mean?"

Val sighed. "Anyone who sees Easter and me gives us weird looks and turns away as soon as they can. It's like we've got the plague or something. Sometimes we catch people whispering too. It's awful, Jem." He shrugged. "It only used to happen at school, and now it's the opposite. Kids at school don't really care. It's everybody else in town that acts like they've got a stick up their ass."

Jemma knew students at Solomon's Cross High already had formed opinions of AJ's mental stability and therefore weren't looking to treat the McCarthys any differently. Nevertheless, her heart sank. She feared the McCarthys would once again become ostracized in the town they grew up in for simply associating with an old woman around whom rumors flew. But what could they do? They needed this job at Gran's Rest, not just because of the money but because being here helped them. Here, they both were happy and felt a sense of purpose. Even Val, who had no interest in magic.

Val sighed. "I just hope the rumors flyin' around won't keep guests from coming."

Jemma's eyes widened. "Do you think that could happen?" Over the past several days, heavy rains had made the roads going up the mountain difficult to navigate. As a result, there were fewer guests. Jemma assumed plenty more would come to Gran's Rest in late spring and early summer.

Val shrugged. "Good chance. People who come to Gran's Rest usually stop in town first, don't they?"

Jemma nodded. Many visitors stopped in town to grab a bite to eat and refill their gas tanks before going up the mountain. The longtime inhabitants of Solomon's Cross often took this opportunity to entice guests with their local businesses and stories of the town's early existence. Now that RJ, one of the longest-standing citizens of the town, had an issue with the owner of Gran's Rest, what would the rest of the folks in town do about it?

Worry showed on Jemma's face. Val paused. "I wouldn't worry about it, Jem. It'll be a hot topic for about a week. That and the ETRAA leaving all of a sudden. Then both will blow over. The town just needs something to talk about since nothing ever goes on here."

This surprised Jemma. Ever since she moved here, everything had been happening. Her life in Solomon's Cross had been the most eventful seven months of her life so far.

"I want to see what's going on for myself," she stated. She had not been to town ever since Mama B suggested they all keep a low profile. "Dad probably has a list of things he wants me to pick up anyway."

"I'm sure Mama B does too," Val added.

They made a plan to go into town on some errands the next day. "Will Easter come?" Jemma asked.

"I doubt it. She has play rehearsals tomorrow," Val answered. Easter's school play was doing their version of William Shakespeare's Macbeth. Val grinned. "I'm starting to memorize lines just by hearing Easter recite them in her bedroom."

The following day, Jemma worked at Gran's Rest in the morning and early afternoon. When he was finished with school, Val came and picked her up. Once in town, everything seemed normal. The main street was lined with cars and customers went in and out of buildings, greeting one another as they pursued their errands. It was busier now that school was out, and work was about to be finished for the day.

Jemma and Val went to Loretta's General Store. There, Jemma picked up some basic household items for her home and some cleaning supplies for Gran's Rest. She had become responsible for inventory at the bed and breakfast. This was something she hoped to delegate to someone else once they were able to hire more people.

They needed a few hardware supplies, but neither Jemma nor Val wanted to go to RJ's, especially since they would be purchasing items on Gran's Rest's business account that Tad had helped Mama B set up. They decided to forgo the purchases and stopped by Harv's Hamburgers and Hotcakes for a quick bite to eat.

The diner was bustling with its normal, late afternoon crowd. Truckers stopping in for a bite before heading out on the road for the night lined the stools at the counter. Booths were full of teenagers having come in after school for fries and milkshakes. Val and Jemma stepped up to the carryout counter to order something to go. Despite it being busy, it still took them a long time to get the attention of a waiter.

Lottie, who normally waited on them, gave them one glance and turned away before hollering, "Be with you in a minute!" Val and Jemma shared a look. While they waited, both noticed stolen glances in their direction. Truckers who had just stopped in for some food barely noticed the two teenagers. Others in the diner who had known Val all his life and Jemma for the past seven months gave them weird looks.

Each time Jemma made eye contact with someone, the other person would look away quickly. Two young women, who Jemma had often seen staring at her father a little too long, made eye contact with her before looking away. They put their heads together and whispered. "What the hell is going on?" Jemma muttered.

She heard someone behind her hiss, "Witch lovers." Whirling, she saw one of AJ's old friends, a football player from Solomon's Cross High. He glared at them and walked by.

Jemma's hands balled into fists. Val's hand on her arm kept her from flying after the young man to scold or punch him or both. "Not worth it," Val told her. "He and his cronies have been saying shit like that all week."

"I thought you said kids at school didn't care."

Val shrugged. "I forgot about them. I try not to run into them if I can help it. They've always got some shit to say."

"And you just let it happen?" Jemma demanded.

"It's not like it's personal, and besides, what can we do about it?" Val countered. Normally, the youngest McCarthy had a shorter temper than Jemma.

Before Jemma could answer, Lottie finally came to take their order. She didn't act like herself, though. Normally, the woman, covered in heavy layers of makeup, smiled and made conversation with them, including sharing gossip she had learned in the diner that day. Today, however, she seemed in a hurry to get their order. She hardly even looked them in the eye.

Once she had taken their order, she told them the price. "I don't think that's right," Jemma told her.

Lottie reviewed the order and found her mistake. "Sorry. Busy day."

Jemma's brows drew together. The diner was no busier than normal. What was making Lottie so frazzled?

It's us, Jemma realized, for she had noticed Lottie acting normal around all her other customers. Lottie left them after taking payment and did not return until their orders were ready. Jemma decided she wasn't going to stand for this behavior. "Lottie, you're acting weird. Everybody's acting weird around us. Come on, tell us why."

Lottie paused, and for the first time since they came in, she looked Jemma and Val in the eye. She sighed and leaned forward. She looked around to make sure no one was paying attention and spoke in a low voice. "It's just that ever since the ETRAA moved out and RJ told all of us about AJ…" she trailed off, again looking around her. She looked back and added, "Well, everybody's a little more on edge, is all. Truth is, Mama B was all alone, and nobody talked to her until recently. Then, as soon as she opens her place up again, weird shit starts happenin.'"

Jemma frowned. "That's not her fault." She wished she could

yell at everyone, telling them the "weird shit" hadn't gotten weirder because of Mama B. She wished they knew how much she had done to save them and their pitiful, prejudiced town. She kept these words in, though, as Lottie continued.

"Sorry for actin' weird." She gave them each an encouraging smile. "You're both good kids. Easter too. Nobody should be actin' cold at ya." Jemma appreciated Lottie's apology but was unsure the rest of the town would follow in the same way. She tried to believe it would all just blow over in a week or so.

They took their food and returned to Val's truck. Neither of them spoke on the way up the mountain. Jemma turned over in her mind how they could restore Mama B's good name. Val seemed to be doing the same because when he pulled his truck to a stop in the drive at Gran's Rest, he turned to Jemma with a light in his eyes. "I know! I have an idea."

Jemma waited to hear it.

"I think it would be good to plan something fun here at Gran's Rest. Something people in town can come to so they can get a break from everything else. Something for the kids, maybe." He got more excited. "Look, there's still snow up here. I think we should plan a sledding day. I'll invite the Cider Creek kids, and anyone else who wants to come can."

Jemma smiled. "Val, you're a genius. That may be just what we need."

CHAPTER FIVE

The sledding day was approved by Mama B and planned by her teen employees. A couple of days later, on Saturday, Jemma was heading out the door when her father appeared from the kitchen. "Off to work again?" he asked.

For the past couple of weeks, the two had hardly seen one another. Jemma had spent most of her time at Gran's Rest. She nodded. "I'll be staying the night if that's all right with you."

For a moment, it looked like Tad might object, and Jemma couldn't blame him. The last time she had told him she would be spending the night with her friends, she hadn't told him the whole truth. Before he could say anything, she explained why by describing Val's plan for the event.

Tad smiled. "Oh, yes. I heard about that from someone in town." The smile on his face told Jemma this "someone" was Linnea Strang.

She wished he would say her name instead of skirting the whole situation. She was halfway out the door when she turned back. "You can stop by if you want. It'll be fun."

Tad's smile grew. "I might. Have fun, Jem."

Jemma biked up the mountain. It was a cold but sunny day.

When she arrived, she found Easter busy preparing cookies and fresh bread with the cook. Val was outside assembling sleds on the back hill. "Where's Mama B?" Jemma asked Easter.

Easter turned, smiling. "Upstairs getting ready, I believe."

Jemma went upstairs, and sure enough, she found Mama B in her bedroom, attempting to pull up a zipper on the back of an old dress. "Here, let me help," Jemma offered.

"You're a dear," Mama B told her.

While zipping her up, Jemma caught the old woman's eye in the mirror. She chuckled. "You seem nervous, Mama B."

"Well, I am." She sounded exasperated after having fought with a zipper for several minutes. "I haven't had the children from my town come to visit me in such a long time." She patted Jemma's hand. "Except for you, Easter, and Val, of course."

Jemma helped the old woman downstairs. They found that many of the children had arrived. Jemma could hear their playful shouting and laughing. Several parents stood in the front hall. Some of them were parents from Cider Creek. They were the ones who weren't working three jobs or passed out drunk in their trailers. Among them, Jemma recognized Esther Green, whose daughter Sharina she had encountered when the children were sick in Johnson City hospital.

The woman smiled as she recognized Jemma. She hugged her. "I cannot thank you and your friends enough for what you did for my daughter. And now this too! Sharina was so excited to come."

Jemma smiled back. "I am glad to know Sharina is doing much better." The last time the teen had encountered the little girl, Sharina had screamed so long that the doctors kicked them out of the children's hospital wing. It hadn't been the girl's fear which had caused the reaction, but instead the presence of a dark spirit reacting to the arrival of a witch. Jemma doubted Sharina would even remember ever seeing her.

Esther turned to Mama B to thank her for the herbal remedy

she'd sent to the children. Some of the children, Jemma learned, were friends of those from Cider Creek but lived in different neighborhoods of Solomon's Cross. Their parents were the ones standing in the hall close to the door, with wary eyes taking in every detail of the bed and breakfast. They began to relax, though, after seeing how much fun their children were having and how normal and hospitable Mama B could be.

Val supervised the outdoor sledding, Easter handed out cookies and hot chocolate in the kitchen, and Jemma took photographs for the website of everyone enjoying themselves. At one point, her father stopped in, and because Tad knew no strangers, he soon became well acquainted with the parents and the children. Jemma was glad to see his kind, cheery manner come out again among these people. No one would have guessed he hadn't been born and raised in this town. Within moments, it was like he had known these people forever.

As the sun began to go down, parents began collecting their children and leaving. Tad tipped his cap to Mama B. "A fine thing you've done here today." He turned to his daughter. "I'll see you at home tomorrow."

Not all the children were going home. Val's seven friends would spend the night. After a hearty dinner of tomato soup and grilled cheese sandwiches, Jemma and Val cleaned up the kitchen while Mama B and Easter took the children upstairs and told them stories before bedtime. After the children had fallen asleep and Mama B had gone to bed, Jemma, Easter, and Val sat for a while in the parlor, taking in the silence. All three were exhausted but happy. They didn't mind planting, weeding, painting sheds, and making repairs, but this part of the job was what they really loved.

Val seemed happiest of all. "We should do things like this more often."

"Do you think it will help? I mean, with things in town," Easter wondered aloud.

Jemma shrugged. "Everyone seemed to have a good time. Let's just hope word gets around." After this, all three headed to their rooms and went to bed feeling warm and happy.

The following morning, Jemma and Easter came downstairs together to find the dining room table laid with an immense and delicious breakfast, including eggs, bacon, sausage, biscuits, pancakes, waffles, fruit, yogurt, juices, and more. How and when Mama B had found the time to prepare such a meal was beyond Jemma. The cook had been given the day off.

A sleepy-looking Val appeared with seven children trailing after him. He had chosen to forgo a room of his own the night before and bunked with the boys instead.

With happy chatter, the children crowded around the table. Jemma, Easter, and Val all ate their share as well. When bellies were full, Jemma insisted Mama B not touch a thing and take the children into the parlor for more storytelling until their parents arrived while she and the McCarthys cleaned up. The old woman was delighted to have so much attention from the young crowd.

An hour later, parents arrived. Easter and Val bid their goodbyes too, and soon enough, Jemma and Mama B were the only ones left at Gran's Rest since no other guests had arrived over the weekend.

"They seem to be doing a lot better," Jemma remarked to Mama B, knowing that the fresh air, good food, and long night of sleep weren't the only reasons the children had looked so healthy and happy this morning.

Mama B shared a knowing smile. "Gran's Rest itself, and this whole mountaintop, for that matter, is a sort of healing locus." She wagged a finger. "Which is why we press this place as therapeutic as much as it is recreational."

Jemma nodded in agreement. Gran's Rest couldn't necessarily cure serious ailments or injuries, but it could help. She began to wonder if this was part of why Mama B was still alive at her age.

And especially when it seems her friends have passed away, she thought. *You know, the ones that didn't stay in Solomon's Cross.*

It was then, though, that Jemma realized she didn't know for sure if Vesna or Josephine had ever died. She had never finished reading the journals. After the fateful, tragic entries about the deaths of Vesna's children, Jemma hadn't been able to carry on. She thought that she might be able to read more now that some time had passed.

Mama B patted Jemma's hand. "Take the rest of the day off, my dear. You deserve a good rest."

Jemma agreed to this after making Mama B promise to do the same. She then went upstairs to the room she and Easter had shared the night before. She had been keeping Vesna's journal in her bag along with her schoolbooks in case an urge to read more came upon her. She felt a certain sense of urgency now as she opened it and flipped past entries she had already read. Most of the pages had been loose and unorganized the day she found them, but she had sorted them out and glued them back into the spine of the journal.

The date on the page she had left off at was smudged, perhaps by the writer's tears. Jemma gripped the journal as she read. Vesna's earlier entries had been precise, detailed, and organized. Often with the writing crammed so close together, Jemma had a hard time reading it. These entries, however, were difficult to read for a different reason. The writing was scattered and scrawled, and many of the sentences were incomplete.

Jemma sensed growing frustration in Vesna's words.

Eloise ignored me today when I—
    I tried to talk with Josephine. Jo won't take a side. She tells me she is sorry about my

Jemma guessed "children" might have come after Vesna's last

word, but that the mother had been hit with too much inner turmoil to finish the sentence.

Today, I received a note. It was in Jo's handwriting, but the words were Eloise's. I could tell.

The last part of this note was bolder than the rest, showing Jemma that Vesna had pressed harder with her pen when writing about Eloise.

They have decided to separate me from the coven. They have betrayed a sister.

Gone were the shaking words of a woman in despair. They were replaced by someone cold and hardened. Jemma's heart thundered. She couldn't blame Vesna. All the woman had known was loss after years of fleeing some unnamed enemy.

More entries followed, but they were obscured by smudges, wear, and blots of ink. Jemma couldn't make out most of what they said, but she caught words here and there.

Tried to go back—
　Eloise—
　My husband is gone—
　Blood in my palms—
　Josephine—
　My Enemy—

Jemma reached the final entry. She paused for a moment, her hands shaking. Part of her didn't want to read how it had ended. She took a deep breath and soaked in the words. The last note in the journal was a rough scrawl, almost too messy for her to make out.

They sealed me. Eloise and Josephine took my power away. I feel empty. Broken. I don't know what to do. I do not know where to go. Wherever I go, I will be in danger. I am no longer afraid of what my Enemy will do. God, I am so afraid.

Eloise will take more from me. I have dreams where she stands over me in my sleep with a knife poised above my heart. I catch her looking at me, a madness in her eyes. If there is anyone who wishes to take my life now, it is her.

Josephine will not stop her.

I fear I'll never write again.

I fear I will not live to lift this pen again. She is coming. I can hear her now. She comes to end this once and for all.

Perhaps I need not be afraid. If she kills me, I can go home to my children. I hope I will not meet flames when I die as they did.

Jemma lifted her eyes from the journal and found they burned with tears. Quickly, she swiped them away. She swallowed hard as she closed the old book. Had Vesna really been afraid Mama B was capable of murder? She needed to know more. The story wasn't finished. Even with Vesna's last entry, she knew she didn't have the full story.

An instinct told her to go into Mama B's study at the end of the hall. Jemma hesitated just outside the bedroom in the hall. She wasn't allowed to go into Mama B's study without the old woman, but she could hear her snoring in her rocking chair downstairs. "It will only be for a moment," Jemma murmured. She just wanted a quick look to see if there were any signs of what had happened to Vesna.

She crept along the hall. The door to the study creaked as it opened. Mama B continued snoring from below. Once inside the study, Jemma looked past the mammoth computer and noticed a trunk covered in dust in the corner. The trunk did not look like it had been cracked open in a very long time. Jemma had seen it before but had left it alone while dusting things in this room and organizing Mama B's books on the shelves Tad had built.

Jemma was compelled to open the trunk. Her heart thundered as she crossed the room. Lifting the lid, she was met with a bellow of dust. She covered her mouth to muffle the coughs. The last thing she wanted was for Mama B to come in here right now. Inside the trunk, she found photo albums much like the one she had discovered at her house. A couple of them had old photographs, and a third was empty. Perhaps Mama B had planned to use it but never had the chance. There were also framed photos, paintings, jewelry, hats, and scarves.

Jemma knew she was looking at a part of Mama B's past. Perhaps a part of the old woman's past she wished to forget. This was a good sign; it meant she might find something. At last, Jemma's eyes landed on a journal that looked similar to Vesna's. Jemma drew it out and blew the dust off the front. Had they all kept their holler witch accounts in similar books? Upon opening it, she found it was not written by Eloise Brickellwood.

Josephine Doire was the inscription inside the front cover. "What are the chances?" She couldn't believe it. She wondered if her instinct to come into this room and find this journal was what Mama B had been talking about when she mentioned Jemma would one day be able to just "sense things" and "just know."

"Am I imagining this?" she wondered aloud as she turned the pages.

Josephine Doire's writings were different from Vesna's. Vesna had documented detailed descriptions of remedies and magical recipes along with paranoid ramblings of the tragic events in her life, but Josephine's seemed to be more of an autobiography. The handwriting was neat, and the dates were clear. This journal would take a lot less deciphering.

Jemma flipped through, passing dates of Josephine's early times in Solomon's Cross to get closer to the end of the journal.

A sense of urgency overtook her; she didn't have much time to read it. Mama B wouldn't sleep forever. She considered stealing it. Would Mama B notice? Jemma doubted it since the old woman hadn't bothered to open the trunk in many years.

I leave Solomon's Cross in a fortnight

Those were the first words that caught Jemma's eye. She remembered that Josephine's son had convinced her to move out of the small town. She hoped moving had done Josephine well. As far as she could tell, Mrs. Doire had been a kind, intelligent woman caught in dire circumstances in which she had no control. The entry went on to explain her son's wish and all the things Josephine would and wouldn't miss about the town. Names and places were listed, none of which were significant to Jemma. There was no mention of either Vesna or Eloise for some time. Finally, Jemma caught sight of their names in a series of questions.

> *Did we do what was right? It was the hardest sealing I've ever done, that of cutting a sister off. Oh, Vesna, could you ever forgive me?*
>
> *Does Eloise wish it had been different? Of course she does, but would she have changed her decision? Would she have driven our sister away from the magic which is so abundant here?*
>
> *I wonder, at times, if my children have discovered some part of the truth. Has Eloise begun planting seeds of one day carrying magic within my own daughter? One day, I hope Mabel reads this and knows the truth. She will. I hope it will not break it. It is a heavy thing for a mother to keep such a secret.*

Jemma's eyes froze to the page. Her heart skipped a beat, and she couldn't help thinking of her own mother and all the secrets she had harbored through the years as she read those last words over and over. She wondered how Mabel had taken it, and if she had even had the chance to read her mother's journal. It was in Mama B's trunk, after all, not in the house where Mabel Doire had grown up.

Jemma skimmed the list of questions once more. With each repeating question, her sense of fear and suspicion increased. Had Mama B been a part of some scheme to murder her own coven sister? Jemma had been able to banish the notion that the old woman was hiding things from her before, but with this new finding, the feeling returned. *You aren't telling me the whole story, Mama B,* she thought with indignation. It only increased as she remembered Mama B's rebuke of what Jemma had done for AJ. As far as Jemma could tell, the rebuke had been the height of hypocrisy.

It's not like I tried to kill him, she thought. *I was trying to save him from the torment of such awful memories.* She couldn't blame Mama B for keeping this journal shut away in a trunk. She was surprised it hadn't been burned.

She looked up and realized it had grown later in the day. In about an hour, the sun would set, and she had agreed to go to dinner with Easter and Val. She closed the journal and the trunk, deciding to take Josephine's account with her. She hoped Mama B would not notice it missing. After collecting her things, Jemma slipped quietly out of Gran's Rest, leaving the old woman sleeping in her rocking chair.

Back at her house, she found Val already waiting for her in his truck. On the way to Harv's Diner, the McCarthys chattered about how well the sledding party and sleepover had gone. Neither seemed to notice Jemma's dismal state. At least not right away. When they arrived in town, Val announced that he was done keeping a low profile. "We live here too. We shouldn't have to walk around like we don't."

"I think what happened at Gran's Rest yesterday will spread some good reputation," Easter added. Once out of the truck, Val was distracted by a man who came over to ask about work Val had done on his truck.

Easter chuckled, turning to Jemma. "Guy things. Let's go inside and wait." There would be a wait anyway since it was dinnertime and Harv's was the only restaurant in town.

"So, Jem, are you going to tell me what's wrong?" Easter asked once they were away from Val. Of course, she had noticed Jemma's change in mood.

Jemma sighed. "I don't even know where to start." She thought for a long moment before she told Easter all she had learned that day, starting with the final entries in Vesna's journal. She did not tell Easter she had stolen Josephine's journal. Easter listened with growing concern.

When Jemma finished, Easter sighed. "Tough to hear, Jem. I don't blame you for feeling down." She shook her head. "I just don't think Mama B could ever murder anyone, especially someone she once considered her own sister. Vesna's writings sound like that of someone gone mad."

"But Josephine—" Jemma began to object.

"Had a hard time of it too," Easter added.

Jemma shifted on the stool she sat on by the counter. "So, after all this, do you still want to be part of this coven thing?" In the past few weeks, the two girls had talked about being in a coven before but in vague terms and in somewhat of a joking manner. The more they talked about it, and Easter mentioned Mama B telling her she had potential for the Art, the less of a joke it seemed to become. Jemma wasn't sure how to feel about it.

Easter shrugged. "I wanna be able to do what you do, Jemma. It's fucking badass for one thing and helpful for another. Think of all the people you've helped. I wanna be able to do that too."

Jemma admired Easter's compassion for anyone hurting around her, but there was a part of her that resented the idea of Easter having the same power she did. Jemma had found something that set her apart from people her own age. Something that made her special. *Before I know it, every girl in Solomon's Cross will want to become a witch.* She knew the thought was stupid and was glad she hadn't said it out loud.

Easter continued. "And just cause some folks mess it up don't mean it's not worth tryin'."

Jemma stiffened for a second but forced a smile and a playful tone of voice. "All right, but you gotta promise me you won't kill me or get depressed or something."

Easter grinned. "Well, you decided to be my friend when I was sicker than a dog, so I don't figure it'd be good of me to turn on you just 'cause you were feelin' blue."

This time, Jemma's smile was genuine. A small laugh followed. "Well, that's a relief." She still felt some tension. Easter, however, did seem to sense any at all. Jemma had shared about Josephine and Vesna's writings in some secret hope Easter might be scared away from the Art. All it seemed to do, however, was encourage her to seek it out more. Jemma's muscles grew tight at the thought.

She knew she had to start facing the reality that a holler witch needed a coven or at least operated a lot better in one. Easter could become a second part. And what about the third? The door to the diner opened, and Val came in, smiling despite the cold having made the tips of his ears and cheeks red. *No,* Jemma thought. *Not Val.* As much as she cared for her friend, he didn't have the touch or seem to have any desire for magic.

Before Val approached them, Easter said to Jemma in a low voice, "We should talk to Mama B about that, though. Just not sure when."

Jemma agreed. She put aside all troubling thoughts and attempted to have an enjoyable dinner with her friends. There were fewer weird looks from customers, and Lottie had returned to treating them with her normal, cheery attitude. They saw no sign of either RJ or his son, and after they ate their dinner and drank their milkshakes, the three decided they would go home and get good rest after an eventful weekend.

"See you later!" Jemma called out to her friends as she closed the back door of Val's truck. Her brows furrowed as she noticed a new car parked outside her house. *Linnea must have driven here.*

Jemma went up to the house and saw that the living room lights were on. Good, her father was home. For the first time in several days, Jemma was glad to see him. She couldn't wait to tell him how well the sledding party had gone.

When she entered, however, she knew right away something was different. At first, Jemma heard low voices coming from the living room. "Dad? You here?" The voices stopped. Jemma went into the living room. She stopped still at the sight of her father sitting on the couch next to Linnea Strang. Were they on a date?

It didn't look like it. Tad and Linnea looked uncomfortable, although they were holding hands and sitting quite close together. Jemma noticed their eyes drifting from her to someone sitting on the other side of the room. In Jemma's chair.

She turned slowly, already sensing who was there. She knew how she smelled. She knew when this woman was in this room. She also remembered now that the car outside had Indiana plates on it.

With her heart lodged in her throat, Jemma locked eyes with her mother.

CHAPTER SIX

Jemma froze.

She couldn't move, couldn't think, couldn't even *breathe* as she took in the sight of Delilah in front of her. Her mother was here in Solomon's Cross after all these years. Jemma had thought her mother was bound and determined never to leave Hendricks, Indiana.

She looked just as she had the last time Jemma saw her. Soft curls of auburn hair framed her face. Each lock of hair was in a specific place. Annie's makeup was perfect. Her clothes, too. They had no wrinkles or spots and looked like they had cost her more than she could afford. The woman's brown eyes met Jemma's.

Am I imagining this? Jemma thought, half-hoping she was stuck in a nightmare. She knew by the uncomfortable expressions on her dad's and Linnea's faces, however, that this was really happening. And then, of course, there was the expression on her mother's face.

Annie looked hesitant as her slow smile appeared. "Hello, Jemma." Her voice was soft and alluring. No one who ever heard Annie's voice didn't like it, but right now, it was the last sound in the world Jemma wanted in her ears.

"Holy shit," came out of Jemma's mouth.

Annie rose, but her daughter turned away. Jemma whirled to her father. "You let her in?"

Tad also stood while Linnea remained sitting, her nervous eyes flitting between the three Noxes. "Jem—" Tad started, but she wouldn't hear it.

"No, no…" She backed out of the room. After all the shit she had learned today, she didn't need to see her mother, of all people.

Jemma turned around, not wanting to see the faces in the living room. She fled to the kitchen and made it as far as the back door before she heard footsteps behind her. "Jemma, wait!" It was Tad. She turned, hand on the doorknob. Tad panted. "Come on, let's talk." He spoke quietly, not wanting the women in the other room to hear him.

Jemma didn't care who heard her. "You might as well have let a robber in the house, Dad! For all she's taken from us!" She glanced past her father to see Linnea still sitting on the couch, looking even more uncomfortable now that she was alone with Annie. Linnea stared down at her folded hands. Annie stood, arms crossed over her chest, and tapped her foot on the floor.

Tad put an arm around Jemma's shoulders. "Let's go outside and talk for a minute." Jemma agreed but only because she felt like she couldn't breathe inside this house. Suddenly, she felt her own home had shrunk, closing in on her from all sides.

Once outside, she sank onto the back step. Tad sat beside her and draped his hands over his knees. He hung his head without a word. "When did she get here?" Jemma finally asked.

"Last night," Tad answered. "We talked. A lot. The whole night, actually."

"And Linnea? When did she show up?"

"This morning after I told her my ex-wife had shown up out of nowhere." Tad smiled weakly. "She came to support me, not because she's jealous or scared I'll run back to Ann—" He stopped himself. "Your mother."

"I should hope not," Jemma grumbled.

"But she wants me to." Tad's words sounded rough.

Jemma snapped her gaze from the ground to her father.

"Not Linnea. Your mother. She wants me back."

Jemma's eyes grew wide. After all this time? She scoffed. "Let me guess, she ran out of bad boys to fool around with back home, and so she's crawling back to you."

Tad nodded. His expression was hard, and until he spoke, his lips were pressed into a thin, tight line. "She's as awful as they come, Jem. To be honest, she first contacted me a couple months ago."

Jemma froze. "And you didn't tell me?" Her heart pounded. How many secrets was she going to unearth today?

Tad shrugged. "What was the point? I didn't answer her. In fact, I blocked her number. Then she sent emails. I sent them all to spam. At first, she just wanted to know how we were doing, and then she asked if you could come visit her for Christmas. Still, I didn't answer. I didn't think it mattered if I told you. I knew what your decision would be."

For once, Jemma was glad her father had kept something from her. During the holidays, she had begun finding a good rhythm in life. She had her friends and a job she liked. She had been doing well in school. All of that seemed like it was teetering on the edge of a precipice now. Delilah had that effect. She could bring Jemma's life crashing down at any given moment.

For a moment, Jemma focused on the changing atmosphere around her. It was dark outside, but the light from the kitchen flooded the backyard. Shadows moved along the tree line. If she focused too long, she would freak herself out. Tad's warm, comforting voice came back to her. "So, after months of ignoring her, she just showed up here yesterday. She was here when I got back from Gran's Rest." He sighed deeply. "I considered calling you and telling you right then and there, but you were having such a good time that I didn't want to ruin…"

A long silence passed. Then, Jemma ventured, "So, what did the two of you talk about?"

"Everything. Nothing. Honestly, it's all a blur to me now. We were up all night. I slept a little bit today, but…"

"It's like having a ghost hang around your house. Hard to sleep when you know it's there," Jemma supplied.

"Exactly." Tad paused a moment, then dove in. "Right off, I told her she shouldn't have come. I told her I was seeing someone I really liked who treated me well." Here, a smile crossed his lips. If they had just been talking about Linnea, Jemma would have found herself happy in the conversation. "I told Annie she had come too late. God, Jemma, she didn't even apologize for anything. She tried to, but I think she's allergic to the word 'sorry.'"

He paused again.

Dread coiled like a snake in Jemma's stomach. "But she found a way in. She always does."

Tad nodded. "You weren't really talking to me, and I don't blame you for not, but before I knew it, I found myself telling her about you coming into your magic. I was pissed off. I blamed Annie for not being here to help you. For not being the mother you needed because clearly, I was failing you."

Jemma felt like her heart might crack open at his words. She didn't have a chance to say anything because he continued. "Suddenly, your mother found herself in a good situation. She could help me out by giving me information on the life of a burgeoning witch. She said she could help me 'figure things out.'"

Jemma scoffed again. "She wormed her way back in. Great." She looked at her father and saw the very thing she feared. "And you're letting her." Any empathy she had felt for her father was replaced by pure indignation.

"Not completely," he replied hurriedly. "It's not like I'm going to marry her again, but she may be able to help you in ways I can't—"

Jemma cut him off with a sharp look. "Mama B has been helping me." She spoke this with confidence, but even that was dwindling after what she had read in Vesna and Josephine's journals. Was it just a trait of witches to lie and keep secrets? Jemma had certainly done her fair share of sneaking around, including taking Josephine's journal. She shoved the thought away. She didn't have room to feel guilt right now.

"What does Linnea think about all of this?" Jemma asked as she stood, throwing her hands up in frustration.

Tad remained seated. "If anything, she's more likely to take your side."

Jemma huffed. "I can't imagine why."

Tad heard her sarcasm but didn't respond to it. He hung his head like a scolded dog. After a moment, he said, "Linnea doesn't want Annie here because she's afraid of her. It's more because… well, Linnea cares about you. She didn't have a great relationship with her mother, either. In a way, she's been in your position before."

"Don't tell me your type is 'witch,' Dad."

Tad laughed. "Trust me, Linnea is not a witch."

Another pause.

"I told her about you and Annie. What you have in common. Not everything, of course."

Jemma stiffened. Tad was willing to be open and honest with his new girlfriend but not with his daughter for most of her life? Or was he just now deciding he needed to be honest about everything with everyone?

"Linnea took it well. She doesn't know what to think, but she's pretty neutral on the whole thing. She doesn't understand most of it, but she knows Mama B is a good person and that everything she's done for the kids at Cider Creek was good."

Jemma remembered that Linnea was the pharmacist who had agreed to send Mama B's brews to the children.

Jemma didn't know what to think. Her mind reeled. Conflicting emotions went to war inside her. She wasn't sure which ones to let out. She wished Mama B or Easter were here. Instead, she felt all alone. Before Tad could say another word, she marched back into the house. "Jem, what are you do—" He was out of earshot the next instant.

Jemma stormed into the living room. Tad may have let Annie into his house, but Jemma lived here too. She went right up to her mother. By now, they were almost the same height, Annie only being a little bit taller than her sixteen-year-old daughter. Linnea watched with a nervous expression. "It's been over a year since you've seen me, and you only try to contact me when you know I'm out of your life for good. So don't come in here acting like you're going to give me advice. I don't want it. I don't want you here." She felt like she was on the brink of exploding.

Tad rushed into the room and attempted to put himself between mother and daughter, but Linnea intervened. She gently pulled Tad away from the others. "Let them talk. They need to." With great reluctance, Tad went outside with Linnea. She suggested he drive her home. That left mother and daughter alone. Jemma was glad for it. She could shout as much as she wanted, and boy, did she want to. She didn't care if the whole mountain heard her.

"You're selfish and stupid and shortsighted. You treated Dad and me like shit when you left and after. God, you stayed in town, so we couldn't get away from you! You made it so we couldn't move on like you had. It was horrible. And *then*, you never bothered to explain this major thing about how I could possibly have magic. Why, huh? Was it because you couldn't stand the thought of someone else, even your daughter, being as *special* as you are? You wanted to be the only one, didn't you? So you hid it from me my whole life!"

As she spat her words, Jemma looked at her mother now as "Annie" once more. Not Delilah. Delilah was the stiff and formal name they gave her. Annie was the free-spirited woman who didn't care what happened to those who had once loved her.

Annie attempted to speak throughout Jemma's speech. Finally, she snapped her mouth shut and let Jemma finish. When Jemma stood there, breathing hard with her hands on her hips and her face flushed red with fury, she spoke. "I'm still your mother." Her voice was calm and controlled. Jemma knew that wouldn't last long. She had gotten her short temper from her mother, after all.

"You haven't earned that title. Not be a long shot. You are feeling old and lonely, so you come around looking for me to make you feel better about yourself. We both know you being my mother doesn't mean much."

"If you would just give me a chance—" Annie started, her pretty, perfect features morphing into an expression of desperate pleading. Jemma couldn't tell if it was an act or not.

"*TO WHAT?* Hurt me more? To let me down again? To make me feel more betrayed, unloved, and alone?"

Annie sighed. "That's all in the past, dear—"

Jemma threw her hands up. She couldn't believe what she was hearing. "No, it's not. It's been my life for three years now, and I've put everything into getting over it. I'm not letting you suck me back into your world just because you can't find any more men who want to spend time with a slut like you."

Jemma didn't expect what came next. Before she knew it, she was staggering back, her face stinging and ears ringing with the sharp slap Annie had sent across her face. Her vision blurred. Then her anger rose, red and hot, sweeping like a fire in a dry forest. She staggered a second longer before she gritted her teeth and swung her fist out, punching her mother in the nose. It was Annie's turn to stumble back in shock. All Jemma saw before she ran out of the house was red blooming on her mother's face and the shocked expression Annie wore.

She was outside in seconds, gulping in as much cold night air as she could. She started walking. In what direction, she did not know. All she knew was that she had to get as far away from her house as possible. The dark trees blurred past. The cold pressed in, but it felt good. It helped quell the fury which had made Jemma's cheeks flush with heat.

She made it far enough down the road for her house to be out of view before she stopped, startled by a sound. It was not the sound of her mother pursuing her. No, Annie didn't like being outside in "the middle of nowhere" while it was dark. She would not be following. It wasn't the sound of her father returning either. The sound came from someone moving among the trees to her right.

Jemma's eyes narrowed. At first, she supposed it might be some animal, but she sensed the presence of a human. Was this a part of the sensing she could do with her magic? With her anger burning hot enough to drive out any wariness, she set off to investigate. Just as she stepped in between the first two trees, a different sense came over her.

It was darker here. Colder. This was not a good idea. The overwhelming feeling that she was in danger gripped her on all sides. She reached into the depths of her being for her magic. The first tendrils of light reached her palms and spread to her fingertips. She prepared to utter words used for defensive spells. They never left her tongue.

She heard something whiz through the air a split second before it hit her on the back of her head. Groaning in pain, Jemma fell to the ground. The magic in her hands vanished. "What the hell?" She reached for the back of her head. It throbbed where she had been hit—by a stick, log, or stone, she didn't know. She couldn't find it in the dark.

Someone jumped out of the brush beside her and ran toward the road. Jemma's heart leapt into her throat and pounded like a bird trying to escape a cage when someone. Still in pain, she scrambled to her feet, gathering her senses enough to give a winded pursuit. The wind lashed at her from all sides as she ran toward the tree line. She came to the road just as she heard a truck sputtering to life.

With a screeching of tires, headlights filled her vision. She couldn't see the driver. The truck tore off down the gravel road. Jemma had to dive out of the way to avoid being run over. The truck made its way down the mountain at an alarming speed, and Jemma was transfixed with horror. *That's RJ Kilmer's truck!*

Had the man been stalking her and hurt her on purpose?

Her head still ringing and full of shock, Jemma knew she shouldn't be alone in the woods anymore, but she also didn't want to return home. She decided she could make the walk to Gran's Rest and just hoped RJ wouldn't come after her again. *I need to call the police,* she thought, but then she realized she hadn't brought her phone with her. It wasn't worth it to her to go back to the house even for that. She could call once she reached Gran's Rest.

She made her way up the mountain, jumping at every little sound. Finally, the lights from the parlor window came into view, and Jemma's body filled with relief. Mama B didn't need Jemma to knock on the door to know she was there.

The old woman met Jemma on the path a few yards away from the front porch. "Come here, dearie." She wrapped Jemma in a blanket, showing a solemn gentleness without asking what had happened. By this point, everything Jemma had experienced that day came rushing in, causing tears to fill her eyes. She didn't care so much about what she had read in the journals anymore.

Mama B led her inside. "I'll make you some tea and something to eat, and then you can rest," the old woman assured her.

Jemma was grateful Mama B didn't ask her what had happened. She wasn't ready to talk about it yet.

CHAPTER SEVEN

Neither Jemma nor Mama B said a word while the old woman prepared food and tea for the teenage girl. After she had finished drinking her tea, Jemma found she couldn't eat. Mama B didn't push her to and encouraged her to sleep in the empty guest bedroom. Jemma lay in bed for a long time, awake and in somewhat of a trance. A hundred thoughts raced through her mind, each one becoming more incoherent the longer she lay there. Finally, her thoughts were so muddled that she fell asleep.

She awoke the following morning wondering if it had all been a dream. It hadn't. As much as she wished it was, she knew the truth. A couple visiting Gran's Rest were enjoying coffee downstairs when Jemma went looking for breakfast. The cook had set aside cinnamon bread for Jemma at Mama B's request. Jemma sat alone at the breakfast nook, nibbling on the bread until the old woman joined her at last.

"Your father called me this morning."

Slowly, Jemma raised her head, her eyes asking the question, "What did he say?"

Mama B sat across from her, still wearing the solemn expression she had had last night. She spoke gently as if Jemma were some wounded bird in need of much care before she could fly again. "He told me about how your mother came back and that the two of you had a fight."

Jemma's face hardened. How did Tad know? Had Annie told him? She assumed this was the only way. Perhaps she had even waited to wipe the blood from her nose until she heard him coming in. Annie had often done that—staged things at the right time to make others feel sorry for her. It had often worked on her ex-husband. Tad was one of the most empathetic people Jemma knew.

And she used him, she thought. She realized Mama B wanted the story from Jemma's perspective but didn't think it a good idea to push. Jemma decided it was as good a time as any. She started with how she had walked into her own house and been shocked to see the one person she had not expected. The rest was blurrier in her memory. All she had known then was rage. Somehow, she got the whole story out. Mama B listened in understanding silence.

When she finished, her listener allowed a moment of silence to pass between them. Finally, Mama B leaned close to her young employee. "Now, I don't approve you hittin' your momma, but I understand why you would. She's done you wrong. Anybody can see that. But it may be best the two of you give one another some time before you do anything else you regret."

Jemma bristled. She didn't have to give her mother anything. *And it's not like I would have punched her if she hadn't slapped me first,* she thought.

The word "regret" rang in Jemma's ears, and she decided to get all of her problems out at once. "You talk about regret, Mama B. I wanna know something about you and regret." She looked the old woman right in the eyes, and although her voice was tight, her expression was earnest. "What happened to Vesna?" She knew it would have been better to wait for Easter since the other girl wanted to hear the story from Mama B as well, but Jemma couldn't hold it in any longer. At this point, she couldn't stand to be around another person who kept secrets from her.

Mama B did not look surprised by the question. Instead, her expression was pensive. "I knew lettin' you keep those damn scribblins wasn't a good idea," she muttered.

Jemma kept staring at her, willing her to spill the story. After everything, she felt she deserved to know.

Mama B sighed. "All right, I'll tell you. It's high time you heard the whole truth."

Jemma couldn't agree more.

"After Jo and I sealed away Vesna's power, the woman became obsessed with finding a way to undo our working. She engaged more in the dangerous, dark magic." Mama B's expression revealed concern. "Which sounds like something your mother may have been dabbling in for a long time too."

Jemma nodded. "I was afraid of that. That's why you have to tell me."

Mama B went on. "While Vesna never found a way, her search got a lot of people hurt, not least of which was Vesna herself. Jo and I, well, we had to keep savin'. After years of it, we grew tired of dealing with all the fallout, and I decided to end it."

"Just you? Not Josephine too?"

Mama B nodded. "I don't want nobody blamin' Jo for what I did." At least she showed some semblance of humility.

Jemma held her breath, waiting for a confession. She wondered if this was the moment when she found out her mentor was a murderer. The thought terrified her. She almost got up and ran out. *No*, she told herself. *Stay. Learn the truth, and then decide what to do about it after.*

"The confusion tonic you used on AJ can drive out some memories," Mama B explained.

Jemma frowned. What did that have to do with anything?

"But there is a more potent magic for locking up memories." Mama B paused and looked Jemma right in the eyes. "I used it to try to wipe Vesna's mind, leaving her with a clean slate. I was trying to help her start over. I erased her memory of everything in her life up to that point, and then I sent her away with a good family a few counties over who owed me a favor. The family was good; they would look after Vesna as one of their own."

She hadn't murdered anyone. For that, Jemma was relieved, but she sensed there was more. The worst part was yet to be told. A sadness came into Mama B's eyes. "I had hoped to give Vesna some years of love and contentment away from all her pain. As it turned out, though, things didn't work out so peacefully. Vesna's mind may have been cleaned out, but something in her soul wasn't. And you can't exactly erase what the soul knows."

Mama B paused as if whatever she had to say next was almost too much for her to bear.

"What happened?" Jemma ventured.

"Vesna became difficult, and then disturbed. Finally, she was a danger to herself and others. She didn't seek magic, of course, but she was prone to bouts of psychosis. The family who took her in claimed they hadn't signed up for that, and they were right. I couldn't blame them for what they did next. They sent her away to a sanitarium, and there..." Mama B shuddered. "There, she killed herself."

Jemma didn't breathe for a second as those four words hung in the air between them.

"It was what finally broke the relationship between Josephine and me," Mama B stated. "Neither of us was able to be around one another without remembering all that had happened. Jo blamed me for Vesna's death. It was my fault, in a way, though I think Vesna would have ended her own life eventually, one way or another. Still, doesn't make what I did right."

She sighed again. "Remember what I told you, girl. Magic don't get rid of your problem; it only moves it to somethin' else. You would have thought I would have learned that after all that time and everythin' we'd been through, but I was still stupid enough to believe otherwise."

Jemma didn't know what to say. She knew she probably would have done the same thing.. At least Mama B had tried to give Vesna a better life. Mama B called it stupidity. Jemma considered it hope—A false sense of hope, yes, but still hope. She kept these thoughts to herself. She didn't think saying any of it would help.

Mama B seemed to want to move on anyway. "Now, let me take a look at that nasty bump on the back of your head. How on earth did your mother get you back there?"

"Oh," Jemma replied, realizing she hadn't told Mama B everything that had happened last night. "That wasn't from my mom."

Mama B looked relieved, then concerned. Standing with her hands on her hips, she demanded, "Well, out with it!"

Jemma told of her encounter with the unseen person in the woods and seeing RJ's truck. "He was stalking our home, Mama B! Think of it! He's gone mad."

Mama B's brows furrowed. "Are you sure it was RJ? Did you see his face?"

"Well, no..."

"And do you think a man as big as RJ would have hurt you more with such a throw? And don't you think he wouldn't have run away so fast?" Mama B questioned.

Jemma scratched her head. "I guess it couldn't have been him..."

Mama B sat down again, sighing. "Did you know that AJ had to sell his nice sports car to help pay for his stint in the hospital? RJ was hoping that, with business booming thanks to his partnership with the ETRAA, he would be able to cover the costs. With the ETRAA pulling out all of a sudden, he had to find another way."

"So, the only thing AJ loved went bye-bye," Jemma replied, her heart sinking. She didn't like AJ Kilmer very much, especially now that she suspected him of being her attacker. Still, pity and compassion rose at the thought of him losing yet another thing he had valued. He'd lost his mother, his best friend, his mental stability, his father's respect, his friends at school, and now his car. "Could be he took his father's truck," Jemma heard herself say.

Mama B nodded. "AJ may not remember what happened on that mountain, but deep down in his soul, he knows you're a part of it."

Jemma wondered if her having glimpses of his memories had anything to do with that. She pushed the thought away. She still hadn't told anyone about that experience and didn't want to. Jemma continued processing these things until the front door opened and her mother appeared.

Both Jemma and Mama B started at Annie standing in the doorway with cotton balls stuffed up her nose. She looked far less put together than she had the day before. There were bags under her eyes, and her hair was a mess. Usually, she made herself look perfect before she went anywhere, but she didn't seem to care today.

"I came to say I'm sorry." She spoke hurriedly before anyone could throw her out. She sounded sorry. Jemma couldn't tell if it was in earnest or just another part of her life-long act.

Mama B bristled and cast Annie a sharp glance. Annie also looked at the old woman, and her eyes widened. Clearly, she had sensed power in the older witch. A change came over her face, one of respect for what the other woman was. Soon enough, Mama B's hardened expression faded away. As much as she didn't like Delilah on account of Jemma's story, she also had to respect someone of her kind of power. Until they went dark, at least.

"Please, Jemma, just let me take you home," Annie begged.

Jemma just sat, unable to move.

Annie went on. "I'll only be around for a few more days, and you don't have to talk to me if you don't want to. It's all up to you." She paused. "I promise." It was the most earnest thing Jemma had ever heard her mother say. The question now was whether or not she could believe it.

After a long, torturous silence, Jemma finally nodded.

Amazingly, Annie was true to her word and remained silent all the way back to the house. The silence was awful, but Jemma didn't want to break it either. She was glad they would be home soon. She stole one glance at her mother, and Jemma swore she saw a tear drop onto Annie's cheek.

Once they arrived home, Jemma couldn't get out of the car fast enough. This was when Annie finally spoke. "I'll be staying at the Pineridge Motel in the next town over." She leaned over and handed Jemma a small card through the window. A number was written on it under the hotel's logo. "Feel free to call me if you want. No pressure."

Jemma watched as her mother drove off, and a pang of old pain resurfaced. She had seen her mother drive off before and hoped she would return. Now, however, she hoped Annie Nox would never come back.

CHAPTER EIGHT

Two days later, Jemma called Easter and Val and told them about her mother coming back. Their reactions were as she expected: a mix of concern, support, and anger on Jemma's behalf. Easter, of course, asked if there was a way to recover the relationship. Jemma didn't answer. The thought of having anything to do with her mother made her feel sick.

Ever since then, both had sent Jemma text messages, trying to help.

Val's message showed his support.

Take your time, Jem. You don't owe her a thing.

Easter's texts were a little different.

Hope today is better. <3

And then another a couple of hours later.

Might not be a bad idea to give her a second chance. We all deserve them. Well...maybe she doesn't. I don't know. Might

not be a bad idea though.

Jemma responded to both friends, thanking them for listening but telling them she didn't want to talk about it anymore.

When she said this, Val didn't reply. Easter's was:

Got it. How's your dad doing?

Truth was, Jemma didn't quite know. Things between her and her father were better. Almost normal, even. He hadn't scolded her for what happened with Annie. When Jemma was dropped off at home by her mother two days before, she found a note from her father.

I have no doubt what happened wasn't provoked by you. Love you, Jem.

Jemma had breathed a sigh of relief. So, she wasn't going to get grounded for punching her mother in the face. Ever since then, Tad had tried acting normal. They had since had two dinners together and plenty of everyday conversations. The whole time, however, Jemma knew Tad was holding back, something he wanted to say. Jemma used to think that Tad was bad at keeping things to himself, but now she knew he had had secrets.

Maybe Linnea or Mama B told him it wouldn't be a good idea to talk to me about my mother yet, Jemma surmised.

Jemma, Easter, and Val had an afternoon off work. They took the opportunity to deliver the last round of herbal remedies to Linnea so they could be included in the Cider Creek kids' last round of medication. Val picked up the jars from Gran's Rest and picked up the girls who were doing chores at Jemma's.

It was a bright, sunny day, and the weather was starting to get warmer. "My play is next weekend!" Easter chirped, smiling broadly as they rode down the mountain into town.

"I wouldn't miss it," Jemma returned, attempting to set aside her current troubles and find something to look forward to.

"You can go with me, Jem," Val told her. "Otherwise, I'll have to go alone."

"Your parents aren't going?" Jemma asked.

Easter's shoulders slumped. "No. They can't. Gotta work."

She tried to sound nonchalant about it, but Jemma could sense her disappointment. She put a hand on Easter's shoulder. "I'll be there. I promise. It's going to be the best play ever."

Easter's smile reappeared. "You must have never been to a play, then." Jemma doubted Solomon's Cross High's production of *Macbeth* would be anything spectacular, but she knew Easter was dedicated to her role as one of the three witches.

Ironic, she thought in light of Easter's current state of magic and how holler witches often worked in covens. Easter's play reminded her of the new information she had garnered from Mama B. *I need to tell Easter.* She waited until Val pulled into a gas station and went inside to pay.

"I talked to Mama B about Vesna," Jemma told Easter.

Easter's eyes went wide, but she didn't speak until Jemma finished sharing the story with her. Jemma spoke in low tones so no one passing by could hear. When Jemma finished, Easter's felt a mix of relief at learning Mama B wasn't a murderer, concern regarding the truth of the story, and annoyance that Jemma had talked to Mama B without her.

"I really wish you would have waited for me," Easter confessed. It was not often that she shared such feelings.

Jemma was taken aback. "Sorry. I know. It just kind of… happened. I know you wanted to be there." She found she only half meant the words. She liked having the special bond with Mama B over their shared magic and felt jealous at the thought of Easter having that too.

Easter forced a smile. "It's okay. I get it."

Val reentered the car and conversation about Vesna's fate was put to rest. Moments later, they arrived outside the drugstore where Linnea worked. The trio hopped out of the car, and as Jemma closed the back door, she noticed RJ Kilmer's truck creeping past. But RJ wasn't driving it.

AJ peered through the truck window with a cold expression. His jaw tightened as their eyes met. He glared for a moment, then slammed his foot to the gas pedal and sped down the street.

"What the hell was that about?" Val asked.

Easter looked at Jemma, noticing her sudden discomfort. "What's bothering you, Jem?"

Jemma slapped her palm to her forehead. "I completely forgot to tell you after I saw my mom again!" As they gathered the seven jars they needed to take inside, Jemma told her friends about her encounter in the woods. "Mama B thinks it was AJ. I didn't think so at first, but now I think she was right."

"He threw something at you and tried to knock you out?" Easter asked, shocked.

"I don't know what he was trying to do," Jemma sighed, "but I know it wasn't good."

Val's expression hardened. "Maybe you should tell your dad. You know, so you can both be more careful."

Jemma shook her head. "If I tell Tad, he'll march into town and knock out all AJ's teeth. I don't need to give RJ another reason to go ballistic on any of us."

"And you don't need your dad in jail," Easter added.

Jemma sighed again. "I'll just have to be more careful. Not take walks in the woods at night and all." The three dropped the topic and went inside. The drugstore wasn't busy, so the trio went straight to the pharmacy counter.

Linnea smiled as they approached. "I expected at least one of you to show up today with the last batch. Seems to have helped, doesn't it?"

The teens nodded as Linnea continued. "I've even thought about asking if we can sell the brew itself as a separate item. It wouldn't have to be prescribed either, since it's all natural."

Jemma liked the idea but wasn't sure how much others in town would like Mama B's remedies being sold in their only drugstore. "Witch's brew," some of them called it. It *was* a witch's brew, but her potions wouldn't cause warts to grow and rashes to appear as many speculated. Easter and Ms. Strang chatted about the possibility of selling the brew. "I'll talk to Mama B about it and see what she thinks," Easter concluded.

At this, Jemma stiffened. Usually, she was the one who communicated with Mama B about such matters. Linnea smiled, and her eyes met Jemma's. "Mind if we talk for a second, Jemma?"

Jemma followed the pharmacist to a back room while the other two waited behind. As she followed Linnea, Jemma's heart pounded. What did she want to talk about? Her father? Her mother? Both? Something else?

Linnea turned to Jemma once they were alone. Her pretty face expressed concern. "I wanted to see where your head is at, but feel free to not say anything if you don't want. Perhaps I'm stepping in where I don't need to." Normally, Jemma wouldn't have appreciated the interference, but Linnea had such a kind way of going about things. She went on. "I don't agree with your father letting Annie come back. More for your sake than my own, but he is just trying to help. He's distressed over it every time I see him. I think he really wants you to have at least one real conversation with your mother."

Jemma could tell there was more. "You mean, without us hitting one another?"

The corners of Linnea's lips twitched as she refrained from smiling. "Precisely."

Jemma couldn't help but grin. Linnea was like her father in some ways. She was friendly, and not a soul in Solomon's Cross disliked her. "Maybe go see her once just to show your father you tried." Linnea shrugged. "I can even give you a ride after work if you want. I can stay until you're done, too, if it helps. That way, you can leave whenever you want."

"You'd do that for me?" Jemma asked.

Linnea produced a soft smile. "I'd do it for you and your father. You're both special people."

Jemma thought for a long time and sighed at last. "I guess it would be better to try for Dad instead of cutting him out like I've cut my mom out."

"That's what I was thinking, too," Linnea replied. She checked her watch. "I'll be finished by six o'clock. I can pick you up right after."

"Sounds good," Jemma returned as she went back out into the drugstore. Easter and Val were waiting for her in the truck.

"What happened?" both asked when Jemma climbed in.

"She just wanted to let me know she's there for me." It was partly true. "Dad told her what happened with my mom." Her friends also knew Linnea had been there for part of the confrontation.

"She's a good person," Easter remarked with a brightened expression.

Jemma had to agree, but the prospect of seeing her mother again tonight dampened her spirits. "I'm starving," she said, attempting to change the subject. "Take me home now, Val?" Her plan was to talk to her father over dinner about her plans for the evening.

When she returned home, she found her father had made a much nicer dinner than he normally did—spaghetti and meatballs, garlic bread, and a Caesar salad. Jemma smiled. "What's all this?"

Tad turned, and his face brightened at the sight of his daughter.

"Not for your girlfriend, I hope? She doesn't get off work for another hour."

Tad chuckled. "No. It's for you. For us. We deserve a good meal, don't we?" He paused. "How do you know Ms. Strang is still at work?"

"I'm pretty sure we both call her Linnea, Dad." Jemma sat down. "And I just saw her. She's uh…she's taking me somewhere tonight."

With brows raised, Tad also sat. "And where would that be?"

Jemma hesitated a moment and then told Tad about the plan. At first, he didn't seem like he believed her, but soon, he smiled. "I'm so glad you're doing this, Jem. I know it isn't easy, but at least you can see what you can learn from a…witch in your own family."

As far as Jemma was concerned, Mama B was more like family to her than Annie was. Nevertheless, Jemma was grateful her father supported the fact that she had magic. It could have been a lot worse. *I'm lucky to have a dad like him,* she thought as they began to eat.

As promised, Linnea arrived at six o'clock to pick Jemma up. They had to drive to the neighboring county where Annie was staying. Jemma found it easy to converse with Linnea. They stuck to light topics, discussing the improvement of the kids at Cider Creek, the sledding event at Gran's Rest, and Jemma's job. She liked talking to Linnea so much that a couple of times, she almost forgot where they were going. For a moment, she was able to forget the dread rising within her. Linnea had a calming presence, and Jemma could see why her father liked the woman so much.

Linnea did not bring anything up about Annie or Jemma being a witch, much to her passenger's relief. She did, however, mention Tad a time or two. Each time, her soft smile appeared, and a light shone in her eyes. *They're happy together,* Jemma realized. "So, my father hasn't exactly told me how the two of you got together. Mind telling me?"

"Not at all." Linnea explained that she and Tad had made

small talk the first few times he had come into the drug. "Then one day, he started telling me more. He told me about you and why the two of you came here. He told me he was uncertain about his future plans jobwise because he wanted what was best for you. That's something I liked about him from the start: he always put his daughter first."

Jemma's heart squeezed, and a lump formed in her throat.

Linnea shrugged. "Then, all of sudden, he asked for my number. A day or two later, we made plans to go out. Talking to one another was so easy. So natural. I've never had that."

"Have you ever been married?" Jemma asked.

"Engaged once," Linnea answered. "He went overseas in the army, and I realized I couldn't do it any longer. I needed someone I could build a family with, who could be in the home as much as I was."

Jemma wanted to know more about Linnea and how she and her father had gotten together, but they had arrived. The motel stood against the darkness. One streetlamp shone over the entrance. Its light flickered over the parking lot that was nearly empty. Jemma hesitated. Could she do this? They had come this far. She knew if she asked Linnea to turn around, the woman would. *But I promised her and Dad I would do this.*

She opened the door. "I'll be right here waiting," Linnea told her.

Jemma took a deep breath and went to the door she knew belonged to her mother's room. She stood in front of it for a moment, trying to gather herself. At last, she lifted her hand, but before she could knock, the door opened, and Annie appeared in a doorway. She had curlers in and a robe on, but this didn't stop her from looking relieved.

"Jemma, I'm so glad you came." Before Jemma could say a word or decide if she wanted to flee, her mother pulled her into a hug. "Come inside, and we'll talk."

CHAPTER NINE

The door to the motel room closed before Jemma could react. Annie let go, and it took Jemma's eyes a moment to adjust to the dimness of the room. The TV was on but set at a low volume. The only other light came from a table lamp between the room's two beds. Everything looked worn and old, and it smelled like a closet full of ancient clothes.

Spooky, Jemma thought.

She shivered. "Damn, it's cold in here."

"Yeah," Annie answered. "Fucking thermostat won't work." She caught herself cursing and turned away, seeming to have forgotten she was talking to her teenage daughter. Jemma stiffened. *Here she goes again, acting like I'm a child. As if I'm three years younger and she's just left me.* Jemma considered turning back, going to Linnea, and asking to be taken home. She wanted to be anywhere but this dingy motel room. She was surprised her mother had chosen to stay in this place. It didn't match Annie's finer tastes. But...

It's probably all she could afford, Jemma thought.

She backed toward the closed door, suddenly feeling trapped in this dark, small room with its yellow light and strange smells. "This was a mistake." She accidentally said it out loud.

Annie turned back, desperation on her face. "Jem, please—" She stepped forward with her hand out. "Please just stay for a moment. Just to talk."

Jemma's hand was turning the doorknob. They'd had plenty of time to talk years ago, and Annie hadn't taken the chance. She had refused to answer Jemma's questions about why she didn't want to live with them anymore. Other questions were more important now, though. Other than Mama B, Jemma had never met another witch. She stopped and sighed. "Fine."

"I know you're cold," Annie continued. She rifled through some of her belongings and pulled out a sweater. Handing it to Jemma, she smiled. "Wear this, please."

Jemma had never heard her mother say please so many times in her life. She pulled the sweater over her head. It smelled like Annie. Jemma wished it didn't. If it weren't for her abundance of questions, she would have denied the gesture and left.

"I'm sorry for being so forward. I will try to restrain myself," Annie added as she sat on the end of one of the beds. The mattress creaked under her weight. Jemma gave the beds a rueful look, doubting they were any newer than everything else in the room.

She kept standing by the door while her mother continued. "I was just getting so low and desperate the past couple of days. You coming here proved to me this wasn't a mistake—leaving home and all." She wore a soft smile. "But I suppose home was never a place, was it? It was people. My daughter and…"

Her words trailed off. Perhaps she meant to say the name of her ex-husband but decided against it. Jemma doubted Delilah had any real love left for Tad. She couldn't tell if her mother's expression was genuine. Annie might have thought this wasn't a mistake, but Jemma was still on the fence.

They were both silent and, desperate not to let awkwardness

settle between them, Jemma sat on the end of the other bed. "I'd like you to start by telling me about our family history and its relationship with magic," she stated in a diplomatic tone. *Get what you need to learn and get out,* she thought.

Annie had been staring at the wall while Jemma sat down, but now she directed her gaze at her daughter. "That's your first question?"

"Well...yeah. Seems important, don't you think?" Jemma returned, feeling confused. Then she realized that Delilah wanted to talk about herself, not anyone else in their family who might have had magic.

Delilah found a way to make the answer about herself. "I was given up at birth, as you know, and I lived in the foster care system for most of my childhood. So, I don't really know much about my family, let alone their history with magic."

Jemma knew some of this from what both Annie and Tad had told her. Tad had even gone so far as to correlate some of Annie's past behavior to her upbringing. Jemma had wondered if her father had made that up as a way of avoiding the truth. Now, she didn't think so. Tad hadn't told any outright lies, just kept the truth from her. Every word that came out of her mother's mouth, however, had to be weighed and examined. How much of what she said was the truth, and how much was simply a grab for attention?

"My connection with magic started in my early teens. Around age thirteen or so, I'd say. I didn't think you had any connection to the Art because, by the time you were thirteen, you weren't showing any signs," Annie explained.

"What kind of signs?" Jemma asked, wondering how similar her mother's coming into magic was to hers.

Annie shrugged. "First, it was just a deeper sense of my surroundings—plants, animals, and people. I could feel things in the life around me that others couldn't. I hated to read as a kid, but I found a book on old spellwork that hooked me. After reading it, I was convinced I might have some connection to the Art.

"I sought out the author, but she was long dead. She had a granddaughter who was still alive, though. Going to her was how I really learned about the Art. She showed me how to connect deeper with what I already knew was in me." She chuckled. "At first, I didn't believe her about the fact that I could be a witch. But then, one day, something happened that convinced me."

She paused, and Jemma took the bait. "What was it?"

"I was about fifteen years old," Annie went on, "and staying with a foster family. They had an old cat named Henry Bogus. One day, I told him to do something, and *poof*, he did. Just like that. I kept trying it, and there was some kind of weird connection I had with him. Over time, I was able to control him more and more." Annie smiled wide. "Until I was eventually able to become *like* him."

Jemma's eyes widened. She couldn't help but become captivated by her mother's story. "What do you mean?"

"I learned to shapeshift into a cat or, at the very least, glean some of his aspects. Night vision, quiet walking, that kind of thing."

For a moment, Jemma wasn't sure if she believed her mother. Mama B had never mentioned shapeshifting or controlling animals as a part of the Art or her future training. Jemma had the notion that Annie's training had gone very differently, that her mother had learned primarily through trial and error as well as her experience with others.

Another question came to Jemma. "Does controlling animals thing have anything to do with the dark side of the Art?"

Annie shook her head. "It's quite common for witches to take on the aspects of animals or control them. Usually, a young witch will start with simple spells such as sealing and binding." She looked at Jemma. "I have the feeling that you've already learned some of that."

Jemma nodded, unsure of how much she wished to share with her mother about her training so far.

"What follows is a greater sense of self and one's surroundings," Annie explained. "This gives one better instincts and allows us to begin knowing things that our five senses aren't aware of."

"So, where do animals come in?"

"Usually, that comes third." Annie had started pacing back and forth in front of Jemma as they spoke but now sat on the end of the bed beside her. Excitement shone in Annie's eyes. "I've learned that the Art is incredibly diverse. More than I ever imagined it could be. All sorts of things can be accomplished with it. I may not know much about our family history, but it seems like we are strongly connected with life, the earth, plants, and animals. You have to understand, Jemma, that not many witches are."

Jemma's brows furrowed. This came as somewhat of a surprise since Mama B and the coven she had belonged to had been so strong in this kind of Art. What did other witches practice? "I know about the plants part of it, but what about animals?" She wondered why Mama B had never mentioned such a thing.

Annie smiled. "With the right spells, you could speak to animals, control them, and even turn into them. And guess what? Humans are animals, just more complex ones. This makes us more difficult, yes, but we can be influenced by our natural surroundings just like any other creature."

Jemma frowned, unsure, at first, if she agreed with this. She found it difficult to accept that she might be on the same level as a bird or a rabbit, but right now, Jemma could relate to feeling caged. She felt trapped in this hotel room in Kalhoun County, too. She wanted to ask another question, but Annie spoke first.

"Enough talk about animals. I want to know more about what Ms. Brickellwood has taught you."

Jemma didn't try to hide her displeasure. "For one, no one in town calls her that. It's just Mama B. For another, I came here asking questions, and I want answers. I want to know more about what you're talking about with animals."

Getting to know a bit more about other kinds of abilities might help me figure out how to repair the damage done to AJ. Or at least stop him from being so creepy, she thought.

Mama B had warned her about seeking out sources of magic on her own and using them without understanding their full impact. *But I don't see another way to fix things.* Magic had done the damage. It would have to provide the repair.

Annie looked at Jemma and sighed. "I suppose you're right." She produced a weak smile. "I should really be meeting you where you're at, not forcing you to get up to where I am." There it was again: Annie subtly making sure Jemma knew she was somehow above her, better than her.

Jemma stiffened, but she couldn't help watching as her mother stood and made her way to a window. She opened the curtains and then the window. A cool night breeze drifted into the chilly room.

Jemma remained on the end of the bed closest to the window and watched with deep interest as her mother leaned out and whispered into the night air. A squirrel sat on a branch nearby, but after Annie repeated the whispered words, it came over to the windowsill. Chuckling, Annie looked down at the bushy-tailed animal. "Come inside, why don't you, and together we'll show Jemma what she will be able to do." The squirrel did as it was told and scampered inside. He sat by the lamp on the nightstand, his tail twitching.

Jemma stared with wide eyes. "He...just listened to you? Did what you wanted him to?"

Annie turned to her. "What you've just seen me use is called beast-tongue magic. The words used are a part of the Art's words of power. I assume you've used some before but only for sealing. With animals, instead of sealing or binding them, it's more like... touching them."

The squirrel looked between the two women, twitching and waiting for his next command.

"I am using my magic now, holding him in place," Annie explained, "but it won't last long. Eventually, a creature will become too used to your touch and discard it. He'll scamper back on out to his favorite branch."

"What should I do?" Jemma asked, desperate to know more.

"Reach out," Annie instructed. "Establish a connection. It may take a few tries, but you'll know when it has happened. It will understand you and do as you tell it."

Jemma wasn't sure how she felt about it, but it was just a squirrel, after all. What was the harm in trying? She did as her mother encouraged. She reached out with the power within her like she would do when attempting to bind or seal another being.

"Be gentler with this than you would be with binding," she heard Annie's patient voice. "Instead of pulling it to you, search for it. Let it come to you. It's like finding a current in the river, only your eyes are closed."

Jemma did this, and after two or three tries, it happened. It was like something clicking into place. She sensed the weak energy of the animal on the nightstand. At first, she expected she might be able to understand its chittering as language as if it could be translated to words she knew, but instead, she had a warm feeling low in her gut and a sense of understanding that wasn't there before. It was only a feeling. For a moment, Jemma doubted if it was real. *What if I am just making up the feeling because I want to be able to do this?* she thought.

What Annie whispered next confirmed that Jemma wasn't imagining any of it. "I've lost connection with it, which means someone else has caught his attention." She smiled. "You. It's you, Jemma." A hint of pride was in her voice. The sound of it warmed Jemma despite her previous reservations.

With the warm feeling of connecting with the animal came some distant sound. Like music playing far, far away in the deep crevices of Jemma's mind. It was happy, sad, and angry all at once. She let go of the magic, not wanting to feel it for too long.

"Wh-what was that? That feeling I had?"

"The squirrel, like all other creatures, is a being with wants, desires, and needs. When you connect with its deepest self, you take on an understanding of those things," Annie explained, giving Jemma an approving nod. "In time, you will be able to hone your intuitive connection even further and be able to speak with the creature. It will become more like a conversation, but you'll never use actual words. That feeling, it will keep coming back."

"How the hell does that work?" Jemma asked, turning to look at the woman sitting beside the nightstand.

"With what both humans and animals have," Annie answered. "Feelings, desires, wants, needs, and interests. This squirrel's desire may be as simple as finding the finest nut, but it is still a desire. That's what you have to connect to." She placed a hand on Jemma's shoulder. "What do you want? Hone that in, create a simple command, and the creature you're connected to will obey."

What do I want? Jemma wondered. *To know more. To see what I can do with this.* She did not voice this aloud, not yet trusting her mother to know she longed for such a thing. A more bothersome thought came to her next, and she voiced it aloud. "C-can this be used on humans?"

It took Annie a moment to answer. Finally, she nodded. "Eventually, you can use it to communicate what you are really feeling or even what you're hiding. You could read these things about others, too. It becomes a pretty good lie detector." Annie laughed. "Once, I even thought your father was cheating on me, and I used it, but he was just hiding a surprise party he had planned for me."

Jemma stiffened. All the good she had felt in the room

vanished. "Around the same time, *you* started cheating. I remember it." It had been the birthday before Annie left them.

Annie stared at the floor, confirming Jemma's words. Had Annie just been projecting her own secret onto Tad at the time? It took a moment for Annie to look up again and revert the subject back. "Be careful with this ability though, Jemma. If you try to read the feelings or secrets of someone who has even a rudimentary connection to the Art, they will notice the connection being made."

Jemma wondered if her mother said this because she still had things to hide and didn't want her daughter, or anyone else, looking too closely. She glanced over at the clock and saw that the squirrel had scampered away. He was on some tree branch outside by this point, she assumed. She had been here for over an hour, and although she had enjoyed the time working with the squirrel, she didn't want to be around her mother any longer.

Does Mama B know what Annie's taught me tonight? Jemma wondered as she stood. *If so, why hasn't she told me?*

"That's enough for tonight," she said aloud as she headed to the door. She didn't wish to be in Annie's presence any longer, and she didn't want to keep Linnea waiting.

"Tonight or forever?" Annie asked in a pleading voice.

Jemma had opened the door, but she paused and glanced over her shoulder. She wasn't sure what she wanted, but she knew for certain that she didn't want to miss an opportunity. "You can stay. For a little bit, anyway. I want to learn more." She closed the door before Annie could tell her goodbye, goodnight, or worse that she loved her. As Jemma headed down to where Linnea waited for her, she wondered if this whole thing was going to turn out to be a huge mistake.

CHAPTER TEN

That night, when Jemma got home, she couldn't stop thinking about beast-tongue magic or about how she never wanted to train with her mother again. It felt like a breach of a contract that she didn't even have with Mama B. What would the old holler witch think of Jemma taking lessons from another witch, even if the other teacher was her own mother? She discarded this concern when she remembered that Annie could teach her things Mama B couldn't...or wouldn't.

Jemma went to bed feeling troubled. Thankfully, Tad conversed with Linnea long enough that Jemma wasn't asked any questions about how it went. In the morning, she awoke with a sense of dread, expecting him to ask soon. She went into the kitchen for breakfast and found her father humming as he buttered slightly burned toast. "Mornin', Jem. Sleep well?"

She had, despite the previous evening's revelations.

"Want toast?" Tad asked.

Jemma looked ruefully at his breakfast. "I think I'll do it myself."

Chuckling, Tad moved over to give her access to the toaster. He didn't ask a single question, but before he left for work, he said over his shoulder, "Your mother says she'll be in Solomon's Cross today if you want to meet up and 'continue what we started last night.' Her words."

Jemma nodded. "I'll bike down later if I decide to see her."

"Whatever you need," Tad answered and shut the door. The silence in the house was almost unbearable. With her father gone, she had no choice but to decide what the hell she was going to do. On the one hand, she didn't want to give in to her mother's wishes to spend more time together. On the other, her curiosity had grown since last night.

I have to work this morning anyway, she thought. She biked up the mountain to Gran's Rest after eating, hoping a day in the sun would distract her from her dilemma. She did not see much of Mama B all day. Jemma worked on outdoor tasks, and Mama B was focused on tending to out-of-town guests.

The work didn't keep Jemma's mind off her recent magic lesson. Working the grounds, she became all the more aware of the life stirring around her. The birds in the trees, chirping to one another and flitting about. The insects buzzing in the brush. The squirrels, chipmunks, and rabbits on the grounds. At any given moment, Jemma could use her binding magic to bring one to her and the methods her mother had shown her to establish a connection. She laughed to herself at the thought of having animals paint a shed for her or weed out a garden.

"I'm not a Disney princess, though," she thought out loud with a chuckle.

Next, she heard a truck rolling to a stop in the drive. Looking up, Jemma spied Val in his truck. Easter hopped out of the passenger side and went straight to the front porch, where she was met by Mama B. Jemma heard their voices but couldn't tell what they were saying. A moment later, they both headed into the forest in the direction of the clearing where Jemma had been trained for the past few months.

"I don't believe it," she breathed. Mama B had started training

Easter, and neither one of them had said a word to Jemma. Were they hiding it, or did they not think it important? A cheery voice rescued her from the thoughts bombarding her mind.

"Watcha working on?" Val ambled over, hands in his pockets. "Want any help?"

"Actually, I just finished," Jemma decided, "and I'm about to go home." She wasn't finished, but she wasn't keen on letting Val see the disappointment on her face.

Val's expression fell. "Oh. Okay." He forced a smile. "Guess I'll find something to do inside."

Jemma retrieved her bike and went back to her house, where she tapped her phone to open a new message to her mother. She hadn't texted her mom in…well, a long time. Why now? Why had seeing Mama B and Easter going to train without her bothered her so much?

I'll learn more from my mother. She'll teach me abilities Mama B hasn't taught me…or Easter.

Before she could regret her decision, she hit send.

In town today? Let's meet.

Jemma's heart pounded as she sat on the porch, waiting for a response. It came a few minutes later.

Pick you up in ten.

Seconds later, Annie added a smiling emoji. It made Jemma groan. She hoped this wasn't a mistake. She imagined Mama B in the clearing teaching Easter the same things Jemma knew. *Guess we aren't the only witches in town anymore,* she mused.

In ten minutes, just as she promised, Annie pulled up. As Jemma got in the car, she glanced at the road leading up to Gran's Rest, half expecting Val to appear in his truck at any moment. She didn't want him to see her with her mother.

"Are you hungry?" Annie asked in a chipper voice.

"Yes," Jemma answered. "But let's find a place to eat closer to where you're staying." She wasn't ready for the questions that would arise if she showed up with her mother at Harv's Diner.

Annie agreed, and they went through a drive-thru close to her motel. When they finished eating, neither said anything. Finally, Annie broke the silence. "What made you change your mind?"

Jemma turned. "Who says my mind changed?"

Annie produced a small, knowing smile. "Last night, you left hoping you'd never have to come back. Didn't you?"

Jemma squirmed.

"It's okay. I'd be on the fence too if I were you."

"I want to know more." Her words sounded and felt like a confession.

"But there's more." Annie's prodding was gentle, and Jemma felt herself opening up despite her reluctance.

"I'm not the only person Mama B wants to train, and I guess I just got…jealous." It felt like admitting guilt. "I also want to learn because I think it could help. Not just me or Dad, you know?" She didn't say who. Ever since being stalked in the woods by AJ, Jemma had been on the lookout. She hadn't seen him again, but she had also avoided going to town where she'd be likely to run into him.

Annie nodded, but Jemma wasn't sure she could agree. Annie hadn't helped anyone but herself as long as Jemma had known her.

Why help me now? Jemma wondered. She was too afraid to ask it aloud and hear rejection again. If she was going to talk to her mother, she was going to get something out of it.

"Tell me about your training so far, so I can understand what's happened," Annie encouraged.

Jemma did as she was asked. She told her mother about the boo hag who had afflicted Easter and how their friendship had spurred Jemma's desire to learn about magic. "I just wanted to get rid of it, and Mama B taught me how." She went on to explain what the ETRAA had been doing and how they had dealt with the nest of haints on Kalhoun's Crest. She skipped telling her mother about Vesna's journal or the holler witch history in Kalhoun County. She didn't mention erasing AJ's memory, either. She didn't need another witch disapproving of her choice to pour a memory-erasing tonic down his throat.

She doubted that her mother and Mama B would agree on much, especially methods of training in magic. What Mama B taught over the course of several weeks, Annie was eager to show Jemma in a matter of days. Her mother was a free spirit in all matters. Her holler witch mentor was duty-driven.

"Tell me more about town. You've mentioned Easter and Val. Any other friends?" Annie asked.

The turn from magic made Jemma wonder if her mother was prying or actually cared about Jemma's new life. She shifted in her seat. "Kind of the opposite, actually. There's this guy…"

"Is he cute?" Annie had excitement in her voice.

Jemma rolled her eyes. "I said 'the opposite.' He hates my guts, I'm pretty sure, and I'm not too fond of him either." She described how AJ Kilmer had been with them on Kalhoun's Crest and gave Annie the same story she had told the police, that AJ had hit his head and couldn't remember anything.

"But his father is irate, and I think AJ has been taking it out on me too." She didn't tell her mother about being hit and chased in the woods. She was afraid Tad would find out and wouldn't let her outside alone for a long time. Worse, he might take matters into his own hands.

The problem had been caused by magic, and Jemma knew her father wasn't the person to fix it. "I'd like to find a new way to handle conflicts, I guess," she amended.

Annie nodded as if she knew more than Jemma had told her. She gave her daughter a broad smile. "Well, then, let's begin."

Jemma put in a call to Gran's Rest, leaving a message for Mama B that she wouldn't be coming to work for the next few days so she could catch up on school. She did have a couple of tests to take, but she also wanted to focus on beast-tongue training. Every afternoon, before her father got home from work, Annie picked Jemma up. They went to her motel, where they sat outside and trained with the animals around them—squirrels, rabbits, birds, and a chipmunk.

Within a couple of days, Jemma could reach out and connect with any of them with ease. Controlling was a little harder. Annie urged her on with patience, supplying the right words for Jemma to say. "Once they understand you, it won't be difficult to get them to do what you want." After another two days, Jemma was able to command a bird to fly from one branch to another and a squirrel to stand on his hind legs at her demand.

"What comes next is the best part," Annie told her on the evening of their fourth day of training. The sun was going down and casting long, dark shadows over the empty motel parking lot. "You've learned about beast-tongue, which will get better with practice, and now I'll teach you about beast shape. First, you will acquire small-scale animal abilities."

Jemma's brow rose. "Like…barking?"

Annie laughed. "You could if you wanted, but I was thinking more along the lines of a dog's hearing and a cat's night vision. If you have any cats or dogs around where you live, you can practice with them. You will need to reach out and connect first, of course."

"I don't know where to look without taking someone's pet," Jemma responded.

Annie rose, smiling. "Come with me."

It was chilly now that night had crept in, and Jemma was not inclined to go very far with her mother, but her curiosity was too much. She followed Annie to the other side of the motel, where she heard the low purring of a cat. The stray calico emerged out of the shadows at Annie's bidding a moment later.

"Your magic is wide and adaptive, Jemma," Annie stated, "but this won't be as easy as the beast-tongue was."

"How so?" Jemma asked. So far, training with animals had been very easy for her, almost like second nature.

"The beast shape requires much more focus. It may feel like trying to keep a muscle flexed when you start. Focus will be difficult to maintain for more than a few seconds."

Jemma found this to be true. After connecting with the motel's stray cat, she reached out, imagining herself as having the same vision and spirit as the animal before her. She would catch it and her surroundings would become more distinct, but in the blink of an eye, it would be gone.

"Try again," Annie encouraged, noting her daughter's irritation.

Jemma tried a few more times, and with each attempt, she was able to keep the sensation longer, but not long enough. After the fourth time, she was worn out.

"It will do that to you," Annie commented. "But cheer up. It will take practice."

Jemma was about to ask another question when her phone dinged, signaling a text from her father.

Still at work?

"Shit." She stood. "I didn't realize how late it was." It was almost 9:30, far past the time she'd usually be home after work.

"I'll take you home," Annie offered.

Jemma hesitated. She wasn't sure she wanted her father to know she was training with her mother. She also didn't want to keep anything from Tad anymore. "Okay, thanks."

When she returned home, it did not pass Tad's notice that it was Annie's car in front of his house. She didn't come inside, and Jemma didn't invite her in. Tad just smiled at his daughter and pulled her in for a hug. "Take your time, Jem. Just tell me when you're ready."

After she stayed away from Gran's Rest for a week, Mama B, Easter, and Val began to suspect Jemma had more than schoolwork on her plate. The McCarthy siblings sent texts to Jemma, asking if she was all right, what she was up to, how school was going, and if she had time to hang out that week. She gave vague responses or ignored her phone altogether, feigning she was busy and distracted when confronted later.

What about Friday night?

Val asked her on Wednesday morning.

Jemma thought about saying no since she was just beginning to get good at holding the cat's vision. She would be moving on to other skills soon. She decided, however, that saying yes was better. That way, she might run into AJ Kilmer and see how he was doing. Over time, she hoped she could find out a way to sense his true feelings without him knowing. *And then fix what I damaged,* she thought.

Friday night, however, lent her no progress. She had to keep up the act of having nothing to do with her mother and spending all her time on chemistry. All the while, she was also searching for AJ through the windows. No sign of him appeared.

"Anything new with you?" Jemma asked Easter, hoping she would hear about her training.

"Nope, not really," Easter replied before she stuck her milkshake straw in her mouth.

Fine. If she doesn't want to tell me, then I won't tell her.

Val didn't seem to notice anything different, which was why Jemma and Easter were being trained in the Art and he wasn't.

Tad remained supportive. He started speaking about Linnea more often when Jemma was home. Now that Jemma was spending most afternoons and evenings with her mother, he started doing more things for himself.

He's been taking care of me in his own way, Jemma thought. Little things here and there showed her that Tad tried to keep as many burdens off his daughter's shoulders as possible. It wasn't until she began splitting her time equally between her parents that Jemma realized his long depression and isolation, which hadn't gotten better until moving to Solomon's Cross, had been, in part, a result of not wanting to start another relationship in fear of putting strain on his daughter.

Tad Nox, however, was a warm, affectionate man who grew lonely quickly without a partner.. When she was with her mother, Jemma didn't ask about Annie's life, and although Annie asked after Tad, Jemma didn't give her any information. Tad deserved a life away from Annie. He could raise the daughter, but Annie could help the witch.

Tad didn't ask any questions until Jemma had been going to train with her mother for eight days. "Mama B called me today. She's worried about you. Says you haven't been to work in a week," he told her when she arrived home that evening. "Anything you want to tell me?"

Tad leaned against the doorframe between the kitchen and the living room. Jemma set her backpack down and turned to her father. "I haven't told Mama B what I've been doing because I don't think she'll like it." She shrugged. "You know, another witch training me and all." More of it had to do with the type of training, but Jemma wasn't sure she was ready to get into that with her father.

Tad shifted, placing his hands deep in his pockets. "Can I give you a word of advice, Jemma?"

She nodded. "Of course."

"Tell Mama B anyway. She only wants to help and support you. Remember, she was the first one to teach you about magic, not your mother."

"But I thought you liked that I was learning from my mother."

Tad scratched his head. "I do, but I wouldn't want you giving up on someone who has a lot more experience and a good track record of having your best interests at heart." He smiled. "Plus, she's your boss, and you've missed a week of work."

Jemma returned the smile. "You're right. I'll go back to work when the weekend is over."

"And tell Mama B what you've been up to?" Tad prodded.

Jemma nodded. "I promise." She meant it.

"Did you have your normal Friday night plans last night?" Tad asked, changing the subject.

Jemma nodded.

"Me too."

Jemma chuckled, knowing her father had spent time with Linnea. "She's good for you, Dad."

Tad seemed surprised to hear the words. They hadn't spoken about Linnea much. "You think so, Jem?"

"I really do." Jemma hadn't seen her father this happy in a long time. Anything that improved his life made hers better too.

Tad seemed to share this sentiment. He pulled Jemma into a side hug. "I hope she'll be good for both of us, Jem."

Father and daughter had dinner together, which ended when Jemma got a call from Easter. She stepped outside to answer the phone. "Hey, E."

Easter, who normally used a cheerful tone when she spoke to Jemma, answered in a tight, cold voice. "Look, Jem, we need to talk. I know you're keeping something from me, and I wish you'd come out with it already. Meet me at the shack down the road. I'll be there in an hour." She hung up before Jemma could answer.

Groaning, Jemma pulled on the sweatshirt. "Going for a

walk," she called to her father. The sun was just beginning to set as she biked down the road to the old fisherman's shed that was set up against a dense clump of trees. This was the place where Jemma first met Easter, Val, AJ, and other teenagers from Solomon's Cross. It seemed so long ago now.

Jemma's eyes widened when Easter pulled up in Val's truck. She had driven herself! She got out, wearing a hard expression. *Here it goes,* Jemma thought. Before Easter could say a word, Jemma stepped toward her. "Look, I know I haven't been the best friend in the last week. I've just got a lot going on."

Easter nodded, her expression softening. She couldn't stay mad for long. "I get that, but the problem is, you would have told me before. All of a sudden, you've gone radio silent on me."

Jemma sighed and sat down on the side of an old fishing boat. "It's my mother, is all."

Easter took her seat beside her. "I figured. You haven't talked about her all week. There's more, though. You're holding back."

Indignation grabbed Jemma. "It's not like I'm the only one keeping secrets."

"What do you mean?" Easter's confusion was genuine.

"I saw you and Mama B going into the woods the other day. Why didn't either of you tell me you were starting training?"

Easter's looked surprised. "I didn't realize we had to tell you. I just assumed that, well, you would know. We've been talking about me learning more about the Art for some time, and..."

Jemma threw up her hands. "Just because I'm a witch doesn't mean I know everything that's going on!"

"I know..." Easter started, but Jemma had already continued.

"After I saw you and Mama B, I decided to let my mom teach me some things, and now I'm getting better. I'm learning things Mama B won't teach me."

Easter remained calm. "Are they things she won't teach you because she can't or because it's not time yet?"

Jemma looked at the ground. "I don't know. I-I haven't asked her. I guess I'm afraid to. I'm afraid she'll disapprove of what I'm learning."

Easter placed a comforting hand on Jemma's shoulder. "I'm sorry for not telling you, and I'm glad you have your mom back in your life a little bit." She sighed. "But regardless of who is teaching us what, we need each other, especially when it comes to AJ. I've been training so we can help him, and my guess is you have too."

Jemma looked at her friend, and Easter produced a smile. "You know me so well," Jemma confessed, laughing.

Easter shrugged. "I do."

The moon was rising into the dark, navy sky as crickets chirped. "I'm sorry too," Jemma said. She turned toward her friend. "I've been away from you all week, and that's my fault. How can I make it up to you?"

Easter grinned. "Two things. Come to my play on Sunday, and after that, tell me all about this new training you've been having." She offered Jemma her pinky. "I promise not to tell on you to Mama B if you promise you'll tell her yourself before too long."

Jemma realized that if she promised both her father and Easter to tell Mama B what had been going on, she had to do it. She hooked her pinky around Easter's. "I promise."

CHAPTER ELEVEN

On the day of Easter's play, Jemma was surprised to see how packed the high school auditorium was. It looked like at least half the town had shown up to see a handful of teenagers yell Shakespeare at one another. It felt strange to Jemma to be inside a high school again after having done school online for so long.

She arrived with Val, and a little while later, Tad and Linnea joined them. They picked seats with a good view of the stage. "I'm already sick of this play," Val murmured to Jemma. "I've heard Easter reciting lines for weeks. I could do her part for her if she got sick." Jemma chuckled, imagining Val dressed up as an old crone.

Val smiled at Jemma. "Hey, thanks for comin'. Easter won't admit it, but she's really sad our parents couldn't make it." He glanced at Tad and Linnea. "I'm glad they could come too."

Jemma felt the same way and leaned over to tell Val this, but just as she moved, the lights dimmed. Applause filled the auditorium as the curtains parted, revealing a set of cardboard pine trees. Against the trees were three figures. The opening scene of *Macbeth* played out just as Jemma had read it, and she sat in the audience with a smile pasted on her face as a hunched-over Easter walked in circles around a fake cauldron.

Jemma and Val had to cover their mouths to keep from laughing when they heard her witch's voice call out.

"When shall we three meet again
In thunder, lightning, or in rain?"

The witches had their interchange, and the scene ended with all three calling, "Fair is foul, and foul is fair; Hover through the fog and filthy air."

Jemma was glad to see her friend doing something she loved so much and watched as she acted her heart out in the first three acts. When the intermission came, Tad and Linnea drifted off to find bathrooms. Jemma took her time observing others in the room. She noticed a figure hunched over a row away from them. AJ's steely eyes were fixated on the now empty stage.

"Surprised he bothered to come," Val muttered when he noticed who Jemma was looking at.

Jemma wasn't very surprised. Was AJ still following her? Did he intend to do her more harm? The young man seemed to sense her eyes on him. He jerked his head to the right and stared into her face. Snarling, he rose and was out of the room before she could react.

"Guess he doesn't wanna see how it ends," Val remarked.

As intermission ended, the lights dimmed once more. For the rest of the play, she couldn't keep her focus during the second half of the play. Had RJ come as well? She doubted it. Who else would be at his store working on a Saturday afternoon? Her thoughts swirled with thoughts of the Kilmers, the rumors that had been started in town, and the threats made against Mama B. Jemma didn't notice that the play had ended until everyone in the audience stood and began clapping.

She also rose, smiling when Easter appeared on stage and took her bow. *That's it,* Jemma thought. *I'm done watching Easter play a witch. I'm going to show her how to be one. One like me.* The sense of jealousy she had had before faded away. Easter deserved the power magic brought. She would not abuse it, Jemma was sure.

The following day, both girls finished their work at Gran's Rest early and headed down the road to the same spot where they had met. Jemma started by explaining to Easter all her mother had told her. Easter listened in rapt interest, nodding along as she took the information in. Her eyes widened. "You mean…you can actually see like a cat can in the dark?"

"Almost," Jemma answered. "I'm still practicing. Go home tonight and try the connection thing I told you about with whatever animals you find around."

"Thanks, Jem," Easter replied with an eager smile. She wrapped her arms around Jemma and gave her a squeeze.

Two days later, Easter texted and told Jemma that it had worked.

It's like turning on a light switch. Easy as that.

Easter, it seemed, was getting a grip on beast-tongue and shape faster than Jemma had. At first, Jemma thought she might feel jealousy over it. But that disappeared when Easter told Jemma that she'd had trouble with the herbal-centric magic Mama B had been teaching her.

"I think animals is more my thing," she told Jemma on Wednesday when they met in the same spot after their work was completed. The week passed in this fashion. After school and work, both girls went to the old fisherman's shack, and sitting on the side of the rusty boat, they both practiced their abilities on the animals surrounding them. It did not take Easter long to catch up to Jemma. Soon, both were able to use feline night vision.

"This would have been helpful when you were ambushed in the woods," Easter remarked.

"Or when we were on Kalhoun's Crest," Jemma added. Looking up, both were able to see the mountain on the other side of town. Neither of them had been there since the nest of haints was dealt with and the ETRAA withdrew their operations. There were other things Jemma still wanted to investigate, like the house owned by Rebecca Willow.

"I feel like there's so much more to discover here," she murmured.

Easter nodded. "I feel things changing, stirring, and I don't know how." A solemn silence passed between them until Easter laughed, attempting to drive it away. "In no time, I'll be sprouting feathers and flying anywhere I want!" They decided they were done with practice for the day. Connecting with the animals and giving them small commands strained them after a while.

Jemma hardly saw her mother during the week. Between work, school, and practice with Easter, Jemma had had little time for either of her parents or even for Mama B, whom she still hadn't talked to about her training. *I want to see what all Easter and I can do on our own first,* she thought, but she hadn't forgotten the promises she had made to her father and Easter.

On Thursday, Jemma didn't see Easter and spent much of her day at Gran's Rest, preparing for weekend guests. Once again, there wasn't time to get Mama B alone. The old woman was distracted by preparations and conversations with staff and guests.

Practice tomorrow?

Jemma texted Easter when she finished work and headed back home around sunset.

Yes

was the reply. And a few minutes later:

I have something to show you.

Jemma's anticipation built over the next day until she met Easter at their spot. "What is it?" she asked.

Easter grinned. "I've been working on it for two days. It takes me a while, but once I'm in it…"

Jemma grew impatient. "In what?" Her eyes widened as she watched Easter stand before her and transform. Gradually, Easter grew smaller until she was small enough to fit in the palm of Jemma's hand. "Holy fuck," Jemma murmured.

Easter's answer was a small chirp since she was not a five-foot-three teenage girl but a bird. Jemma recognized it as an American Kestrel from one of her father's bird books. Easter was arrayed with blue, orange, and yellow feathers. She had tiny, bright orange talons and black spots on her wings.

Jemma wondered if she was imagining things. "Can you fly?"

Easter chirped again and took flight. She was unsteady at first but gradually gained confidence. She flapped her wings and rose past tree branches. She could not yet soar or dive, but she remained in the air for a few minutes. Jemma laughed in disbelief. "What does it look like up there?"

Although Jemma couldn't understand Easter's chirps, she could tell her friend felt good. For a moment, Jemma imagined what it might be like to have the vision and hearing of a bird, to feel the wind on its wings. One day, she was determined, with lots of practice, she would do the same thing. Easter was able to master the connection to wildlife quickly since she had such a deep connection to the Art and had lived near an abundance of magic all her life.

The bliss of Easter's flight was interrupted by the screech of an animal from above. Jemma jolted when she saw an eastern golden eagle crest the trees. Normally, such a sight would leave her marveling, but she was terrified because this eagle wanted Easter.

"Easter, come back!" Jemma cried. If she didn't move fast enough, the much larger bird would descend on its prey, not sparing a single second to gather the American Kestrel in its claws. Easter's wings flapped faster, and she descended to the ground, crashing into the gravel. In a blink of an eye, she had transformed back into her normal self. Jemma rushed over, laughing nervously with concern in her eyes. "You were almost eaten, Easter! I sound crazy just saying that."

Despite the averted danger, Easter uttered a shaky laugh as Jemma pulled her up from the ground. "It feels so good, Jem. Thank you for teaching me." She paused, wiping dust and dirt off her clothes. "For now, can we just keep this between us? Like, don't tell Val? I want a chance to tell Mama B first."

Jemma nodded. "Let me tell her, please. That way, if she gets mad, she won't blame you. I've been teaching you anyway."

Easter agreed, and both decided they had had enough practice for the day. Within the next couple of weeks, the eagles would be a little farther north, and Easter could fly around all she wanted.

Jemma went home excited about what she had just witnessed. She wanted to tell Tad the incredible story, but she remembered her promise to Easter. Jemma planned to tell Mama B as soon as the weekend was over when there were fewer guests to distract her.

What if she doesn't like it? Jemma thought. What if Mama B decided Annie's teaching was too close to a dark part of the Art. Was it worth the risk? *Mama B thinks I should stay here forever, though.* Jemma made her way inside. *I shouldn't be tied to this place. It's not right for anyone—magic or no—to have to remain in one spot forever. I tell magic where to go, not the other way around.*

Jemma stopped short as she realized these thoughts were not her own but words her mother had spoken to her in the past couple of weeks. "Shit," she muttered. She was starting to sound like Annie, even if it was just inside her head. She remembered what was at stake: Kalhoun's Crest, the magic stirring beneath it, and the friends she had made. It didn't have to feel like her home yet for her to give a damn about it.

She sighed. It wasn't as simple as it had been when she first moved here, wondering if this town in the middle of a mountain could become a home to her. Shifting sounds from the kitchen alerted her to the presence of her father.

Tad walked into the living room wearing a broad smile. "Evening, Jem. I'm glad you're here. We have something very important to talk about." From the way he smiled, Jemma didn't think her father wished to discuss anything serious.

"Yes?"

"It's your birthday next weekend, and we haven't made any plans yet. Big seventeen!" he chortled.

To Tad, every birthday was big.

Jemma laughed. "Honestly, I had forgotten about it with everything going on."

A sober expression came over Tad's face. "Well, let's have a day next Saturday where nothing is going on but celebrating you. What would you like to do?"

Jemma thought that having some sort of get-together would help repair the distance that had grown between her and her friends over the past couple of weeks. "I'd like to hang out at Gran's Rest. You, me, Easter, Val, Mama B, and you can bring Linnea too if you want."

Tad beamed at the mention of his girlfriend, then grew sober. "What about your mother?"

Jemma hesitated. "I'm not sure that's a good idea." She recalled how her mother's words had started appearing in her thoughts.

"Did anything happen?" Tad asked. "You haven't seen her at all this week. Did she go home?"

Jemma shook her head. "No. She's still here. I just think

taking a break is a good idea for me. In fact, I think I'm going to call off lessons with her for the time being. Until I can talk to Mama B, at least." Part of her felt guilty for even thinking this. She felt guilty that Mama B didn't know yet about what she and Easter had learned to do. She also felt guilty for dropping lessons with her mother after so many successful days. Regardless, she still felt this was the best decision.

Tad didn't push for more information, and just as Jemma finished speaking, her phone rang. "That's her now."

"Are you going to answer?" Tad asked.

Jemma nodded and stepped outside onto the porch. She hesitated a moment, knowing her mother would want to know why she hadn't come for several days. "Hey, M—" Jemma started and then stopped. *Since when did I start wanting to call her* Mom *again?*

"Jemma, are you all right? I haven't seen you in a few days."

"Yes, everything's fine. I've just been busy. Actually, I was thinking it might be a good idea for us to—"

Annie didn't seem to hear Jemma, or perhaps she sensed what was coming and wanted to put a stop to it. "It's going to be your birthday soon, Jem, and I wanted to do something special for it. I was thinking you and I could go out tomorrow night in Johnson City for some fun. Plus, it would be a good chance for you to start testing your beast-tongue on humans. It will just be innocent stuff. Just getting a feeling for interacting with people and such."

Jemma had a twisting feeling in her gut, something that told her this wasn't a good idea. "I don't know—" she started.

"Oh, come on, Jem. It'll be fun. We haven't had fun, just the two of us, in so long."

Jemma's next words escaped her lips before she could stop them. "Yeah, and whose fault is that?"

Annie sighed. "I know. I'm to blame, and I'm sorry. Let me make it up to you."

One night out in the city was going to do very little to make up for several years of absence, but at least it was something. More than anything, Jemma wanted the opportunity to learn beast-tongue on humans so she might at least get some insight into AJ. *He's still lurking around, just being more careful,* she thought, remembering that he had been at Easter's play.

"If it makes you more comfortable," Annie added, "you can invite Easter too."

Jemma smiled. "All right, that sounds good. Tomorrow night?"

Annie sounded excited. "I'll pick you up at six."

CHAPTER TWELVE

For many years, Delilah Nox was late anywhere she went. Her tardiness was considered endearing by those who fell for her charming explanations. As Jemma grew older, she saw her mother's tardiness as another small way Annie garnered attention. "Fashionably late" was what she called it.

"Better than being on time or early and missing out on being the star of the show" was what Tad called it later on after she left them.

Since she'd come to Kalhoun County, Annie had been on time for everything. Jemma wondered if Annie's on-time arrivals were part of the same sort of act she'd pulled before when arriving late. It certainly drew Jemma's attention. It did the same to Tad. Glancing out the window as she pulled into the drive, he commented to his daughter, "She's been consistent. Never would have dreamed. Do you know why?"

"She's trying?" Jemma guessed as she and Easter headed to the door. Tad held his daughter back. "I'm glad you and your mother are on somewhat good terms again, even if it's for your…witch lessons. But be careful, Jem. People can change, but…" His words trailed off as if saying what he really thought would sound too harsh.

Jemma finished for him. "But not her. You're right, I think."

Annie beeped her horn. "See you later tonight, Dad."

Annie gave both Jemma and Easter cheery hellos and suggested they go back to her motel first to get ready for their evening. *But we're already ready*, Jemma thought. She made no objection, however, and the motel was on their way to Johnson City anyway. Jemma found she was looking forward to their night out. A night in the city usually wasn't her type of thing, but she hadn't been to Johnson City since dealing with the ETRAA, and she was looking forward to seeing it in a different light.

"We should be in Johnson City by seven!" Annie chortled as they entered the motel room.

Jemma's brows rose. Johnson City was thirty minutes away. What were they going to do for a full hour? Then she saw it. The bed was covered in makeup, hair products, clothes, and shoes.

Damn, had Annie brought her entire fucking closet?

She glanced down at her outfit and then at Easter's. Both girls had worn their best jeans and nice shirts and called it a day. This was when Jemma realized Annie didn't know they were ready to go. The preparation hadn't even started.

"Uh, what's all this?" Jemma asked.

"For you two, of course." Annie beamed. "I pulled everything out. Use whatever you want. You and I are about the same size, Jem, so you should be able to wear my clothes."

I'm already dressed, she thought, frustrated. Both girls idled near the bed, trying to figure out how to tell Annie they weren't looking to wear her expensive clothes. Knowing her mother couldn't afford the clothes, Jemma took a closer look. Sure enough, many of them still had tags on them. Either Annie had come across new money, or she planned to return the items tomorrow.

"This is nice and all, Ms. Nox," Easter started.

"Please, call me Annie," Annie interrupted.

"Okay, Annie," Easter started again. "Thank you for offering us your clothes, but I think we're fine."

Annie gave their outfits a rueful look, expecting a punch line. Then, realizing the girls weren't joking, she laughed anyway. "Oh, you both look beautiful, of course, but I was thinking more of a wine and dine night out. Nothing like your scrappy diner in town."

Both girls stiffened. Harv's had become one of their favorite places. They glanced at one another and shared the same thought. A sly smile spread across Jemma's lips. "All right, we'll make a deal."

Annie had been curling her hair while they were talking. She paused, turning away from the mirror. She turned slowly, almost as if she were dreading what Jemma would say next. "What's that?"

"We'll go out with you tonight, but next Friday, you have to join us at Harv's and eat every greasy thing we give you."

Annie hesitated, and Jemma wondered if she should have said anything. Taking her mother to Harv's would raise questions. No one would doubt who Annie was. From appearances alone, it was obvious she was Jemma's mother.

Slowly, Annie smiled. "I suppose that's fair. It's a deal. But now both of you have to pick out something else to wear. Only the finest for us three ladies tonight."

Jemma had the feeling her mother was trying to get them into the spirit of a girls' night out. What both selected at first, however, wasn't going to cut it with Annie. who despised anything neutral and bland. "No, no, try this." She handed Jemma a shimmering, teal cocktail dress with long sleeves and a pair of heels.

Jemma stared at it. "Looks a bit…grown up, doesn't it?"

Annie shrugged. "Isn't that the point?"

Jemma sighed. "It won't hurt to try it on." She did so, and, looking in the mirror, she couldn't help but admit she looked good. Too grown up for her liking, though. This was what Annie wanted, not her.

No other girls her age would be out and about Johnson City dressed like this. *So, this is what she does instead of treating me like a little girl,* Jemma thought. *She'll turn me into a grown-ass woman instead.*

"Fine, I'll wear the dress, but not the heels. I hate those things."

Annie didn't bother to argue with Jemma on this. Although Jemma didn't allow her mother to give her anything besides natural-looking makeup, she did agree to let Annie curl her hair. Annie turned her attention to Easter next, suggesting the dark-haired girl wear a dress that hugged her curves and gave her more flare than the oldest McCarthy would have ever chosen on her own. Not wanting to disappoint Annie, Easter did as she was encouraged.

"She's such a pretty thing," Annie told Jemma while Easter changed in the bathroom. "All that glossy dark hair."

Jemma thought of how much healthier Easter's appearance was now. She had become fuller, and there was color in her complexion. Her hair had grown back, although she still wore hats for style.

An hour after arriving at the motel, the three were ready. Before they left, the teenagers stood in front of the mirror together.

"I don't know how I feel about this," Easter confessed in a whisper.

Jemma just nodded in agreement.

"I just feel like it's…too much. For my age, ya know? Looks like I'm trying to grow up too quickly."

Jemma nodded again, feeling the same kind of pressure.

Easter shrugged and put her usual positive spin on it. "Maybe it'd be more fun to try it your mother's way. Won't hurt, anyway."

All Jemma could think about, though, was she would have

thought about this a month ago. So much had changed in such a short period of time. Never would she have imagined a month ago, she'd that she'd be reunited with her mother and go out on the town dressed like her.

Annie had done it again. She'd wormed her way into someone's life despite their better judgment. Jemma brushed away the thought, hoping this time letting Annie into her life would turn out different.. Learning about beast-tongue and shape had already made it worth it.

"So, where are we going?" Easter asked as they piled into the car. Having been to Johnson City several times for medical treatments when she was sick, she was familiar with the downtown area.

"There's a live music event I'd like to take you to," Annie told them.

Jemma shifted in her seat. Annie didn't even know her taste in music. How would she know if she would like to go to something like this?

Annie played the radio all the way into Johnson City, humming and talking to herself. Gone was much incentive to engage the two girls in conversation. Jemma had seen it before, of course. Annie just wanted to have fun, and she would have it with whoever she could drag along. They arrived as the sun began going down and realized the live music event was just a concert on the back patio of a bar.

"So much for wine and dine," she grumbled to Easter as they were led up to the patio. It was a pleasant view of the downtown area with mountains in the distance, but they were distracted from this by the loud music and the heavy press of a crowd gathered near the stage. It didn't take very long before they realized this was not going to be a place where they sat down and ate.

"What do you girls want to drink?" Annie asked.

"Just water, I guess," Jemma answered.

Annie laughed. "No, silly. Like, alcohol."

Jemma's mouth fell open. "I'm sixteen."

Annie tapped her shoulder. "Almost seventeen."

"Which is not twenty-one," Jemma replied.

"So?"

"So, I don't drink in bars," Jemma objected. She had sipped a few beers and seltzers from time to time, but drinking wasn't a regular thing for her. Easter hadn't touched a drop of alcohol during her many months of taking medication.

"I still want water," Jemma told her mother.

"Me too," Easter chimed in, trying to maintain a cheerful tone despite her increasing discomfort.

Annie shrugged and sighed. "All right, if that's what you really want." She disappeared toward the bar and the two girls were left to examine their surroundings. Everyone here was at least five years older than them, and Jemma wondered if, later in the night, someone would stand at the door checking IDs.

"I don't like it here," Jemma told Easter.

"I agree." Her friend sighed. Annie returned moments later with two waters and a cocktail for herself. As the night wore on, the crowd became rougher. Intoxicated young people got louder and pushed one another around. People danced near the stage. Jemma's stomach grumbled.

I'm so fucking hungry.

Other than sparse bar food, there was nothing to eat here. She was just about to tell Annie that they wanted to go when her mother pulled them both toward the center of the patio. "It's a girls' night. We should be dancing!"

Dancing was the last thing either of the girls wanted to do. "If you're not going to dance, let's at least practice beast-tongue," Annie added as she turned to survey others on the patio. She pointed to two young men drinking at the bar. "What about them? They're both cute."

"They're both at least five years older than us," Jemma objected.

Annie eyed the girls. "You don't look younger than twenty-two the way you're both dressed." Her eyes sparkled, and Jemma realized this had been her mother's intention the entire time. If Jemma couldn't be Annie's baby, Annie wanted her to be her grown-up BFF.

"Come on, just try it. Go up to them and just start talking. They're drinking, so it won't be hard to establish a connection," Annie encouraged. Jemma knew her mother was referring to a magical connection, but she was sure Annie wanted them to flirt a little too. Annie had made the two girls look older than they were and had dressed herself to appear younger on purpose.

"No, I won't do it," Jemma stated flatly. *I won't become like you,* was what she was thinking. She didn't want to be the free-spirited flirt Annie was, picking up drinks from whoever was dazzled enough by her to buy her one. Or two. Or three and a night in a sleazy apartment and whatever else came with hooking up with guys like that.

What would Dad think of this? Jemma wondered. *If this had been my choice, I would be grounded. For. Ever.*

Annie turned to Easter. "What about you? Are you game? Your abilities will grow stronger, that's for sure."

For a fleeting moment, Easter considered it. It was the training. Easter was drawn in by the Art and her connection to it. Or was Annie using beast-tongue to influence her? Jemma moved between Easter and her mother. "Come on, don't push her."

Annie shrugged and downed the rest of her first drink. Brushing Jemma aside, she smiled at Easter once more. "It'd be fun. Just push their buttons a little. Make them wonder if you're a mind reader." She winked.

A slow smile crept across Easter's lips, but before she opened her mouth to do as Annie asked, Jemma jerked her mom away by her arm. "You're using it on her!" She turned to a startled Easter. "Come on, E. We're not staying here anymore." She didn't know what she would do. Call her father or Val.

Whatever. She didn't care. She just didn't want to be here anymore.

"N-no, Jemma! *Wait!*" Annie's voice was panicked.

Jemma whirled, not caring who saw or heard them. "What, so you can use it on me? No fucking thanks."

Annie followed them out of the bar onto the street, her expression and voice pleading. "Okay, okay. I promise no more grown-up stuff. No more bars, and we don't even have to use magic if you don't want." Her shoulders slumped, and she made her face look crestfallen. Jemma couldn't tell how much of it was an act. "Please. I just wanted to make this night special."

Jemma looked at Easter before she sighed. "Fine. What did you have in mind?"

Annie's smile returned. "We could get a hotel. A nicer one, and just do girl things. Watch movies, eat snacks, that kind of thing."

It sounded much better than barhopping. "I guess, but I'll have to text Dad first and tell him we're not coming back tonight."

Annie clapped her hands and squealed. "Great! Tell him we're at Staybridge Suites if you want."

Jemma and Easter shared another look. Annie had already chosen a place to stay? She typed the message to her father, hoping he wouldn't worry. *I'll tell him what Annie really wanted us to do later.* She knew it would worry him, but she also knew keeping it from him would only make things worse.

Annie claimed she was sober enough to drive, and they went a couple of blocks to the nearby hotel. Getting out of the car, Annie told them, "I have a surprise for both of you inside."

Jemma stopped short. "You planned to come here the whole time. Hell, you already have a room."

Annie shrugged. "What's a good night out if you know everything that's gonna happen?"

That made Jemma warier.

Annie saw it on her face and drifted closer. Jemma could tell her mother was wearing expensive perfume. Later she would probably break the seal and return it, claiming it was that way when she purchased it. "Look, I just want to help. What I have inside is going to help both of you with what you're learning, but no drinks or boys or anything like that involved."

Easter stood by, giving no opinion on the matter, but Jemma sensed that she was reaching out with her power to soothe her. Easter was on her side, no matter what Annie had waiting for them.

"Fine," Jemma replied. "But we go home first thing tomorrow morning."

Annie beamed. "It's a plan!"

Sure enough, when they went inside, it was confirmed Annie had already reserved a room. She even had a key. *Why did we go to her motel first?* Jemma wondered.

The hotel was much fancier than Annie's motel. Maroon carpet lined the hallways. Gold light fixtures and chandeliers decorated the main lobby. Annie directed them to a room at the end of a hall. She placed the keycard against the sensor, and the door swung open. The lights were already on in the room, filling it with a warm golden glow. The beds were big, with fluffy pillows. The wallpaper wasn't peeling, and everything smelled fresh and clean.

For a moment, Jemma was almost happy to be here. Then she stepped into the room and froze. Someone sat on the bed, someone tall and large and familiar. She knew his face. Jemma's heart pounded. "What the fuck?"

Easter gasped. The man was sitting on the end of the bed with his huge hands on his thighs. He looked at the floor, not noticing them enter.

Jemma whirled on her mother. "What the fuck is RJ Kilmer doing in your hotel room?" She wondered if he had figured out they were staying here and had gained access. Was he stalking them too?

Annie explained hurriedly. "Calm down, Jemma. It's all right. I brought him here. You see, after you told me about your troubles, I made it my mission to use the power I can teach you to wield on someone who...needed to stop bothering you."

"So, you brought him here?" Jemma demanded to know. She threw her hands up. "I didn't even tell you it was him! How did you know—" She stopped short, shaking in anger. "You used your beast-tongue shit on *me* to find out, didn't you? All those days of training, and you were just trying to read me."

Annie folded her arms on her chest. Gone was the amusement in her eyes. She didn't deny Jemma's claims. Jemma couldn't believe she had let her mother in. Of course something like this had happened.

"Will you just let me show you first and then get mad about it after?" Annie asked, her voice deadly calm instead of the pleading tone she had used earlier.

Before Jemma could say, "Hell, no, we're leaving right this second," Annie turned to RJ and commanded him in a hard tone. She only spoke one word. Jemma wasn't familiar with it. It wasn't English, though it sounded like it. As soon as the word was out of Annie's mouth, RJ went rigid. He lifted his head and stared at the wall with blank eyes.

"Stand," Annie commanded. He stood.

Jemma felt like she was going to be sick. The sight of a huge man being controlled by the much smaller woman's words was unnerving. However, despite the dread curling in Jemma's stomach, her power responded to it. It was like a warm tug deep in her being. It made her want to do the same thing to RJ. Make him do what she wanted, even if it was as simple as standing up.

Easter hadn't spoken since their arrival at the hotel, but her words came out in a trembling voice as she backed toward the door. "This is all kinds of fucked up."

Jemma pulled out her phone, preparing to text her father to come get them and maybe even call the police. How would she explain what had happened? How had Annie gotten RJ here? It was difficult to think. Further, the longer RJ stood in a trance before Annie, the harder Jemma felt the tug deep within her. She hated how it felt. She hated that it made her want to do what her mother was doing.

Out of nowhere, a voice cut the air. It came from behind the curtains. No one had noticed the window was open. The curtains parted, revealing a menacing face and bared teeth. AJ Kilmer's eyes flashed at Annie, and he demanded, "So, was that how you did it? Pulling strings? Was that what your daughter did to me?"

CHAPTER THIRTEEN

Annie's calm demeanor was gone in an instant. Anger turned her pretty features into something threatening. When AJ stepped out of the curtains, her eyes blazed. She lashed out. The words she used sounded like forceful beast-tongue magic. The force of the words filled the room, sending Jemma and Easter reeling back against the wall.

Jemma's mouth hung open. The beast-tongue was much more powerful than she realized, but Annie had been practicing it for a long time.

AJ, however, seemed unaffected. He remained where he stood, hands in his pockets, and laughed. It was a strange laugh that Jemma had never heard from him, and it startled her.

"That's not going to work on me." He brushed off her command like dirt off his clothes.

Jemma's eyes widened. How was that possible?

"I can feel you doing it, though," AJ added. "But it won't do nothin' to me like it did to my father." He turned to Jemma and smirked. "Or like it did to her."

Even AJ could tell Jemma was under the influence of the beast-tongue. But how? How could he tell when she couldn't?

She whirled on her mother. "How long have you been doing this? How long have you been controlling me?" Her voice rose to an infuriated pitch.

Annie's angered expression remained. She ignored Jemma, turning back to RJ. She opened her mouth to utter another command, but Jemma cut her off. "AJ, I didn't use this shit on you. You have to believe me! I didn't even know about it when we were at Kalhoun's Crest. I can tell you the truth but right now—" She ran out of breath, and AJ's expression faltered. For a fleeting second, it looked like he almost believed her.

But just like that, his hardened expression returned. "You really expect me to believe—"

Another angered voice added to the mix. "AJ, go home. Take your father with you and go home." Easter had stepped between AJ and Jemma.

Much to everyone's surprise, AJ listened, and not because Easter had used magic on him. "Yes," Jemma chimed in, "and when I get back, we can talk all about what I did to you, but we'll also discuss your stalking." She turned on Annie. "But first, I need to have a conversation with my *mother*."

Annie opened her mouth as if she were about to stop them, but seeing the fury in her daughter's face, she gave in. With less anger, she told RJ he could get up and go with his son. On their way out, she grabbed RJ by the arm. Annie's small hand barely covered the width of the huge man's forearm. "Remember, don't tell a soul about this."

Jemma hadn't even thought about that. She hadn't thought about what the town would think of Annie and all the damage she was doing. But if RJ didn't say a word, it would remain covered. AJ could talk all he wanted, but no one believed he was sane anymore.

It all felt so heavy. The Kilmers left, and the close of the hotel room door jolted Jemma out of her semi-trance. "Should I go too?" Easter asked.

Without looking at her friend, Jemma shook her head. "I'd like you to stay to make sure I don't beat my mother to a fucking pulp."

Before either Easter or Annie could stop Jemma, she tore into her mother with more heat than she had done the day Annie came back. "How long? How long have you been doing this?" It could have been before they started training or much, much worse...for years. Annie could have been manipulating both Tad and Jemma for a very long time. Jemma realized the damage her mother caused them ran much deeper than the abandonment.

"You know what I think?" she stormed. "I think it was so *fucking hard* for me to move on after you left because something else had gone, and I didn't know how to deal with it. It was this magic, this pull you had over me."

Easter's eyes widened as she realized what Jemma was thinking.

"How long?" Jemma demanded again.

Annie backed up against the dresser, her angry expression replaced by something desperate and pleading. "I-I don't know when it started! I just started using it one day, and it got easier until I didn't know the difference between—"

"Well, give me a ballpark, then!" Jemma yelled.

Annie threw her hands up. "Years. Okay, years, Jemma. Is that what you wanted to hear?"

Jemma's heart thundered. She felt like she was going to be sick. So much made sense. Tad's depression, how hard it was to move on, Annie staying in Hendricks, Indiana instead of leaving. It had still been going on, even then. All Annie had to do was see them every once in a while to re-establish the connection. It hadn't gone away until they moved to Solomon's Cross.

Jemma turned away. She feared if she saw Annie's face for another second, it would send her into a rage she couldn't come back from. Her expression of disgust and revulsion cut Annie to the quick. Jemma had always known her mother to be an appearance-conscious person whose greatest fears were being despised or exposed. Jemma had done both at the same time, but she wasn't sure she cared.

Annie spoke again, the fury in her voice gone, replaced by something that sounded brokenhearted. "I just wanted to love you and you to love me. That's all I ever wanted, and I guess I got desperate. I tried to hold on as best I could."

Her actions of leaving and controlling her daughter and husband made these words meaningless. Jemma wanted to shout that fact, but Annie already knew it. Saying it out loud wouldn't do a damn thing to change what had happened. Annie couldn't change. Jemma and Tad had concluded this very thing themselves earlier in the day.

"Please, Jemma. Listen to me. I love you. I love you so much."

For a moment, the words ate away at Jemma. Was Annie, for once, telling the truth? She began to doubt her own anger. *Give her another chance...* A muddling sensation came over Jemma's mind, broken only by Easter's sharp voice.

She turned Jemma toward her and looked in her eyes. "Jemma! She's doing it again!"

That was it. Jemma was done trying to talk—or yell—it out with her mother. She reached into her purse. She found some herbs she had brought just in case and crushed them in her palm. Whirling on Annie, who was still stuttering out a half-assed apology, she struck her palm into her mother's face, driving the herbs into her nose and mouth.

Annie staggered back, gasping at the pain and sensation. She gagged next, bending over as if she would throw it up. The shock broke Annie's concentration enough for the web of beast-tongue Art she had worked over Jemma to peel away. Annie scratched her face, screaming. Jemma saw that the herbs were having the effect she wanted them to, causing Annie's face to itch intensely.

Meanwhile, the sense of confusion fell from Jemma like a heavy blanket. Images of trauma flashed through her mind, some from her childhood, and others were memories she didn't even know she had. They were all related to the woman standing in front of her.

The controlling, she understood, had begun again during their first conversation when Annie returned. *Before I hit her the first time,* Jemma realized. She wondered if Annie's slap that day had been part of her working magic. Of course, she didn't know her daughter well enough to expect Jemma to return the attack and go off into the woods alone.

She staggered for a moment, feeling suddenly lighter and like she couldn't stand up on her own. Easter reached out to catch Jemma before she crashed to the floor. This gave an enraged Annie a chance to react. She emitted a low snarl. "I'm still your mother, and you don't treat me like that!"

This would have sent Jemma flying into another rage if it weren't for the fact that something else was happening to Annie. The transformation was quick, not the gradual overtaking Easter had shown Jemma when turning into a small bird. In a matter of seconds, Annie stood before them not as a woman but as a large bobcat. Her black-spotted fur bristled, and her pointed ears laid back as she bared long, sharp teeth.

Jemma and Easter gasped. Yes, after years of being a pathologically manipulative bitch dabbling in dark magic, it had finally caught up with her. Was this really happening? Would she really be willing to kill her daughter in a rage? Before Jemma could think of what to do, Easter also transformed. It took her longer, but she became a sleek-coated red wolf. Annie, in bobcat form, didn't notice the wolf until she went to pounce on her own daughter, snarls filling the air. Letting out a low growl, the wolf intercepted the bobcat.

The two witch-turned-animals tumbled together into the wall where the curtains hung. Scrambling out of the wolf's grasp, Annie, in her cat form, clawed the curtains, bringing them tumbling down upon them. Easter let out a yelp as the rod crashed on her head. She wasn't too hurt, though. Not until Annie pounced on the wolf. She scratched and tore, not hesitating to bury her teeth in Easter's red fur. Easter yelped again and Jemma scrambled for her fallen purse, knowing it was up to her to end this. She pulled out more herbs. Thankfully, she had enough to cobble together what Mama B called one of her surprises.

With shaking hands, she tossed the herbs on Annie's furred back as she pounced on Easter, prepared to sink fangs into the back of her neck. Jemma's heart thundered. When the powdered nettle and thistle hit Annie's fur, it started growing white fibers that would reach beneath her skin and have the stinging potency of a nettle. It would go deeper after that and spread all across her body like an invisible net.

Annie yowled, then dropped off Easter and writhed on the floor. The fur dissolved, leaving a woman shaking on the carpet in pain. As soon as her beast shape was gone, the thistles fell off and shriveled up. Easter also had returned to her normal form and now stood beside Jemma, panting for breath. Both girls looked at the woman on the floor in disbelief. Jemma had thought learning beast-tongue and shape was going to give her the most power when all she'd needed to win this fight was what Mama B had already taught her.

"You just tried to fucking kill me and my friend!" Jemma cried.

Annie just lay there, cowering and cursing. She pulled herself into a corner and began crying. Jemma wasn't sure if it was an act or if she was still experiencing the stinging sensations.

Jemma bent over her mother, shaking and sweating. "Leave, Delilah. Never come back." Her voice grew colder. "I don't need you, and I don't want you. If I ever catch you lurking around Kalhoun County again, that little nettle trick I just used will be the least of your worries."

Annie's reply was a low whimper. She seemed beaten. Jemma

rose and took her things from Easter, who had gathered them up. "Let's get out of here," Easter insisted in a shaking voice. Jemma couldn't agree more. She could see it was quite dark outside. Damn, how many guests in the hotel had heard the commotion? They had to get out of here before anyone came. Hearing a big cats growl and scream was probably not very normal in this establishment.

Before they were at the door, however, Annie's shaking voice came to them once more. "You're an ungrateful little bitch. You know that, Jemma? After all I've tried to teach you." Her voice turned into a snarl. "And your work is cut out for you. Someone else is pulling your stalker boyfriend's strings. You know that?"

Jemma froze. It made sense. If AJ wasn't affected by Annie's magic, it meant he was already under the influence of someone else's. Who was it? She knew it wasn't her, Easter, or Mama B. Was there another witch prowling around Kalhoun County? Jemma muttered to Easter that they should just leave. Allowing Annie another word was not in their best interest.

Once they were outside the hotel, they realized it was almost two in the morning. The ordeal inside the hotel had taken a lot longer than they realized. With a shaking hand, Easter lifted her phone to her ear. "Val? I need you to come pick us up. Something's happened."

Val was frantic on the other end, but Jemma couldn't hear his words.

"We're fine. We're both fine, but we need you to come get us." She hung up a second later. "He'll be here as soon as he can," Easter told Jemma. They decided to wait on the other side of the building, away from the lights. Jemma concluded it was better for Val to pick them up than Tad. She would have to tell her father what had happened eventually, but she wasn't sure how the hell she was going to explain it.

I have to tell him the truth, no matter how much it will hurt him, she thought. She also had to tell Mama B. More than ever, the holler witch of Kalhoun County needed to know what its other witches were up to.

"And we're not the only ones," Jemma breathed out.

Easter heard her and didn't need an explanation. Annie's words played over in her mind. She shivered. "Someone else is working the dark Art in these mountains."

CHAPTER FOURTEEN

As promised, Val came to pick up the girls. He listened with wide eyes as Easter told him all that had transpired, from being taken to the bar to the fight she had had with Annie in the hotel room. At the mention of Easter turning into a wolf, Val slammed on the brakes. No one else was on this rural road in the middle of the night. "You're telling me this magic stuff you've been learning has given you cool abilities?" He glanced at Jemma in the back seat. "No offense, Jem, but what Easter did sounds way cooler than your plant nets."

Easter gave her brother a hard look. "If Jemma hadn't used her 'plant nets' as you so irreverently call them, I would have been killed, so shut it."

"Sorry," he muttered before his mouth snapped shut.

Jemma saw it as going both ways. Easter had saved her by changing form, and Jemma had saved Easter by thinking quickly with the nettle. It was just as Easter had said; they needed one another.

Val resumed driving while Easter described what they had been practicing over the past couple of weeks. The whole time, Jemma remained quiet. She was both too tired and too stunned by the recent turn of events to speak. When Val dropped her off, Easter got out too and pulled her into a tight hug. "I'm glad you're all right."

"You too," Jemma choked out. The weight of everything came crashing down upon her again. Once more, Annie had proved herself more selfish than Jemma could have imagined, and now AJ was out there planning who the hell knew what. Jemma crept into the house, hoping she wouldn't wake her father. She tumbled into her bed and was asleep before any more troubling thoughts could grip her mind.

Jemma slept into the following afternoon.

When she awoke, she found sunlight streaming through the parted window curtains. She had fallen asleep wearing the dress her mother had loaned her. Now, she not only wanted to take it off but also burn it. Before she got a chance to change, she heard a commotion downstairs. She went down and found her father with a worried expression on his face. "I heard you come in late last night, Jem. When I went to see if you were all right, you were already fast asleep." He noted her disheveled appearance. "What happened?"

Jemma sank onto the couch, and Tad joined her. "A fucking disaster is what happened, Dad."

Normally, Tad would have called her out on the cursing. But he let it slide since the trouble Jemma had been through the night before was evident.

"What is it?" he pressed. "What did your mother do?"

Jemma began to explain. She told him about getting all dressed up before going to Johnson City. "She told us we were going to a nice restaurant, but we ended up at a sleazy bar with a band."

Tad stiffened, his hand tightening on the arm of the couch, but he didn't say a word.

Jemma continued. "Sh-she tried to get us to use our magic on strangers, but we wouldn't." She realized she needed to explain to her father what kind of magic she was talking about. "You see, she's been teaching me this new kind of thing. Beast-tongue and shape. Magic pertaining to animals."

Tad nodded. "Yes, she mentioned being able to understand animals before."

"Oh, but it's much worse," Jemma replied. She sighed. This was going to be a tricky conversation. If she told Tad her mother had attacked her, it would send him raging after Annie, and none of them needed that. She also wasn't sure how to reveal to her father that he had been under Annie's controlling influence for most if not all the time he'd been with her. Jemma wasn't sure when her mother had started controlling Tad. Annie had described learning the beast-tongue as a child. It could have been well-developed by the time she met him. The question was, how much of a controlling bitch had she been by that time?

Jemma decided to dive in and leave out the part where her mother transformed into a bobcat. When she finished, Tad sat on the couch, staring at the floor. He sat perfectly still, in shock. After a moment, he shook his head. "I can't believe it. I just can't..." He turned toward her. "Why didn't you call me?"

"I-I was in shock when we left," Jemma answered, "and the next thing I knew, Easter had called Val. But I'm home now. That's what matters."

Tad continued shaking his head. "I knew when you texted me saying you'd be back in the morning that something wasn't right. Not that it's your fault." He sighed, the weight of Jemma's revelation bringing up old wounds and new hurts.

Jemma wondered if she should not have told him. She didn't need her father sliding into another episode of depression, especially after their lives had gotten so much better in Solomon's Cross. A lot more eventful, Jemma acknowledged, but better.

"I don't think it would be a bad idea to go to Mama B and have some of her Art worked over us," Jemma told him. "If there's any remnant of Delilah's control left, we need it wiped off." From what she knew of beast-tongue, an animal or person could still feel some of the effects even after the witch who'd controlled them was gone. It had taken Jemma all the months she lived in Solomon's Cross before Annie showed up to finally feel free. She just didn't realize it until now.

Tad took some time to think this over and finally nodded. "I would like to do that, especially since things are getting serious between Linnea and me."

"What do you mean?" Jemma ventured.

Tad leaned back, and a small smile changed his troubled expression changed. "I think I want to marry her, Jem."

She froze.

Tad dragged a hand through his hair, a sign that he was stressed or nervous. "I'm still working up the courage to ask her. Not because I think she'll say no, but because…well, I really want it to be right this time."

Jemma felt a stab of anger. Marry Linnea this soon? Hadn't they only been together for a couple of months? Or had it been going on for longer, but Tad hadn't mentioned it in fear of burdening his daughter?

Jemma wasn't sure if the anger she felt came from her mixed feelings or if Annie had put it there. It wouldn't have surprised her to discover that Annie had planted resentment toward Linnea in Jemma. After all, Annie wanted to control Tad too. She had come here thinking that she could win her ex-husband back with charm, looks, magic, and shared memories. She had arrived to find Tad with a woman who was worlds better than her—a wrinkle in Annie's otherwise perfectly ironed plan.

This is why Mama B never taught us this, Jemma thought. The dangers of beast-tongue included the difficulty of differentiating between where the magic ended and real emotion began. Without intensive counter magic, could it ever be untangled? It was just as Mama B had told her. Magic didn't make problems go away; it just made them move elsewhere.

My problem was I got jealous of Easter and Mama B, she thought. What had once felt special to her didn't anymore, so she had gone to someone who would use that jealousy as a weapon. No doubt Annie had sensed it in Jemma and guessed the reason. Perhaps that was why she suggested Easter come along with them. She had hoped Jemma would want to show off her abilities to her friend.

Tad looked at his daughter and saw there was much weighing on her mind. "There's more, isn't there?"

Jemma nodded and sighed. "I don't know what the Kilmers are going to think of all this."

"There has to be a reason Annie knew about them. Have you been having any troubles with AJ recently?"

Jemma shifted uncomfortably and decided she could tell her father about RJ's threat to Mama B without mentioning that AJ had been stalking her. "Thing is, though, I never told Annie who had done it. I never gave her a name." A realization hit her. Had RJ threatened them because Annie influenced him to do so? She hadn't influenced AJ to stalk her, though. That was someone else's dark magic at work.

Tad sat in stony silence.

"We should go to Mama B today if we can," Jemma told him. She shuddered. "I want whatever sick magic is on me gone."

Tad nodded. "I've never been one much for magical remedies, but me too."

Jemma knew it would be good for Easter to have an herbal cleansing as well, despite her not having been under Annie's control for very long. A couple of hours at the most, which was nothing compared to the years Jemma and Tad had been under the influence without their knowing.

Jemma explained to her father that the preparation might take some time. "Go on ahead with your friends," he told her. "I have to finish up work, and I will join you when it's ready." It was a relief to hear this since she determined she would need to explain everything to Mama B first. She feared rebuke and didn't want her father there for that. This was another reason she wanted Easter there—for moral support. Val decided he would join as well since he was already going to Gran's Rest for work.

When they arrived, they found, much to their relief, that many of the guests had checked out, leaving the bed and breakfast almost entirely vacant except for some of the staff. Sensing the troubling thoughts occupying the minds of the three young adults, Mama B dismissed them for the day, saying they had had a busy weekend and deserved rest.

"Well, come along, you three. I can tell you have one hell of a story for me." The old woman led them into her parlor, where she gave them tea and cookies. Val ate some, but the girls wanted to talk first.

Mama B eyed Easter, then Jemma. "All right, out with it."

Jemma recounted what had happened, beginning with her visit to Annie's motel and all she had learned that night. She looked for a reaction when bringing up beast-tongue, but Mama B gave none. The woman continued wearing an unreadable, neutral expression when Jemma got to the point about RJ being Annie's captive in her hotel room. Easter picked up with the part about transforming into a red wolf.

Mama B's eyes widened. "Ah, so you've progressed quickly. I thought that might be the case with you."

"It was Jemma who thought fast, though," Easter insisted, then described the nettle-net that had stopped Annie from attacking further.

Mama B observed the two girls and then nodded to herself. "You did just as you should have. You worked together, and without each other, I doubt either one of you would have gotten out of that...without severe consequences."

Jemma knew the word alive should have been used there, but Mama B seemed as though she didn't want this conversation to weigh on them any more than it had to. Jemma half-expected her to fly into some lecture about why they should have never dealt with magic they knew nothing about.

To her surprise, Mama B remained calm. "While I can tell you it was not right to dabble in the magic you did, I cannot fault you for it entirely. Another witch, quite practiced in the Art, told you that you could." Her expression softened as she directed her full attention to Jemma. "And from your own mother, as well. I don't blame you one bit."

Val broke into the conversation. "What if Jemma's mom tries to come back?"

"I will keep an eye out for her," Mama B assured them, "but I doubt such an opportunistic witch will come around here any time soon. She has little to nothing to gain now, from what I can tell. Especially with the girls on their guard." She gestured toward Easter and Jemma. This was followed by a deep, resigned sigh. "I expect Ms. Nox was kicked out of whatever screwed-up coven she found after leaving your father. She might have come around here looking to get something from him while she rebounded, but she found something else."

Mama B looked at Jemma again. "A young witch coming into her magic from her very own blood. A precious thing to a witch who is also a mother." Jemma wondered if Mama B thought about her old friends Josephine and Vesna when she said this since she had not had children of her own.

"Do you think she thought she could start her own coven with Jemma?" Easter asked.

Mama B nodded. "I believe it came to her mind, yes. She might have even sought to include you, Easter. Any witch with any senses around them could tell you have a connection to the Art."

"You all keep saying that," Val chimed in, "but I don't get it. What's it even like?"

"It's like every time I'm around a living thing, be that a person, plant, or animal, I feel a tug within me. Sometimes it's light. Other times it's hard," Easter explained.

Mama B nodded. "The longer you have it, the less you notice it. Until it is gone, of course." A shuddering sigh escaped her lips. "And then, I suppose, it feels like you've been stripped of everything. No wonder it would make anyone go mad." Jemma knew Mama B had Vesna in her mind as she spoke these words.

"How much did you know?" Jemma asked the old woman. "While it was going on, I mean. Did you know my mother was training me?"

Mama B laughed, which made the three sitting opposite her share questioning looks. "Know? Oh, know is a big word. If you were to say guessed, I'd say near to all of it. But when you get old enough, there is little that surprises you." She tapped her chin. "And yet, when you get *really* old, you find what can surprise you often matters a lot, so you'd be wise to let it show itself before you go makin' an ass of yerself."

Jemma wasn't certain what Mama B was saying, but the old woman continued before she could ask questions. "As for the beast-tongue, of course I know about that. I feared teaching it to you girls for the very reasons you have told me today. Though I will admit to having used it from time to time to get news from creatures about the goings-on in Kalhoun County." She chuckled. "I wasn't clueless about what people thought of me."

"But you've never controlled any?" Easter asked.

Mama B shook her head. "Never. Even simple animals. I refused to. There are other ways to get what you want without controlling someone or something." A small smile appeared on her lips. "For instance, I bartered with them, often food or shelter for their services. It's funny how much a chipmunk likes marmalade if you offer enough of it." She sighed, her amusement fading. "But I knew if I taught you, you'd figure out its uses to manipulate and control. And, well, that was once my greatest regret."

Again, Jemma knew she referred to Vesna.

Val had sat through this whole conversation, not understanding the full depth of what they spoke about. He stepped in now with a concern of his own. "Okay, but what about the Kilmers? AJ's going to be even more pissed off after what happened."

"That's what I wanted to talk about, too," Jemma remarked. "I think it would be good to do an herbal cleansing for me, my dad, and Easter. AJ could probably stand to have one too, after everything."

Mama B nodded. "A ritual would have to be done to throw off any magic still clinging to any of you."

"But what?" Easter asked, sensing there was more to it.

"But such rituals require a coven," Mama B answered.

Jemma and Easter shared a look. Neither of them understood what the problem was. "Don't the three of us make a coven?" Jemma asked the older woman.

Mama B shook her head. "Just because there are three witches in one place doesn't bind them together. It would be as silly as thinking the two of you were in a coven with Ms. Nox just because you spent time around her."

Jemma figured that made sense and wished she had thought of it sooner.

"For the three of us to be in a coven," Mama B continued, "we would have to bond ourselves. I think I am too old to take on any more bonding. I believe it would do me in. Besides, my magic is much older than yours. Stiff, almost arthritic. My magic feels like it is fossilizing and will soon crumble."

"Would we have to form a coven with someone whose magic is newer like ours?" Easter inquired.

Mama B nodded once more. "That would be the wise course of action if it can be done. My coven sisters Josephine and Vesna, as the three of you might remember, have been gone for quite some time, and since they left, my magic has not felt the same. Sadness can do that to magic. Either it makes you wilt away or sends you into madness."

Had it been sadness or some other negative feeling that made Annie dabble in the darkness of the Art? Anger and sadness, it seemed, were things Jemma needed to keep in check. A bitter smile came to Mama B's lips. "My magic was withdrawing just before you showed up, Jemma Nox. You woke me up enough for me to realize I needed to pass on what I had learned. Clear out the old growth for new green things to grow, you could say."

"For me and for Easter," Jemma finished.

The old woman nodded slowly, and her eyes glazed over with tears. She sniffed away her emotions. "And someone else," Easter added. "But there might be someone. Just…not someone we want anywhere near us."

At last, they shared Annie's final words to them with Mama B: the revelation that AJ Kilmer was under the magical influence of someone who was close enough to keep control over the young man.

Val cleared his throat, and all heads turned to him. "I dunno if I should say this, and call me crazy if you want, but didn't you say AJ wasn't affected by Annie's magic?"

"Well, yes…" Easter started.

"Annie explained that AJ was under the magic of someone else."

"Okay, that explains why it didn't work on him," Val went on, "but he still knew what she was doing."

Jemma and Easter's eyes widened. "That's right," Easter murmured. "He knew what was being done, which means…" Her words trailed off. She was almost afraid to utter the rest of the sentence aloud.

"Trust me, I hate the thought as much as you do," Val remarked.

AJ had been drawn into all this supernatural business time again, which hinted that he, too, had a connection to the Art.

"But that doesn't make any sense," Jemma said, shaking her head. "I didn't think boys could be withes."

"The Art isn't just for witches," Mama B explained, her expression and voice far graver than they had been before. She also didn't seem pleased with the idea of AJ having a connection to the Art. "It is for many kinds of people and creatures. Perhaps it runs in his family too."

For a moment, Jemma couldn't breathe. She didn't know if she wanted to deny the idea or embrace it fully. Whatever it was, she knew one thing for certain. "We need to get to him before it's too late."

Mama B's expression remained somber. "I'm afraid it may be too late for that. Someone else has their magical talons dug into him."

CHAPTER FIFTEEN

For as long as anyone in Solomon's Cross had been there, the Kilmer family had lived a little south of the town on a stretch of acreage called the Old Farm. It was an oversized produce garden rather than a true farm, but it had been owned and harvested by the Kilmers for decades. Years ago, they had run Kilmer Produce before RJ Kilmer lost his wife May to sickness. Doctors hadn't been able to explain the cause of her death.

Kilmers dying seemed to be a pattern. RJ had lost all three of his older brothers before he turned thirty. People had warned his wife before she married him about taking on the last name. Folks said it was a bad omen. People who had it died young.

When she'd died before her forty-fifth birthday, many in the county called it a real shame. "She was such a pretty young thing," and similar remarks were made. RJ's wife had always looked much younger than her age. Her death had come about three years before Thaddeus Nox and his daughter traipsed into Solomon's Cross.

Working the land wasn't the same without much of his family around. His daughters had moved out of the county, and his only son AJ didn't have any interest in working the land.

RJ had purchased the empty post office and turned it into a store. He took to selling hardware instead of produce. May's cousin Henry Dover was the assistant manager.

Folks in Solomon's Cross still talked about Mary Anne Kilmer as if she were not only still alive but one of the most beloved people in town.

Some who pitied AJ more than they taunted him thought what a shame it would be if May knew how far her son had fallen. For some odd reason, everyone wanted to act like AJ was the black sheep of the family or that he was the only bad apple when, in truth, he had always been May's favorite.

Although the family had lived near Solomon's Cross for a long time, the town's residents seemed to have forgotten about AJ's three older sisters. That's how it worked in a town like that—once someone left, people liked to forget about them.

After Jemma, Easter, Val, and Mama B had had their conversation, the old woman put in a call to RJ's house. "No answer," she muttered after trying a couple of times. She called the hardware store, but no one picked up there either. This was strange because RJ wasn't the only one working there. Someone else could have answered. But nothing? Was the store closed?

"We could go down there and see if he's there," Val suggested. Jemma wondered if RJ had even gone back to work after being put in the trance by Annie. AJ certainly wasn't going to run the store. That left Henry Dover as the only option.

"Might as well," Easter agreed.

While Val drove them down into town, Easter related all she knew about the Kilmer family. "Weird how AJ's mom died right when mine decided to leave me," Jemma murmured.

"It is strange, ain't it?" Easter echoed. "You would have loved Mrs. Kilmer. Everybody did. Except, a lot of people still called her Ms. Dover. Those who watched her grow up, that is."

"Were the Dovers in Solomon's Cross before the Kilmers?" Jemma asked.

Easter nodded. "Long before. The Kilmers became a part of town when they started selling what they'd grown on the land. That was probably four or five generations before RJ."

"That long?" Jemma asked.

Easter chuckled. "Around here, that's not very long, Jem. Everybody else has been here for much longer."

"Not Jemma," Val remarked.

"Thanks for making me feel like an outsider again, Val," Jemma cut in.

Val was ready to apologize but then realized she was joking. "Hey, stop pulling my leg." The sun was beginning to go down when they made it into town. They wasted no time making their way to RJ's Lumber and Tools. The place was eerily quiet. Not a soul was in sight. They put their faces up to the windows and peered in. All was still and dark.

"Guess it's closed," Val murmured. He checked his watch. "Shouldn't be for another hour." He checked the front door to see if the hours had been changed. No new signage had been posted.

A small gasp from Easter brought Jemma and Val back to the window where Easter had kept looking. "There's someone in there!" Sure enough, Jemma spied a shadowy figure moving to the door. She nearly jumped out of her skin when the door was wrenched open, and a face appeared.

After a moment, she recognized the man as Henry Dover, the assistant manager. He was a little older than RJ with a full gray beard and light-blue eyes. He was normally a quiet but friendly person. Right now, he looked harried and concerned. "What do you kids want?"

"We're looking for Mr. Kilmer. Have you seen him?" Easter inquired.

Henry looked down at his feet and shifted his weight slightly. He looked nervous. Why? Jemma wondered if he knew something. Finally, he looked back up. His expression changed to one of deep concern. "I got here this afternoon and found the shop closed up. RJ never told me it was gonna be closed today."

"Did you call and ask?" Val ventured.

"Of course," Henry answered. "No one answered. So, I called AJ too. Same thing." He scratched his head. "So, I've been waitin' here hopin' one of 'em will show up, but they haven't. I'd go out to the Old Farm, but it's a forty-five-minute drive, and I've gotta be home 'for long 'cause my wife gets herself all worked up."

"Have you seen or spoken to RJ this past week?" Jemma asked.

Henry sighed. "Yes and no. It's ain't like RJ to not pick up the phone, but he's been actin' strange ever since he took up with that gal from out of town."

Jemma's brows rose. She was surprised to learn that others in town knew about Annie Nox. Perhaps they had never heard her name. "Who was she?" she asked, fearing that people would connect RJ's stranger with her and her father.

Henry shrugged. "Dunno. He didn't say, but he sure seemed taken with her. Wouldn't come to work for a couple of days. Went and stayed in some hotel in Johnson City, he said. I called the hotel, but they said there was no RJ Kilmer staying there."

Jemma's heart sank. Annie had done plenty of prep work before coming to Tad and Jemma. It made her all the more furious at her mother. Annie either planned every single detail out, or she flew by the seat of her pants. Both did damage, and Jemma hoped she would never have to deal with it again.

"All right, well, thank you anyway," Jemma told Henry.

"Sure thing. I'll let you know if I hear anything," Mr. Dover responded. He then locked up shop and made his way home, looking more worried than ever. Jemma considered telling the man she had seen RJ the day before, but then an explanation would have to follow.

"What are you thinking, Jem?" Easter prodded after seeing the troubled expression on her friend's face.

"I just hope no one in town other than RJ actually met my

mother. She looks a lot like me, and I don't need my mother's sudden appearance to put me on the outs even more."

Val patted her on the back. "We're on the outs as much as you can get. We'll stick with you."

Jemma could have argued Easter and Val were more in with the residents of Solomon's Cross than she or Mama B was. She mustered a smile for them anyway. "Thanks, guys. But what now?"

Easter and Val shared a look as if they also shared the same idea. "What is it?" Jemma prodded.

Val grinned, but Easter remained solemn. "Well, we could always go out to the Old Farm."

"It'd be an adventure, that's for sure," Val stated.

Easter looked less than comfortable. She rubbed her shoulders as a chilly night wind coursed through the main street. "Well, we used to go all the time when we were friends with AJ. Ya know, as kids growin' up and stuff, but we've only gone once since May Kilmer died and, well…"

She hesitated, so Val finished for her. "The Old Farm gives E the spooks, and I don't blame her. It's got a different kind of presence out there now."

"A magical one?" Jemma asked.

"Yes and no," Easter answered. "Yes, because everything in this place has a magical presence to it. The ground is, like, soaked in it. But no, because Val senses it too."

"Yeah, and I'm not all high and witchy like you two are," he stated with a chuckle.

"You guys really think we should go?" Jemma asked.

Easter shrugged. "It may be worth a try. I don't wanna go now, though. Not while it's dark."

Jemma checked her watch. "I can't go now, either. My dad won't be too happy if I'm out late, especially if it's because we went to the Kilmers."

"Tomorrow, then?" Val asked. "We could go after work at Gran's Rest."

This was agreed upon. "I'm gonna bring our rifle and a few extra rounds just in case," Val said as he dropped Jemma off. "And if you've still got that bat Mama B ensorcelled, that'd be great."

Jemma grinned. "I think you just want to hit someone over the head with it again."

Val shrugged. "I might. I might not."

The following day was Friday, and the three teens decided it would be best not to tell anyone exactly where they were planning to go. Their plans were disrupted. Mama B wanted more help from Easter and Val with repairs inside the bed and breakfast, and Tad insisted Jemma go with him into town to pick up supplies for the big day.

"Honestly, I forgot all about it," Jemma said with a sigh when she called Easter to tell her the news.

"Forgot about what?"

"My birthday."

Easter squealed with delight. "Eee! Wait, when is it?" Jemma confessed that it was on Sunday, and her father had planned had a little party for them at Gran's Rest the following day.

"I hate you, Jemma Nox, you know that? I hate that you waited this long to tell me," Easter said.

"I'm sorry. If you can't make it…"

Easter laughed. "No, I hate you because I have no time to buy you a present." The McCarthys agreed to be at Gran's Rest the following day for festivities.

"You know, now that I'm thinking about it, this might be good," Jemma mused before they hung up.

"How so?" Easter asked.

"AJ might not have given up stalking me just yet. If we tell enough people in town that it's my birthday tomorrow, he might come up to see what's going on."

"I don't think getting stalked on your birthday is the best gift, but it might work. He did come to my play to keep you in sight, after all." So, yet another plan was set. Easter would make mention of Jemma's birthday while she went shopping in town for a present. If AJ didn't show up to Gran's Rest, they would assume he had given up. *Or something worse happened,* Jemma thought with a shiver.

Saturday morning was almost joyous enough to make Jemma forget all the unfortunate events of the past week. She awoke to a row of five pancakes, each with a letter of her name cut out. "Ta-da! Been working on them all morning!" Tad announced when she walked into the kitchen, still rubbing sleep from her eyes. Jemma laughed and sat to wolf the pancakes down. All the while, Tad hummed *happy birthday* to himself. She knew she'd be sick of the song by the end of the day.

"I know there will be gifts up at Gran's Rest later, but I wanted to give you mine first," Tad told her before they prepared to leave. He beamed as he handed her a box. From the way it was wrapped, Jemma knew he had not done it. He blushed. "Linnea helped me."

Jemma grinned. "Pick it out or wrap it?"

Her father shrugged. "A little of both. Now, I know this isn't normally your kind of thing, but I thought that since you're growing up and everything, it might be nice to have something a grown woman would have."

More eager than ever, Jemma unwrapped it and slid off the top of the box. Peering inside, she glimpsed a silver chain with an oval charm attached. Drawing it out into the light, she saw the letter J carved into it. At first, she didn't think the necklace was original, but then Tad told her to turn it over. Doing so, she saw something else on the back. A date was inscribed. Jemma looked up at her father, confused.

"It's the day we moved here, Jem. I figure that since coming here was a fresh start for both of us, this might be a good reminder. No matter where we end up going in life." He smiled as he said these words.

The date inscribed on the back made the necklace much better.

Tad blushed again. "Though I will say I used the idea first for Linnea. I got her a necklace with an L and the date we met on the back. She thought you might like on like it."

"I love it," Jemma told him, and she meant it. She slipped it around her neck. She seldom wore jewelry. Most of hers had been frivolous gifts from her mother, and she wanted nothing to do with them.

Tad clapped his hands. "All right, let's go get this party started!"

Jemma felt dismal as they rode up the mountain. She had expected her mother to text or call, wishing her a happy birthday and was disappointed that it hadn't happened. She also hoped Annie would stay out of her life. *I don't need her to have a good day,* Jemma thought.

The rest of the day passed in a globe of golden warmth. The sun shone, and Easter had helped Mama B set up a picnic on the slope behind the bed and breakfast. Mama B had made all her best recipes. Val and Linnea were also present, and Jemma received presents from everyone. Easter gave her a new, leather-bound journal, and Val had purchased an ivory-handled pen to go with it.

"With all the journal reading you've been doing," Easter told her with a smile, "we figured you should have one of your own."

Jemma smiled back. "It's perfect."

From Linnea, she received a new pair of shoes and a keychain. "For when you start to drive." She winked. "I'd be happy to teach you if your father is too busy."

"I'm not too busy," Tad protested, "just not fond of the idea of my daughter driving around on roads like these—"

It was Val who objected to his argument. "If you're going to keep her here forever, she's gonna have to learn sometime. Nobody wants to ride an old, rusty bike all the time."

Jemma grinned at her friend. "My bike is less rusty than your truck."

Laughter ensued until Mama B presented Jemma with her gift: a wooden case full of jars. "All the herbs and ingredients you need for your own spell casting, dear. At least for a time." Everything Jemma would have needed was separated into small jars. It was clear Mama B had spent a lot of time preparing it.

"Thank you," Jemma breathed as she stood to hug the old woman.

"We have one more gift," Easter announced. "Val and I were able to convince Mama B to make only *one* online purchase a week, so you don't have to sort through packages every time you come into work."

Jemma's brows rose. "Wow, you must have had to do a lot of convincing."

Val rolled his eyes. "Don't even get me started."

Mama B sniffed. "I don't see why it was ever a big issue in the first place—"

Seeing an argument would soon ensue if it wasn't stopped, Tad clapped his hands and suggested cake. The group sang to Jemma as the sun went down, leaving the hillside bathed in pinks and oranges. As the festivities came to their conclusion, she found her heart overflowing with joy. Even in the midst of trials and tribulations, she could just be a teenager.

The adults went inside to begin cleaning up. "Look, there's one more gift you forgot to open," Val stated after they'd eaten cake. He had found it on the table with all the food. He tossed Jemma a small package.

"Who's it from?" she asked.

Everyone shrugged. "No one here, it looks like," Easter remarked, her brows furrowing.

Jemma unfolded the newspaper wrapping and found nothing

inside. "Is this a joke?" Then, she realized something was written on it in bright red marker. The writing was hurried.

I know what you are doing. Stay away from me. I won't follow you, and you won't follow me.

Seeing Jemma's worried expression, Easter and Val crowded around. Easter gasped. "Do you think—"

Jemma nodded. It wasn't signed, and she had never seen AJ's handwriting before, but she knew it was his. "I won't follow you, and you won't follow me," she repeated.

"I guess he's done stalking you?" Val queried.

"That would be nice," Jemma answered. "But..." She looked around to make sure no one was listening. Jemma was glad her father wasn't out here to learn AJ had been following her around.

"But we really need to go out to the Old Farm," she finished. "Tomorrow if we can."

Val and Easter nodded. Val spoke. "We'll tell our parents we're having dinner at Harv's since we missed Friday night."

Jemma agreed that would help. They had decided they wouldn't be allowed to go if they told anyone. "I'll leave a note for Mama B in her office in case anything goes wrong while we're gone," Easter suggested. She pulled Jemma up and hugged her. "But let's not worry about it until tomorrow. It's still your birthday, Jem."

CHAPTER SIXTEEN

Jemma didn't know what to expect from the Old Farm belonging to the Kilmers, but it certainly wasn't this. From how RJ had run his store and the careful perfection with which AJ had kept his sports car, she had not expected to find it so disorderly. Ramshackle was the word she would have used. Easter called it a mess. It hadn't been like this before.

Val took on a more personal approach. "Turned this place into a steaming pile of shit." No doubt coming back here had brought up fond memories of his childhood with AJ that he did not wish to remember.

After work that day, around four o'clock, the three friends piled into Val's truck and took the forty-five-minute drive through Solomon's Cross and past Cider Creek and the adjoining town before reaching farmland that stretched for miles between the mountains. It was a warm day. The late afternoon light made the road shimmer like gold and the ponds dotting the fields look like silver. All around them, life buzzed. Birds, insects, and smaller animals darted to and fro. It would have been a pleasant ride if it weren't for the troubles occupying Jemma's mind.

What would they find at the Old Farm? She almost expected

the worst. A strange feeling stirred in her gut. She didn't know what they would find, but the magic within her seemed to. They knew they had arrived when they saw a dented, red mailbox on the side of the road with the name "Kilmer" imprinted on it alongside the address number. The "m" in Kilmer had fallen sideways and was hanging off the mailbox, barely seeming to stay on. This was only the first sign of disorder. The second was the fact that they couldn't even see the house from the road.

So many weeds had grown in front of the house, blocking it from view. Vines crawled over the narrow walkway. Val frowned as he pulled the truck into the field beside the house. They decided they didn't want to pull into the drive and alert anyone who may have been home. It would be best to approach the house quietly and scan it for danger, then see if anyone was home.

"It never looked like this before," Val murmured. "Place has turned into a shit hole."

Although Easter didn't feel as strongly as Val did, she nodded in agreement. "RJ always took good care of his land. He was the kind of guy who mowed every Saturday. They used to have a nice garden, too."

"Mrs. Kilmer did the gardening," Val explained. "I guess this started when she died."

Jemma presumed the disorder on the Old Farm had gotten worse in recent weeks. They hopped out of the truck and trudged through the tall grass to a low stone wall on the edge of the yard. They stood behind it and peered over. Val had his family's rifle strapped over his back concealed beneath his jacket. He also held the bat belonging to Jemma's father that Mama B had inscribed with sigils, making it more powerful than an ordinary piece of wood. Easter was prepared to transform, and Jemma clutched her satchel in case she needed to pull the nettle out.

From the stone wall, they got a good view of the house. It was a large, sprawling home, not because of its grandiose design but because generation after generation had expanded and added on to it. An extensive screened porch surrounded the building. The three-car garage appeared to have rooms over it.

The yard, house, and garage were surrounded by trees. Beyond the house, there were more trees, then the cleared acres of the Old Farm. The field had gone fallow, though its borders, unlike the yard, had been maintained. A nearby barn was also in good order, though it was in need of a fresh coat of paint.

The place perplexed Jemma. It looked dearly loved and taken care of but also disorderly and abandoned at the same time. The only sound they heard was the creaking of some door. She assumed one of the barn doors had been left open. No voices or sounds of movement. Not even of animals. No sound of cars being worked on. All of the sounds which might have been expected on the Old Farm were not present. It was too quiet.

Maybe the Kilmers weren't home, but they also weren't in Solomon's Cross. Where were they? "Do the Kilmers own any other land?" Jemma asked in a low voice.

Easter shook her head. "Not that we know of. If they do, it's a well-kept secret."

Well-kept secrets were the name of the game in Solomon's Cross. Jemma had learned to expect anything.

"Well," Val decided, "let's check the house." He scrambled over the wall but remained quiet as he neared the side door of the house. Jemma and Easter followed, the former with her hand inside her satchel.

"Just in case," she breathed.

Once they reached the door, they found it hanging open, the top hinge broken. "Mr. Kilmer?" Val called in. No one answered. Not a sound besides the wind. Val held the baseball bat behind his back, but he gripped it tight as he made his way into the house. Once again, the girls followed.

What they found inside reflected the disorder of the yard. The kitchen looked like it hadn't been cleaned in weeks. Dirty dishes were piled in the sink. The sink was running and almost overflowing with water. Easter turned it off. Someone had been here recently. Why had they left the water running?

"AJ?" Val called this time. None of them expected the answer. A low whining sound reached them from behind a small door. Val opened it carefully to reveal a pantry, the contents of which were all overturned. They looked down to find what had made the whining sound. A dog lay on the floor. He lifted his head and looked hesitantly at the newcomers.

Val bent down. "Hey there, Benji. It's your old pal Val." They had known this dog when they came here years ago. After a moment of sniffing, the dog came to Val and eagerly accepted petting and praising. Easter bent down to give him attention too.

"Where's everybody?" she asked the dog. After a moment, Jemma realized Easter was using her beast-tongue abilities to communicate with the animal.

"Anything?" Jemma asked as her heart pounded.

Easter's brows furrowed. "He's hungry. That's all he knows."

Jemma found an almost empty bag of kibble and a dirty dog bowl. She cleaned it before pouring the rest of the food in for him. The speed at which he ate told the trio that he had not been fed for a couple of days at least. "What the hell is going on?" Jemma muttered.

Just then, a door slamming shut made all three jolt out of their skins. The door sounded like it had come from the garage. AJ Kilmer smiled in the kitchen doorway. "Howdy, folks. I was wonderin' when you'd come around."

At first, Jemma expected a sinister look from the young man or, at the very least, a displeased expression. There were no glares from AJ Kilmer. In fact, he seemed pleased.

And very much unlike himself, Jemma thought, feeling uneasy.

He walked farther into his house, and Val backed up to hide the bat from view. Benji whined when AJ bent down to pet him. *He knows he's been neglected,* Jemma realized.

She remembered the note she presumed AJ had written for her birthday. Had he forgotten, or had she been wrong about it being from him? He straightened and smiled at each of them. "Anybody hungry?"

None of them were, but AJ didn't seem to notice their silence. He ambled through the kitchen, collecting ingredients to make himself a sandwich. His voice and expression seemed detached, Jemma noticed with keen but wary interest. When he finished making his sandwich, they followed him into an adjoining dining room. From there, Jemma could see into the living room and a staircase leading to the second floor.

Everything was cleaner in this part of the house, though it still appeared abandoned. "Hey, AJ, is your dad here? People in town are startin' to get worried since they haven't seen him at the shop." Easter attempted to sound cheerful, but the worry in her tone came through.

AJ shrugged. "How should I know?"

"Have you heard from him?" Jemma pressed.

"I hear lots of things," AJ replied in a wistful tone.

Easter, Val, and Jemma exchanged looks. What now? Jemma almost wished angry stalker AJ was back. This version of him was a lot scarier. AJ, normally lean in body, had shriveled into a gaunter frame. None of this—the house, his weakening body, or the absence of his father—seemed to bother him in the least.

AJ finished eating his sandwich and wiped off his mouth with the back of his hand. "Oh, wait. I remember." He stared out the window for a long time, seeming to have forgotten he said anything.

Gently, Easter approached him. "Yes? What is it?"

AJ turned back. "Oh." He laughed. "I forgot. My father is here. Follow me!" Jemma's heart pounded faster. The longer they stayed here, the stranger it got. She wondered if she were stuck in some weird nightmare. AJ escorted them into an adjoining sunroom where there was a little breakfast nook with a big bay window that overlooked the back of the Old Farm. Sitting in the nook was RJ. He had a cup of coffee clasped between his two large hands, but he wasn't drinking it. He just stared into it with the same dazed expression he'd had in Annie's hotel room.

Whatever she had done to him, it hadn't gone away.

"Hey, Mr. Kilmer," Easter tried in her gentlest voice.

He didn't look up.

Jemma turned to AJ. "Was he like this before... You know, before my mom." Just thinking about it again made her skin crawl.

AJ didn't seem to mind. He shook his head. "He's been this way for a little while, and he won't snap out of it." A disappointed tone came into AJ's voice.

"I'm sorry," Jemma told him. "I really am. If I'd just believed my mother was still a lying bitch, this wouldn't have happened." Deep down, she knew Annie had been at work on RJ before she'd involved Jemma.

AJ turned to her, his gaze still detached as he asked, "Are you apologizing because your mother did it or because you had a part in it? Like what you did to me?"

Jemma realized she owed AJ an explanation despite his stalking. *Maybe that wasn't all his fault either, like all the shit he did when the haint was hanging around him,* she thought. Her heart filled with pity for him.

"No..." she started, but AJ shook his head. A hard look came into his face. Everyone, except maybe for RJ, felt the tension ratchet up.

Val stepped forward, prepared to defend Jemma. Jemma put a hand out to him Val and gave AJ her sincerest look. "I am sorry for what my mother did and for what I did, but I want to help you and your father. That's why we're here. To help."

She half-expected him to refuse in anger, but much to everyone's surprise, AJ just nodded. "I appreciate it." A small, crooked smile lifted his lips. "Maybe I do believe you. I know things between us have been really fucked up." He shrugged. "But I've learned from it, and I don't regret nothin' about it because it's helped me out, you know? Thanks to you, Jemma, I've reconnected with my momma."

At first, Jemma couldn't believe what she was hearing. At the mention of his momma, the trio of friends all became alarmed. Jemma wished they could get the hell out of here as soon as possible. Screw help. She wanted to save her skin. Something, however, kept her rooted to the spot.

It was the fond look in AJ's eyes and the soft way he spoke. He went on, "It's a blessin', ya know? Me and my momma are gonna make everything right. Just wait and see. Hear that, Dad?" He glanced at RJ with a knowing smile.

Jemma knew something was very wrong. Whatever magical thing had taken hold of him had convinced him that his mother was alive, or at least not dead.

What if this momma AJ's talking about isn't his real mother? Jemma wondered. The thought came at the same time as a warm, tugging feeling deep in her gut. It was something her magic knew and told her mind. Jemma somehow kept her voice from trembling as she asked, "AJ, can you tell us more about your momma? How'd you see her again?"

AJ smiled. "I can show you instead." Before anyone could react, AJ walked out of the house and into the side yard. Everyone, including the dog, followed him as he made his way to the barn at the back of the property.

At first, the interior of the barn looked like any other. There were no animals, but there were plenty of tools. A mower sat on one side, and something big covered in a tarp sat on the other. Jemma assumed it was a vehicle.

The longer she stood in the entrance and soaked in the details, however, the more aware she became of the strangeness in the barn. In the center, a circle had been drawn with chalk. It was faded, but it gave Jemma a bad feeling. It looked like a ritual had taken place here. What the hell was this, a debased magical laboratory? It felt like magic—the wrong kind.

Something abnormal was stagnating in the vats, and the smell of blood was in the air. There were scribbles and scrawls carved into some of the surfaces—walls, floors, even machinery and doors. Squinting in the dim light, Jemma realized she recognized some of them. The cramped writing was all too familiar. A shock shot through her, and she froze to the spot. *Vesna Soucek's handwriting!*

Why the hell was Vesna's handwriting on the walls of the Kilmers' barn? Her heart pounded erratically. All she wanted to do was bolt. That wouldn't be easy, though. As she was examining the markings, AJ stepped to the doors and slid them shut with a shuddering creak that filled the whole place. Jemma jumped and spun toward him. Val and Easter looked on with suspicion.

"AJ," Val started in a warning tone. His hand tightened around the bat. Jemma reached for her satchel.

A crooked smile grew on AJ's face as he held up a match in one hand and the matchbox in the other. A rasping whisper filled the air beside AJ, but it wasn't him. Gradually, a figure appeared. Jemma's skin crawled. *Run, run, run!* was the thought racing through her mind, but she couldn't move. She could hardly breathe as the figure came into full view. It was a hunched, filthy, ragged, skeletal figure of a woman, and she was the one whispering.

She lifted her head and strings of black hair fell away from her face. Jemma wanted to deny it, but she knew that face. Only from photos in an old album she had discovered in her house, but still...

Vesna.

How?

Mama B said she died!

AJ nodded at the woman. "Yes, Momma. Sorry, guys." He

seemed almost regretful as he struck another match. Jemma screamed, but it was too late. He tossed it onto a pile of oily hay. It caught in an instant, and a blaze filled her view. He turned to the closed entrance, and a cross bar fell across the doors.

They were trapped, and the barn was going up in flames.

CHAPTER SEVENTEEN

Val ripped off his jacket and threw it on the fire, but it was too late. Since the fire had started on a stack of oily hay, it could not be put out easily. It got too big fast. Everything inside this damn barn was flammable. Jemma glimpsed Easter bending to the floor to pick up something, but Jemma couldn't tell what it was. Whatever it was, Easter was determined to rescue it from the spreading flames.

Crackling filled the air. It got unbearably hot. Sweat slicked Jemma's body. She was struck with such shock she could not move. They had to get out, but how? The door was sealed, and Jemma saw no other exit. They would have to make one by sheer force.

AJ stood by the barred door, which was further blocked by the fire that had sprung up between them. Smoke rose, stinging Jemma's eyes and filling her lungs. It blocked AJ and the woman standing next to him from her view. She could no longer see the McCarthys, only hear their sputtering coughs. A *thud* sounded. An alarmed cry rang out. *Easter!* Had she fallen or collided with something?

Jemma's heart pounded faster. Fear had her in an iron grip. For a fleeting moment, she thought about her father and Mama B and the shock and despair that would come over them when they learned she was...

No, she determined. *I'm not going to die just because AJ's gone fucking insane!* She would escape out of pure spite. They would find a way out. Even as she thought this, despair filled her.

The flames had swept up one side of the barn. Hay in the loft above sizzled. "Move!" Jemma screamed, sensing what was about to happen. She dove to a part of the barn that had not yet caught flame and slammed into Easter. They sprawled, wincing as they hit the hard floorboards. Seconds later, the loft above them crashed down. It missed them by inches and sent debris into the air.

At first, the fallen hay and wood put out the fire, but the flames were not smothered for long. It erupted anew, filling the barn with heat and light.

It was hard to breathe. Jemma thought that if she didn't die by the fire, she would die by suffocation. "Come on," Easter choked out, hauling Jemma to her feet. Where was Val? She heard coughing that sounded like his, but she couldn't see him.

She was distracted from her search for him when a great crashing sound came from the other end of the barn. Shards of metal and glass came flying toward them, some of them on fire. Jemma screamed and pulled Easter down. They landed hard once more, this time in an effort to evade becoming collateral damage to an...

Explosion? Jemma wondered. It had sounded like one. Some of the arcane laboratory equipment had exploded, it seemed, though she wasn't sure what it was or what, exactly, had caused it. There was all kinds of weird shit in here. The explosion sent up thicker, darker smoke. As it filled Jemma's vision, she could hardly see anything else. All she could feel was the pressing heat and Easter's hand gripping her own.

"Val!" she rasped, then attempted to cover her mouth and nose. He did not answer. Where the hell was he? Jemma felt panic at the thought of him lying elsewhere in the barn, unconscious or pinned beneath something from the explosion. He hadn't yet burned, for they had not heard his screams. They needed to get together and find a way out of here.

Jemma glanced at Easter. Her face was ashen, and her lips quivered as tears gathered in her eyes. Jemma squeezed her hand, a silent command to stay with her, to keep fighting. Then, through the smoke, she glimpsed a flashing blue light. The ensorcelled bat! With the markings Mama B had put into it, it glowed blue, and could do much more damage than any regular old bat. The light appeared again. Val was swinging it. At what? The following sound told Jemma. The crash of the bat against the weakened barn wall filled the air.

"Come on!" Jemma cried to Easter. Between them and where Val stood at the wall was the pile of hay AJ had set on fire. The hay was almost gone, and many of the floorboards had caught fire. They could not run across the barn without becoming engulfed in flames.

Jemma remembered when she had participated on the track team for one semester in ninth grade. She had quit because she hated running, but right now, what she had learned was going to become very useful. Yanking Easter with her, she took a running leap. She was in the air for half a second, Easter with her, and the fire was below them. She crashed down a second later, safely beyond the flames. She rolled, wincing as she put out a flame with her jacket. It burned through her clothes to her skin, but it hadn't covered her whole body.

She hurried to her feet so she could clear the area before the fire swept to this part of the barn. Easter groaned in pain.

Coughing, Jemma staggered over to her. "Easter," she choked out as she reached down to pull her up.

Easter let out an agonized scream as Jemma touched her arm.

Jemma also cried out because Easter's right forearm was puffy and blistering. Burned. She pulled Easter up by supporting her under the arms. "Come on. We have to get out of here," she told her friend. She didn't know if Easter heard her.

Val continued bashing the wall. A crack followed. Soon he would have a large enough opening.

A cackling laugh sounded behind them. Jemma whirled, but she couldn't see Vesna or AJ. For a split second, she considered going back, finding AJ, and pulling him out with them, but he had set the barn on fire. He was more trouble to them than ever before.

With one more loud cry, Val swung the bat into the wall, and a large enough opening for them to stagger out appeared. Easter went first, still coughing. Val pushed Jemma through and followed last. All three had to tear past sharp shards of wood to get out. They stumbled into the yard, choking up smoke and trying to clear the area as fast as they could.

While they had been inside, night had crept in. The sun was down, and the barn blazed against the dark sky. The cool night air filled Jemma's lungs and soothed her skin. It was little comfort, however, given what stood behind them.

Jemma staggered back, her eyes stinging a little less now so she could take in the full, harrowing sight of the barn on fire. The whole thing was engulfed in flames by now. The wood turned black, and angry red flames danced around the building like ferocious spirits summoned to end them. She whirled, searching for the others. Val and Easter still stood behind her, but AJ and Vesna...

Was it her spirit they had seen? Something else?

Whatever it was, she and AJ were nowhere to be seen. Had he gotten out, or was he going to die in the fire?

"We need to get the hell out of here!" Val shouted, his voice shaking. He pointed beyond the house. Across the street was another farm. Its occupants would, no doubt, see the smoke and call the nearest fire department. At once, Jemma knew why Val demanded they leave. If they lingered any longer, they would be suspected first. The barn blazed, and no one was there to say they had been invited onto the property.

The complex nature of their relationship with the Kilmers was the talk of the town now, too. It wasn't going to help matters. The three of them scrambled over fallen debris in the yard. Reaching the house, Val sprinted ahead to get over the wall and to the truck. Easter was a little farther behind, tears streaming down her face as she clutched at her burned arm. Jemma was just behind the house where the bay window overlooked the back portion of the farm. She skidded to a halt. RJ still sat inside, staring into nothing. A pang of guilt filled her chest. "Fuck you, AJ. Fuck you for doing this."

She didn't know how much of this was his fault. Had he found out about Vesna Soucek from town resources and found a way to bring her back? Or had Vesna come back herself and found AJ, a likely candidate for whatever trouble and tragedy she wanted to brew in Kalhoun County?

"Jemma!" Val shouted after her. He had just helped Easter over the wall. Jemma took off at a run, following them to the truck. They scrambled inside. Val searched for the key. "I lost it!" His voice was panicked. "Fuck, fuck, fuck!"

"You must have dropped it somewhere!" Jemma's voice held equal panic. They didn't have much time. She just hoped the key hadn't fallen inside the barn. Val rushed back to the yard to search for it. The wails of sirens reached them. "Val, hurry!" Jemma screamed.

He returned seconds later, waving his hand. He had found the key in the grass between the barn and the house. The sirens grew closer. Val could hardly put the key in the ignition, he was shaking so hard. The truck sputtered to life seconds later.

"Don't go out on the road!" Easter told him. "They'll see us and think we were just here."

She was right, so Val veered toward the woods at the back of the farm. He hoped the fire department would not check the adjoining field and see tire marks. By the woods, there was a smaller road. He pulled onto it and drove at an alarming speed away from the farm. Eventually, this unpaved road would lead out to the highway they had taken to get here.

Val pulled to a stop a couple of miles from the farm. The sounds of sirens could still be heard, but they were farther away now. A whimpering sound directed Jemma's attention to Easter. With tears still in her eyes, Easter pulled back her arm. Several welts had formed. Her right arm was burned from her wrist to her elbow.

"We need ice," Val murmured, shock still in his voice. All three sat, stunned, trying to process what had just happened and the fact that they were still alive and hadn't been caught. *Yet*, Jemma thought. Plenty of evidence of them being there was left behind, including tire marks in the side yard and…

"Val, where is the bat?"

Val swallowed hard, his eyes almost bulging out of his head. "I-I dunno. Dropped it."

Jemma waved the subject away. It would do no good to worry about it. If the fire department found it, fine. The magic wouldn't reveal itself unless someone tried to use it. Jemma hoped no one would give the bat a second glance.

She reached into her satchel and pulled out herbs used for soothing burns. It was a concoction of aloe, garlic, and a red seed. Easter winced as Jemma applied the rub. "We'll get ice on it as soon as we get back."

Val started the truck again. A *ding* on Jemma's phone alerted her to a text message from her father.

Was just in town. Didn't see you. Everything good?

She had told him they were eating at Harv's, which had been

their plan for after investigating at the Kilmers. Jemma looked down at her clothes. There were burn marks and she was covered in dirt, dust, and ash. Easter and Val didn't look any better. There was no way in hell they could stop in town now without being accused of committing arson.

"Shit," Jemma muttered as her fingers hovered over the keyboard. Lie to him so he wouldn't worry or tell him they had just escaped a fire started by a legitimately crazy person and the spirit of a woman who'd died decades ago?

Yeah, heading to Gran's Rest. I'll be home after.

She knew that as soon as her father saw her, he would know something had gone wrong.

Her answer was truthful enough. They had to go to Gran's Rest. Jemma's voice was tight when she told her friends, "We have to tell Mama B who we saw. We have to tell her Vesna isn't gone like we all thought she was." She swallowed hard, imagining the old woman's reaction.

The three drove to Gran's Rest in silence. When they arrived, Mama B was in the kitchen, brewing something up in a pot on the stove that didn't smell like food. In fact, it smelled very bad. The three came in through the back door in case there were any guests still in the front of the bed and breakfast.

Mama B turned, her brows pulled together, showing worry on her face. "What in stinkin' hell have the three of ya gotten up to this time? I swear you'll make all of my hairs turn gray—" The very gray-haired woman stopped short as she took in the sight of the trio, covered in dirt and ash and wearing singed clothes. "Oh, you poor dear," she murmured when she saw Easter's burned arm. Jemma and Val also had burns, but they were minor and didn't need immediate attention. Mama B tutted as she had them sit down. "I had a feelin' I should make a brew with everythin' good for burns in it. Couldn't figure why, just had a feelin', and as always, it was right."

All three remained silent as she applied the brew—a thick green paste that smelled heavily of garlic and aloe—to Easter's arm. She also selected an ice pack from the freezer. Then Mama B prepared tea for all of them.

"Now, tell me what's happened. You look like you've seen a ghost."

Jemma gulped. "W-we might have." The heaviness of what all had occurred finally hit her. The adrenaline had worn away, leaving her exhausted. Val, who was a little less stunned by the appearance of Vesna since he had not read her journals, explained what had transpired.

Mama B listened in keen interest. When Val reached the part about Vesna, he stated, "And there were weird drawings and writings all over the inside of the barn, and AJ lit a match, and that's when we saw her. A skeletal, scary-looking woman…thing beside him. He called her Momma, and she told him to light the fire." If Jemma hadn't been there herself, she would have thought Val was describing some freakish nightmare he had had.

Jemma wished she was a little girl again, waking from a bad dream and crawling into her father's arms. She was older now, though, and the nightmares were a lot more real.

At the mention of the woman, Mama B's frown deepened. Her voice shook as she asked, "Did this woman, or whatever she was, say what her name was?"

Jemma's hand shook around the teacup Mama B had given her. "No. She didn't have to." She locked eyes with the old holler witch. "It was Vesna. I swear it on my life."

Mama B shook her head. "It can't be. Vesna died. I saw her body. Went to the funeral and everything. She was as dead as anything."

"Well," Easter croaked out, "she found a way to come back."

Jemma had not seen true fear in Mama B's face until now. She had seen regret, yes, disappointment, and even anger. But never fear like this. She could see it in Mama B's eyes as the old woman weighed the gravity of what this portended. A shuddering sigh escaped her lips a moment later. "If what you say is true, then something much worse than a barn fire is in the making." Mama B stared into her own teacup as if the dregs at the bottom could give her answers. "If it were up to Vesna Soucek, she'd burn down the whole of Kalhoun County."

How could Vesna, whose own children had died in a fire and who had lost her mind as a result of that tragedy, be the one who had led AJ to commit arson. It took everything in Jemma not to shudder at the irony. If anything, this Vesna controlling AJ was not the same woman who had wept while writing of her children's deaths.

Finally, Mama B looked up, staring longer into Jemma and Easter's faces than she did at Val. "You girls are going to have to put everything you know to work. If a crazed witch the likes of Vesna has found a way to come back, or worse, faked her own death – body and everything – then this is more than some petty vengeance." She looked into her cup once more. "Though that would have been enough."

"You think some bigger plan is in the works?" Easter asked.

Mama B nodded. Jemma felt like her throat might close up. Haints had been difficult enough to deal with. But a witch coming back from the dead? Or one who had never died at all but made it seem so?

"If only you could have read what was written on those barn walls before it was destroyed," Mama B lamented. "If you had, we could have some clue as to what she is planning."

"I might be able to help with that," came Easter's voice. All eyes turned to her. "The walls weren't the only thing she had written on. There were papers too. I just didn't see them until the fire started."

Val sighed. "Doesn't help too much now, does it? Everything

in that damn barn is gone. At least the fire department won't find—"

He stopped short as Easter pulled something out of her jacket pockets. She laid scraps of paper, burned at the corners and wrinkled from being in her pockets, on the table. Jemma gasped as she stood. "Easter McCarthy, I think you just saved our asses."

CHAPTER EIGHTEEN

All of them stared at the scraps of paper.

Some were too torn or burned to be legible. Nonetheless, they tried to make out what they said. "How the hell are we supposed to know what an old, possibly dead witch's writing says?" exclaimed Val. "I mean, just look at it! Looks like a three-year-old's drawings."

Easter scowled at him. "You sound stupid, you know that? What you're looking at is the writing of someone who dealt in magic for a very long time."

Val shut his mouth. "He has a point," Jemma stated. "Vesna's writing, the longer she dealt with the dark side of the Art, became erratic and almost unreadable. Like this." She pointed to the scribbles on the scraps of paper. "Trust me; I've read her journal a couple of times." The older entries in the journal were far more legible than more recent scribblings. Recipes of herbal remedies were easily deciphered, but what Vesna wrote of her personal life was more difficult to read.

Mama B stared at the papers without saying a word. It wasn't until she let out a deep sigh that she said to them, "It's her writing, that's for certain, but I've never seen it like this. So scattered. So mad."

"Well, you shoulda seen *her*," Val muttered, the gravity of what they were looking at still lost on him. "Would've made this writing make a lot more sense."

Mama B scooted her chair up to the table. "With Jemma's knowledge of Vesna's handwriting and mine of her magic, we should be able to work it out. There's just one problem. Not all of it is written in English."

Jemma's brows rose. "What do you mean? Is there a witch language?"

"Not exactly," Mama B replied. "You remember she came from Eastern Europe?"

Jemma and Easter nodded. Val continued to frown at the scraps with his arms folded across his chest.

"Some of this is Russian, and some is Lithuanian. Now, I know a lot, but I sure as hell don't know either of those."

"Then how do you know what languages they are?" Val asked.

"Because I've seen what Vesna wrote," Mama B explained. "She switched between the three languages. I don't have to speak a language to know which one it is."

Jemma's brows furrowed. She had never seen anything but English and a few weird, scribbled codes of figures and numbers in Vesna's journals. Easter pulled out her phone. "While you two try to figure out the English part and the scribbles, I'll use Google." She grinned in an attempt to shake off the horror she'd been through in the past couple of hours. "Internet search might be the most useful magic this time."

Val grumbled something about how it didn't take a trained witch to use Google, but the girls and Mama B ignored him as they set to work. He stood by, watching as anticipation built. Jemma peered at the cramped writing, trying to distinguish between where one word ended and another began. To make this even harder, the words weren't written in a straight line across the paper but in spirals and shapes that looked like snakes. What the hell had Vesna been trying to do? Furthermore, many of the phrases were repeated. Jemma asked Mama B why this might be.

"Could be an incantation or some other ritual saying. She might have had to write something down a certain amount of times before…" She stopped short, her eyes wider than they had been before. She picked up one of the scraps and placed it with a few others so they formed one whole page. She pulled back, squinting her eyes. The swirls of words seemed to create a large shape. "Snakes," she muttered. "What the hell did she need snakes for?"

"Maybe we could count them?" Easter suggested, her eyes still darting between the papers and her phone.

Jemma counted. "Twenty-three snakes, if that's what they are. Anything about snakes in what you're reading?"

Easter shook her head. "Nothing, but there is this one word repeated over and over. It means 'ritual.' Here, see?" She slid the paper over, pointing to the word and then at her phone.

Mama B began shaking her head in disbelief.

"What is it?" Jemma asked.

But Mama B pointed at the word beside the one that meant ritual. "And what does this say, dear?"

"Hold on one sec," Easter replied as she typed it into her phone. She frowned. "It's weird. Never heard of this word. Ouroboros?"

Mama B nodded this time and sank back with a deep sigh. "Just as I thought. The Ritual of the Ouroboros, otherwise known as the summoning of a vengeful spirit in the ultimate act of spite. A witch must be in the deepest aspects of dark Art in order to attain such knowledge. The ritual has, for many hundreds of years, been buried in the ruins of old civilizations, only known to the oldest minds of our order."

Jemma and Easter shared a look. What did this mean? Val's brows furrowed in confusion. "So…" he started, "you'd have to be a really bad witch to do this, and that woman is. Okay, so what now?"

Mama B continued explaining as she pointed to the twenty-three snakes. "These words are the incantation written in snake form to represent a serpent encircling and then devouring itself. In a way, that is what Ouroboros does." She pointed at the papers Easter had been translating. "I suspect what she wrote here are instructions on how to carry it out or more about it, whereas this," she pointed at the snakes formed by cramped writing, "is the incantation."

"She had it written all over the barn's walls," Jemma added. "She wrote it so small, and there were so many that it just looked like scribbled drawings."

Easter's voice quavered as she asked, "What's the ritual do?"

"A witch calls up a haint using this magic," Mama B explained, "and has to agree to enact terrible vengeance. This makes it so the haint can have its bloody way with the witch who summoned it, thus making both witch and haint more powerful than before. The haint gains all knowledge the witch has of magic, and the witch gets to work within the bounds of a realm beyond our own. She can sink into the dark recesses of the earth and survive."

Here, Jemma recalled the darkness writhing beneath Kalhoun's Crest.

Mama B's expression remained grim. "It is the ultimate kind of vengeful magic and is only used by those who are truly willing to get revenge." She paused, shaking her head. "No matter the cost."

"This magic is very old, then?" Easter asked.

Mama B nodded. "Quite old. As old as ancient Egypt, if I was to guess. Those who practice it have been doing so for a very long time."

Jemma had to suppress a shudder. She didn't know much about magic from ancient Egyptian or anywhere beyond the realm of Kalhoun County, for that matter. "What does this say, though?" she asked, pointing once more to the words which formed the snake.

"In the beginning, there was the serpent," Mama B recited. She knew the incantation without having to read the writing but knew it would do no harm unless she had the proper magical properties, location, and, of course, access to the dark Art. "I know about it well enough though I've only seen it done once." Her words held weight as if the memory of whatever she had seen before was more than she wished to dwell on. It was in these moments that Jemma remembered how old Mama B was.

"Sounds ominous," Easter answered dryly.

"It's in reference to the world being made for the sake of death, not life," Mama B explained. "The serpent devouring its own self shows this. And so, through the summoning of the haint, Vesna will devour her own self. I am surprised she has much of herself left to devour."

Val stepped back into the conversation. "I'm confused about all this shit. I thought the two of you," he gestured at Mama B and Jemma, "bound all the haints under the mountain."

Mama B patted his arm in a patronizing manner. "Sweet boy, those are just the haints beneath the mountain trapped from before men walked this earth."

A chill darted up Jemma's spine at these words. Mama B said them as if this were common knowledge. The old woman continued. "But the blood that's flowed over these hills is more than enough to have some godawful haints lurkin' in some dark places. The top of that old mountain ain't the only place trouble can brew."

"When you talk about blood flowing in these hills, do you mean of people who have died?" Easter asked.

Mama B nodded. "All those who have died in these mountains, yes. First, those poor souls who once lived here, Indians or Native Americans or Firs People or whatever I'm supposed to use now. That's blood enough, but then you have the cruelties of the Klan, the War between the States, Prohibition days, and so on. Anyone who came bringin' greed and chaos could've gotten a haint's attention. Any one of those has spawned haints aplenty, and it'd only take one, and not even the worst of 'em, swollen by this magic to wipe out most of the life in Kalhoun County, yours truly included." She glanced up. "Ever heard of Roanoke?"

Easter's eyes widened. "You don't mean..."

"Again, this is a matter of guessin', not knowin'," Mama B continued, "but I passed by there once in the old days, and I'm more than fairly convinced the Ol' Wyrm curse was part of it."

Jemma had to pull from her memory of history reading to understand what Mama B was referring to. A lost settlement of a hundred and twenty people among another range of mountains in Virginia. Vanished. Gone, just like that. "By Wyrm curse, you mean this snake ritual?" Jemma asked.

The grave look in Mama B's eyes answered her question. Yes, and it could happen again to this town. To Solomon's Cross and everyone who lived in it. It could be happening now, evoked by Vesna's need for vengeance.

"We've got to evacuate the town," Jemma heard herself say. Before they all met the same fate as Roanoke, whatever it was that had happened.

"By telling the town what?" Val interjected. "That AJ Kilmer and a witch who should have died half a century ago are going to summon a dark spirit? Solomon's Cross is Spooky Central, but I'm not sure anyone will go that far. Ain't nobody in this town want to leave where they've always been. Some of 'em will want to stay here no matter what happens, even if they see the dark spirit themselves."

And wonder if Mama B and the rest of us had anything to do with it, Jemma thought. *We're in really deep fucking shit.*

Easter stated her thoughts. "If this is Vesna, how is she

controlling AJ?" Addressing Mama B, she added, "Didn't you seal her off from her magic before you wiped her memory?"

Mama B shrugged. "I did, and I wish I knew how she'd done it since maybe it'd help us stop her. But we can worry about that after you catch that Kilmer boy before he works the curse. Ain't no way he died in that fire. Vesna needs him now more than ever. It's mighty difficult for a witch who's supposed to be dead to find somebody else to inhabit. Stoppin' AJ is the only thing that can stop what's comin'. We'd better hope there's enough of him left in there to pull out. He's gotta figure out how to stop what's darkenin' inside his own sacrificed self."

"Sacrificed?" Jemma echoed.

"That's what the ritual entails. Somebody's sacrificed. Not carved up on an altar all bloody and such, mind you," Mama B told them, "but sacrificing their mind and memory. If he ain't stopped and saved, he won't ever be the same."

Jemma placed her head in her hands, doing little to hide her distress. "He could be hiding in one of a thousand places in these hills."

"The question is," Val said, "what does he need to do the ritual?"

Mama B had the answer. "Traitors. Three of 'em, to be exact. If Josephine was still here and she had a third, Vesna would've used me, her, and whoever that mighta been. She don't, though, because the men who tried diggin' into these hills all those years ago are dead now. AJ's got to cut the throats of three people who betrayed him to empower the ritual and the haint that takes him up on his offer of blood and death."

Jemma's mouth went dry. "Sacrifice."

Mama B nodded, her lips pressed into a thin line.

"So Vesna poured her sense of vengeance into AJ?" Easter asked. "And he has to kill three people who have betrayed him?"

Jemma felt a chill. Val said what they were all thinking. "Us?"

But Mama B shook her head. "Not the three of you. You ain't

betrayed the boy. Think of somebody who would've been close to him but decided not to once he got all caught up in this haint nonsense. The fire in the barn could've been his way of stopping you, not sacrificing you. If he thought you three were traitors, he would've slit your throats."

This wasn't a comfort to the three who bore burns from the fire.

Easter had another question. "If you have three traitors to kill, why would you need more vengeance?"

"For some," Mama B started, "there's not enough blood in all the world."

Flashes of descriptions Jemma had read in Vesna's journal of World War Two came into her mind. Blood-bathed battlefields. Cities destroyed by bombs. Broken bodies and ashen faces. Vesna had faced so much blood in her life, most of it not her fault or responsibility.

"Who the hell would AJ think is a traitor?" Val wondered aloud.

Three faces came to Jemma's mind. AJ had had friends before the town deemed him crazy. Those guys had rejected him, pushed him to the outside the way he had once done to Easter and Val. "Those guys who always shit on us at the diner. What are their names?" she asked.

"Oh, yes!" Easter exclaimed. "That's it!"

Val listed off their names. "Dougy Butcher, Clide Griswalk, and Phil Shell."

"You think they're his targets?" Jemma asked, wanting to be sure.

Both siblings nodded. "Makes sense," Val stated. "They cut AJ out right away after he went to the mental institute. Said they wanted nothin' to do with crazy people."

While none of the three Val had mentioned was nice, Jemma didn't think they deserved to be part of a ritual sacrifice in which their throats were slit. At the very least, their families, who also lived in Solomon's Cross, didn't need to go through such loss. Committing such a heinous act would only further damage AJ. He'd be going somewhere worse than the mental institute when people found out.

And if we save them, we save the rest of this town, Jemma thought. That was, if AJ hadn't lost his life in the fire. She had a feeling he hadn't. He had barred the barn doors, knowing he had a way out. The fire was to hurt or stop them, not kill himself.

Her phone dinged, jolting her from her thoughts. A text from her father showed on her screen.

Getting late. Everything good?

Far from it, Jemma wanted to tell him, and she would, but not yet. She could be honest with him, she decided, but on her own time. They had a lot of witchery to conduct that he wouldn't be too happy about. *Might have to leave Dad out of this one until we've figured more of it out,* she thought. Once again, a secret would have to be kept by her, Easter, Val, and Mama B.

And AJ Kilmer, as much as she didn't like it.

She typed a message back to her father.

Okay with you if we spend the night at Gran's Rest?

A minute later, he responded.

Sure. But let me know if you go anywhere else.

Jemma knew he was just worried after everything that had happened, and he didn't even know about the fire yet. He would soon, though. Word spread faster through town than the fire had through the barn. It was going to be a long week. Rumors would spark and spread, and all the while, Vesna would continue her magic from behind a dark curtain. That was how Jemma imagined it, anyway.

"We have to save them," Easter said, breaking through Jemma's thoughts.

"But first, rest," Mama B ordered as she stood. "I'm not sendin' the three of you out after such work without some preparin' first."

CHAPTER NINETEEN

The following morning, Jemma and the McCarthys wanted to hurry. They were frustrated by the slow pace at which Mama B prepared them. She told them she had been up all night preparing, but when they awoke and joined her in the kitchen, It wasn't clear exactly what she'd accomplished.

"Breakfast, anyone?" she asked them when they appeared. Her cheery voice gave the impression that she had forgotten everything they had talked about the night before.

Easter used her gentlest tone. "Mama B, we really have to go."

Jemma wasn't so gentle. "Like, yesterday!"

Mama B glowered at her. "Not dressed like that! You'll have the whole town talking!" She gestured to the burned clothes they were still wearing

"We'll stop by my house first. Easter, you can wear my clothes, and Val…" Jemma eyed him. "Well, my dad's clothes will be too big, but they'll have to do." Tad was a lot taller than Val, though the latter was just as lean. They didn't have time to go to Cider Creek before they went to town to begin their search.

Mama B insisted on giving them breakfast to go, at least. She also handed Jemma her satchel, which she didn't know had been taken from her before bed. It was fuller than it had been the night before. "All loaded up for you, dear," Mama B told her. "You will find some new concoctions inside that might come in handy." She didn't give Jemma a moment to ask what those might be. "And one more thing."

She scuttled over to the corner and picked up a baseball bat, which she handed to Val. Surprise came over his face. "How'd you get it back?"

"It's not the same bat, silly," she told him with a frown. "You lost the other one, didn't you? Well, I found this one in the basement, and I ensorcelled it just as I did the other one." She grumbled something else under her breath. "Took me all night!"

"B-but," Val sputtered, "if you had this the whole time, why did we need the other one?"

Mama B looked at him as if he were missing the point. "It wasn't there the whole time. One thing you have to understand, young man, is that sometimes things turn up when you need them. Otherwise, they clutter up the place!"

At this, all three of Mama B's employees exchanged significant glances. Mama B was the queen of clutter. The cardboard boxes from her online orders took up a lot of space. She had been doing better in past weeks thanks to the admonishment of her younger peers, but it came as no surprise to any of them that she had found a spare bat in her cellar.

"We're wasting time," Jemma groaned. Everyone else agreed, and the trio piled into Val's truck. As it sputtered to life, Jemma texted her father.

Easter, Val, and I will be running errands for Gran's Rest today.

It wasn't a lie. *More like we'll be saving this whole damn town today. If we're lucky,* she thought. Knowing her father would not be home, they stopped by her house to pick up fresh clothes. She hoped Tad had not caught wind of what had happened the day before, but she was certain that word of the fire had spread around town very quickly.

When they arrived in town, she discovered she was right. The streets were busier than ever, and clusters of people had gathered outside buildings to discuss recent events. This wasn't normal. Usually, gossip was spread in Harv's Diner or the hardware store. But today, it seemed the residents of Solomon's Cross couldn't wait to be inside before they began discussing recent events.

"Let's split up. Cover more ground," Val suggested. They agreed Val would go to RJ's hardware, Jemma to the drugstore, and Easter to the diner. If nothing turned up, they would try other places.

As soon as Jemma walked into the drugstore, she saw Linnea behind the counter with a line of customers waiting for her. She decided to take a quick glance through the store to see if any of the boys were there. She considered whether she should wait to talk to Linnea, but she was distracted when, from around the corner on a shelf, she heard two older women talking to one another.

"Heard about the fire, have ya? Well, I heard 'bout it last night. Soon as it happened! Richard came home and told me the Bensons saw it from their farm across the street. And on top of that, my grandson works for the fire department, you know."

"Oh yes. Heard RJ had a psychotic break. Was wonderin' when it would happen after all he's been through." Jemma glanced at them and saw the second woman shake her head. "First his wife dies, then his daughters desert him." She lowered her voice, and Jemma had to listen harder to hear what she said next. "And now AJ has gone missing. You know what I think?"

"What's that?" the other woman asked, her voice shrill despite trying to keep it low.

"Those McCarthy kids and their new friend from out of town have been hangin' around Anthony as of late."

Jemma stiffened. After nine months of living here, some people still thought of her as the girl from somewhere else. She supposed no amount of time would make the older folks in town consider her anything but a pesky teenage outsider. *Well, you're peskier,* she thought. Here they were, standing in the middle of the aisle, blocking other people from the heartburn gummies while talking nonsense about people they barely knew.

Another voice joined the women. This one belonged to an older man who had just approached them and seemed to know both of them well. He wasn't looking to shop but to join the gossip. It was infectious. Everybody in town couldn't seem to get enough of it.

"Yeah, and those kids hang around with that old witch on the mountain. I ain't one ta believe much in witches and all that nonsense, but she's always been a strange old lady." Jemma dared to glance at them once more. The balding man shook his head. "Bad things always seem to happen around her."

One of the women gasped. "You think those kids are responsible for the fire?"

"Dunno," the man replied, but there were tire tracks in the yard next to the Kilmer's land. Fresh ones. Somebody was there and made a quick getaway."

"Shit," Jemma muttered under her breath and then hoped no one had heard her.

"You know RJ was with some new woman too?" the first woman asked.

"Oh yes, heard about her. Pretty thing, ain't she?" the second woman replied.

The man spoke next. "I saw her myself. Somethin' 'bout her made me feel like I'd seen her before."

"What was her name?" the second woman asked.

"How'd RJ meet her?" came the first woman's question.

"Dunno," the man told them, "but she's gone now."

Knowing they were speaking about her mother, Jemma

swung into the next aisle just as the trio walked in her direction. She pretended to search the Band-Aid selection and thought it might not be a bad idea to grab some gauze strips and tape. She didn't want to be seen, so she hid behind a shelf until they were gone.

She watched as the line of customers dwindled. The last one, a middle-aged woman, leaned over the counter and asked Linnea, "You know anything? You've been datin' that Tad Nox, haven't ya?" She shook her head. "Be careful, dear. Datin' men you ain't grown up around can be hard."

Jemma's heart sank. Was the town really going to turn on one of its own because of who she wanted to date? Or maybe it could turn around for them. Maybe Tad marrying Linnea, as he had told Jemma he wanted to do, would help the Noxes fit into Solomon's Cross.

Do I even want to fit in here? Jemma wondered after hearing all that had been speculated about her. If these people didn't want her, then she didn't want them. It wasn't until Linnea gave the woman a forced smile and finished checking her out that Jemma remembered not everyone in town was so unpleasant. Tad had chosen the kindest one of all to date.

A few minutes later, the line of customers had cleared, and Jemma found herself in the pharmacy section alone. A voice called out to her. "Jemma, you can come out now." Jemma emerged to see Linnea smiling at her from behind the counter. "Mind telling me what's going on?" the pharmacists asked her.

"Everybody's talking," Jemma stated. "I don't like it." She slid the gauze and tape onto the counter.

"I don't either," Linnea confessed. She placed the items in the bag without scanning them. That was for the best since Jemma had forgotten to bring her wallet in with her. "But do you know anything? About the fire, I mean?"

Jemma shook her head. She didn't want to lie to Linnea since she liked her so much, but she didn't see what good it would do to tell her the truth right now. "I'm trying to find AJ, though," she stated instead. "I was trying to find his friends to see if they knew where he was." She listed their names, and Linnea said she hadn't seen any of them in the store that day.

Jemma turned to leave. "Well, thank you anyway."

Linnea called her back. "Wait, just one second, please."

Jemma turned back.

"I'm sorry things didn't work out too well between you and your mother. Maybe I shouldn't have helped or encouraged you to try again."

"It's okay now," Jemma replied. "I am glad she's gone, though."

Linnea smiled, and a relieved look came onto her face. "I feel selfish saying it, but I am too. A small part of me was scared that she might get your dad back."

Jemma understood but decided it wouldn't be good to tell Linnea that Annie might have eventually done just that with her controlling magic. She didn't want Linnea to have a bad impression of magic like a lot of the town did toward Mama B. She smiled at Linnea in return. "I get that. None of us would have been good with that."

Jemma left the drugstore and joined up with Val at his truck. Easter was not there yet.

"Anything?" he asked.

"Nothing but gossip."

Val sighed. "Me too. It was like almost every man in town was in there talkin'. RJ wasn't there, of course, and Henry Dover was more beside himself than ever." Val described some of the things he'd overheard.

"I bet ol' RJ finally snapped and laid his boy low and burned the barn to cover it up."

Jemma thought it was a harsh thing to say. RJ wasn't a murderer, especially of his own child.

Val shared what another man had stated. "If them fire

marshals dig deep enough, they'll find AJ's burned bones in there."

Another had speculated, "I heard AJ was into meth. Probably blew himself up cookin' it in his daddy's barn, and now poor RJ's broken heart can't take it."

Jemma remembered seeing no evidence of meth or any other kind of drug in the barn. *Unless dark magic counts,* she thought. She mused that perhaps the dark side of the Art could be addictive enough. She also wondered if her mother had gotten just a taste and then couldn't stay away. Were she and Easter and any other witch capable of dabbling in it without becoming a slave to it?

Her thoughts were interrupted when Easter joined them.

"Any luck?" Val asked her.

"I'm not a very lucky person," Easter replied, but then a grin appeared. "But today, I guess I am." They got back into the truck as she explained, "Lottie overheard them talking about going to the bridge." Val and his sister shared a significant look, but Jemma was lost.

"The bridge?"

"Its real name is Sleepy Stream Bridge, but no one calls it that anymore. Anyway, it's over a river at the other end of town past the high school," Val explained.

"When Lottie said that, it jogged my memory. AJ and his friends used to go there all the time. I guess they still do," Easter stated.

"It's their favorite drinking spot," Val added.

Easter nodded. "Yeah. They get their booze the most illegal way they can. They buy moonshine off Dougy's cousin Ray-Ray Butcher. He brews a few gallons every spring."

"Has anyone done anything about it?" Jemma asked.

"No," Easter replied. "Either the police can't catch them, or they don't care."

"I don't think they care much. A couple of 'em like the moonshine, too," Val interjected. He looked nervous.

Jemma noticed. "What's wrong, Val?"

He shrugged. "Well, I used to hang out with 'em too. Went down there and drank and everything. I hated it even then. AJ kind of hated it too. All he ever wanted was to fit in with other guys, and after his mom died, it was the only thing he wanted. That was when he bought his sports car and all that shit."

What he didn't add was what Jemma already knew—AJ had ditched Val as a friend and spent all his time among the other boys in Solomon's Cross. The boys whose favorite pastime was drinking illegal moonshine under the bridge.

If it was their favorite drinking spot and AJ used to go with them, he might have already found them. A renewed sense of urgency came over Jemma. "We've got to get there as fast as we can."

CHAPTER TWENTY

The isolated county bridge was officially called Sleepy Stream Bridge, but everybody who knew anything about it called it Gallagher's Gallows. Long before the McCarthys were born and told the tale, a Samuel S. Gallagher was found swinging from a rope tied to the crossbeams under the bridge.

He had made many enemies during his time in Solomon's Cross by scamming the town's residents out of thousands of dollars. People speculated that someone had killed him, but others thought he might have done the deed himself out of guilt over his years of embezzlement.

The rumors had become an entangled mass like the ivy that grew all over the bridge. Some said he was possessed by the ghost of his late father, an alcoholic who had hidden his addiction for years with his charming manner. When he died, his eldest son Samuel made it a point to expose his father's addiction and vices. Many thought Samuel might break the cycle, but by the time he was thirty, he had stolen money from two of the town's more prominent residents, including his stepmother.

Samuel and his wife had no children, and the town was glad about it. As far as they were concerned, the Gallaghers were bad seeds, and anyone who had that name died young or of poisoning in their liver.

The McCarthys shared this story with Jemma as Val drove out to the bridge. Few from town came out to the bridge because of its gruesome history, though the stream was placid and the fishing good. It was a prime spot for the younger crowd looking to drink or smoke or do whatever else in private, but even the teens who hid here did not stay at Gallagher's Gallows past dark.

In the days when Val came with AJ and the other three, he claimed that as soon as the sun went down, spooky things began to happen. It got a lot colder, even in the middle of summer, and there would be no wind, but voices would sound out from under the bridge.

"The spookiest shit I've ever heard," Val muttered as his hands tightened around the steering wheel. This made Jemma look up at the sky. It was late afternoon. She hoped they would have enough time to deal with AJ's old friends before it got dark. She didn't want to be stuck out here if the ghost of old Samuel Gallagher was prowling around.

Val parked the truck far enough away from the bridge itself so they could approach on foot without being seen. "Just in case," he stated. All three made their way to the bridge, grim-faced and expecting the worse.

As they neared the bridge, Jemma's eyes scanned the vicinity. She noted how overgrown everything had become. Weeds and brush had sprung up alongside the road all the way down to the stream. Clusters of trees grew close together, making the greenery so thick that it was difficult to see anything beyond. Val chose the narrow path right to take to get under the bridge. It was very muddy, especially in the springtime when heavy rainfalls were frequent.

The bridge itself was covered in ivy, and potholes had become home to various wildflowers and other weeds. It was clear no car had come over this bridge in quite some time. The only sign of human life was trampled down grass leading to the path which wound under the bridge. Standing at the top of the path, they heard three male voices coming from under the bridge.

Jemma had only encountered Dougy, Clide, and Phil a couple of times before, but she still recognized their voices. The sounds made her stiffen. She had an ongoing list of people in Solomon's Cross she didn't like, and these three were pretty close to the top. *Doesn't mean I want them sacrificed because a vengeful old witch has come back to town,* she thought.

"Well, I think it's time to go say hello," she told her friends. The McCarthys shared a glance, both seeming a little nervous.

They made their way down the path. Val whacked aside the tall grass with the bat Mama B had given to him. When they reached the end of the path, Jemma's shoes were already caked in thick mud. She drank in a new sight. The concrete slabs, which lay between two pillars supporting the bridge at either end, were larger than she thought they would be, leaving plenty of room for anyone to enjoy themselves.

She spotted a bonfire built on a sandbar on the left side of the bridge. This was where the three boys were. The fire was small as if they had just gotten it going. Did this mean they planned to stay here after dark? Since they had lived in Solomon's Cross all their lives, they knew about Gallagher. Either they were crazy, or they were being idiotic teenage boys.

Just as they expected, the boys were well into their drinking. "Good afternoon!" Jemma hollered out, knowing her presence would be unwelcome as soon as they registered who she was. Not only was she an outsider, but she was also invading their favorite private space.

Clide, who was the leader of the three, rose to his full height. He was a little taller than Jemma. He had bright green eyes, and a sour expression almost never left his face, even while he was drunk and laughing. "What in hell are you girls doin' here?" He sneered. "Ain't no girls welcome here. Boys only."

"Well, then maybe you won't mind if I stay," Val said, stepping up beside Jemma. Easter lingered a little behind.

The boys ignored Val. They bent around the fire together and muttered among themselves for a moment. Then, they lifted their heads, and Clide spoke again. "As a matter of fact, we've changed our minds. Two pretty girls like you are welcome. Come a little closer, Easter! We won't bite." The other two boys snickered. "Well, Phil might," Clide added.

"Hey!" Phil objected, but he laughed. He said something else, but he was too drunk to make any sense.

Jemma noted that there were two empty bottles lying by the fire. Dougy held a third, and he wagged it at Val. "You can drive on home now, Val. We'll take care of the girls just fine on our own." Val opened his mouth, but Jemma put out a hand to stop him. Dougy spied the bat in Val's hand. "What's that for? Wanna play some baseball?" The others joined him in laughing loud enough to scare any animals that were nearby.

"Yeah, yeah, bash 'im in the head with it!" Clide chortled.

It took everything in Jemma not to snap at Dougy and Clide or clock them in the face. Phil was a little less threatening, especially drunk. He was smaller than Jemma, almost smaller than Val, and went along with whatever the other two boys told him. Easter was beside Jemma. "I don't really wanna hang out here," she said. "We were hopin' we'd find you and could go somewhere else." When Easter wanted to, she could put on a good act.

A slow smile crept across Clide's face. "Nah, but we like it here. We don't wanna go anywhere else." He sidled close to Easter and nudged her with his elbow. "Besides, the sand's nice and comfy with the fire next to it once it gets dark."

Easter frowned. "You aren't gonna be out here after dark, are you?"

Clide shrugged. "Why not?"

Easter pointed at the bridge's crossbeams. "Gallagher, duh."

Clide waved a dismissive hand. "We've been here plenty of times, and nothin's ever happened to us."

Phil, however, began to look disturbed. "I forgot 'bout that. Ol' Samuel Gallagher's ghost and everythin'. Maybe McCarthy's right."

Clide punched Phil in the shoulder harder than he meant to. "Oh, don't listen to her."

Phil rubbed his shoulder. "That hurt."

"Well, drink more, and it won't," Dougy encouraged.

Jemma's hands formed into fists at her sides. How the hell were they supposed to convince the boys to come with them if this was how they were acting? "It's not safe here," she told them at last. "We should go before it gets dark."

Clide frowned at Jemma. "You know, you'd be a lot prettier if you kept your mouth shut."

Jemma almost sprang forward. Easter stopped her. "None of us will be pretty when we're out here after dark getting attacked by a fucking ghost or whatever it is."

Clide's frown deepened, and he crossed his arms over his chest. The stare he leveled at the new arrivals held strong suspicion. "Say, why did the three of ya come here anyway?" He didn't wait for an answer. "Either you can stay and drink with us, or you can get your asses home." He still stood close to Easter, and he reached out to touch her backside.

"Get your hands off her!" Val shouted, anger making his face red.

Clide snickered. "Val, I told you to go home. Why don't you ever listen?" He gestured at their surroundings. "It got a lot more fun 'round here when you stopped comin' around. AJ got cooler too, but now he's not. Do you know what I think?"

Dougy sauntered away from the fire, coming closer to the group. "What I think is that AJ was cool until he started messin' around with all of ya." He pointed at Jemma. "Especially you. I don't know what shit you've brought into this town, but we were better off without it."

Val had had enough. Before either Jemma or Easter could stop him, he swung out, smacking Dougy across the jaw with his fist. Val had grown up quite a bit over the winter, gaining a least a couple more inches in height and a bit more weight and muscle too.

"Val!" Easter cried out. "Don't!" But he swung again, this time with the bat, and knocked Dougy down by hitting him across the shins. Dougy howled.

From there, it only got worse, just as both girls knew it would if any of them started fighting. Seeing Dougy staggering back with blood flowing from his nose, Clide and Phil sprang into action. They weren't very coordinated due to their drunkenness, but three intoxicated boys were plenty to take on one Val. In a matter of seconds, the four of them tumbled into a pile of limbs and rolled into the shallow water. None of them seemed to care how wet they were getting as all four shouted and swung arms and legs. Val sputtered in the water as he attempted to find his footing. In the middle of the fight, Val lost hold of his bat.

Great. We have to fucking deal with this first, Jemma thought as she and Easter waded into the water. They called out to the boys to stop, and Easter went as far as to grab Val's arm so she might pull him away. Val tore away from her and dove for the nearest boy, which happened to be Phil.

Val slammed Phil into the water. This pissed off Dougy and Clide even more. "Get the hell off!" Jemma shouted as she trudged through the water. She was able to latch onto Clide's arm and yank hard, but he barely moved. Instead, she stumbled back and landed in the water. Easter wasn't having much more luck. In a matter of seconds, all six of them were soaked and floundering in the water. Since it was still spring, it was ice cold. The sun would be down soon, and the fire wasn't going to help any of them very much.

At the thought of the fire, Jemma turned. Then she froze.

Standing beside the small flames was AJ. He had a whimsical smile on his face as he warmed his hands, unaware of the fight going on in the stream. He wasn't alone. Beside him stood Vesna, her hair hanging in her face.

AJ looked up, his gaze sliding past Jemma to the boys who had not yet noticed him. He spoke in a loud, firm voice but remained calm. "Dougy, Clide, Phil." The boys spun at the sound of AJ's voice.

"What the fuck are you doing here?" Dougy began, but AJ just smiled.

"Momma says you need to come with me. Come on, now." The boys looked at each other in bewilderment. Their drunken state did not help matters.

"The fuck—" Phil started.

"No way, we wanna stay right—" Clide began, but they all stood still. It had taken them a moment to see Vesna. When she'd first appeared, Easter and Jemma had seen her before Val did. Magic, it seemed, made her visible.

Phil's lips and pointed finger quivered. "Wh-what's th-that?"

The other two backed away.

Jemma's heart thundered. Vesna kept her head down, but her hand tightened on AJ's shoulder as she whispered to him.

AJ's eyes slid away from his old friends. He peered into Jemma's face. She saw a blankness in him. What he was saying came from Vesna, not him. "The rest of you should get out of here. These woods aren't safe, and we wouldn't want you getting hurt." A sly smile spread his lips. "You escaped last time, but if you don't go now, you won't escape again."

CHAPTER TWENTY-ONE

AJ's words sent a chill up Jemma's spine. Easter and Val froze, wondering what Vesna would do through AJ next. The three other boys, however, burst out laughing.

Jemma couldn't tell how much of their amusement was due to the alcohol and how much was from jittery nerves at the sight of the skeletal woman on the sandbar. Everyone was confused and more than a little unnerved, but AJ's old friends seemed to be handling it with laughter.

They had expected the woman to vanish. When she did not, Phil pointed to her again, shaking even more than he had before. "That's not your momma!" He jeered at AJ but stepped backward into the water like a scared animal about to bolt. "Your momma's dead, remember? Three years!"

Jemma half-expected rage to leap into AJ's face at his friend's declaration, but a slight smile appeared on his lips. His voice remained eerie and distant. "I thought so too, but it seems Momma just got turned around and was lost for a time." Without looking at Vesna, he added, "But she found her way back home to me."

Lost where? Jemma wanted to scream, hoping it would break

through the wall of magic between AJ's mind and the reality Vesna had created. Was there some parallel realm where other creatures roamed? Had Vesna gone there and found her way back? If so, it was possible she had died. It was also possible she had gone into the other realm, leaving her body behind and faking her own death. She had learned from Mama B that this was possible but only with years of work in the dark Art.

"You've gone batshit-crazy," Clide muttered.

"Yeah!" Dougy hollered. "We ain't going anywhere with you an-and—" He stuttered, his attention once again on the spooky woman who had her hand on AJ's shoulder.

"Come on, now! Get out of here!" Phil shouted as he picked up a stone from the bottom of the stream and hurled it at AJ. The rock missed, but his actions, along with the moonshine, gave the other two courage. They had taken Val three to one, so they assumed they could take AJ too.

All three picked up rocks, growing belligerent as they hurled them across the stream at AJ. "Go home, now! You and your creepy momma bitch!"

They advanced on AJ as one staggering, drunken force. They weren't coordinated in the least. All of their stones had missed their mark, and AJ had stood on the bank beside the fire, unfazed by their antics. Jemma felt like she was watching three toddlers throw a tantrum at another kid who had taken their toys away from them. They floundered out of the water toward AJ and Vesna.

It took a few seconds for Jemma, Easter, and Val to gather themselves. They had stood by, panting for breath after their fight in the water. "No!" Jemma cried. "Stay away from him!"

The three boys were shouting, though, and didn't hear her. Or they ignored her. As far as they were concerned, Jemma and the McCarthys had disappeared. AJ and the spooky woman were all they cared about.

Jemma, with Easter and Val behind her, rushed toward the

sandbar, but it was too late. The boys reached AJ with more stones in hand. In a flash, AJ withdrew a buck knife and slashed, cutting Dougy's thigh. With a howl of pain that echoed off the walls under the bridge, Dougy collapsed to the sand. Blood dribbled onto it and into the water.

"AJ! Stop!" Val screamed. Easter had been holding the bat since retrieving it from the water, but before she knew what was happening, Val snatched it from her. He leapt from the water, swinging it at AJ in a way that should have knocked the knife from his hand without battering him too badly.

This didn't go as planned. Jemma knew what was about to happen, and she yelled. It wasn't warning enough. Val's shriek filled the air a second later, and he dropped the bat again. He stumbled back, holding his right hand with his left and moaning in pain. AJ had slashed his hand, causing him to drop the bat before it could hit him.

"Val!" Easter cried as she ran to him. With Dougy injured and crying on the sandbar and Easter trying to help Val up and get him away from AJ, Phil and Clide had lost their nerve and began running in the opposite direction.

"Cowards," Jemma muttered. She wanted to run too, and she couldn't. Vesna's hand snapped AJ's shoulder to the right, and with it, his whole body. A look of menacing anger overtook his expression and he stalked toward Val, who was kneeling in the water with his bleeding hand. Easter was bent over him. She had picked up the bat but was too focused on Val to think of swinging it at AJ as he advanced.

Jemma knew it was up to her. "Shit, Jemma, think!" she hissed at herself. She knew she could make the growing things around her move if she wanted to. If she could just think of the right word…

It came to her mind a second later, just as she had wished for it. Like a fire being ignited in her mind, the words to command the ivy growing along the bridge came to her. She uttered them, and they sounded like whispers all around her. Her voice grew, and so did the ivy. It crawled down from the bridge, growing faster.

AJ stepped toward the siblings with the buck knife held tightly in his hand. He lifted it, snarling. Vesna whispered something to him. Jemma cried out, and at the sound of her voice, the ivy plunged forward, wrapped around AJ's arm, and jerked it back so he dropped the knife. It sank into the water, out of sight. More ivy tore loose from the bridge, causing pieces of it to plummet into the water. The ivy wound around AJ's other arm and his legs, too.

Vesna did not seem to notice. Her hissing whispers increased until Jemma couldn't hear her own words. She leaned closer to AJ. He tore one of his arms loose from the ivy, having been given the strength by Vesna. More vines came. Jemma had to keep uttering the words so they would not stop. She had to buy them time to get out of this place.

"Easter, Val, come on!" The ivy slackened for a second. She uttered the words again, and the vines tightened. More came, wrapping around AJ's ankles and jerking him to the ground. He growled, clawing at the sand as he attempted to escape.

Easter scrambled to her feet, pulling Val with her. Phil and Clide had run toward Val's truck. They had to get there before the boys drove off in it. Jemma bounded toward Dougy and pulled him up. He kept crying and could barely walk on his own. Jemma threw his arm around her shoulder as she kept uttering the words.

A dark, unsettled feeling came over her. It came over the whole area. It wasn't just because the sun was almost down, and night had crept in. Easter's eyes went wide as they met Jemma's. She could sense it too. Vesna's working of the dark Art filled the air. Jemma wanted to throw up. "Come on, Dougy. Walk with me." It was no easy task to get up the muddy path with the injured boys.

Their flight gave AJ enough time to tear loose of the vines and come after them. He didn't have a knife in hand this time, but with Vesna's magic, he was powerful anyway. When they reached the top of the bank, they saw Phil and Clide bolting for the woods. "No!" Jemma called after them. "Not that way!" She wanted to curse them for leaving their friend behind, but they wouldn't listen to her, not as drunk as they were.

They skidded to a halt, turned, and gave her confused expressions. "This way!" She nodded in the direction of Val's truck and shuffled to the truck with Dougy. Easter and Val were not far behind. Val was still groaning as Easter helped him into the driver's seat and used her bandana to bind his bleeding hand.

"Can you drive?" she asked him.

Val gritted his teeth. "I'm gonna have to."

Jemma yanked Dougy into the back seat. Phil and Clide scrambled in behind him. Jemma was the last one to climb in, and there was barely enough room for her. They all smelled like sweat, stream water, and fear. None of them put their seatbelts on. They had to get the hell out of here and fast. "Val! Step on it!" Jemma commanded.

"I'm trying!" He shook as he attempted to place the key in the ignition with his injured right hand. Easter looked over her shoulder and saw AJ tearing up the path. Darkness had descended over the hillside and the road. Vesna's power wasn't just in AJ but was coming from the wildlife around them. The trees swayed, wind tearing through the branches. The sky showed no clouds.

Dark magic was in the air, prowling out of shadows and engulfing the life around it.

"Hurry!" Easter shouted. She took the key and plunged it into the ignition. The truck roared to life, but when Val stepped on the accelerator, it groaned in place.

Panic overtook his voice and face. "It won't move!"

"It has to!" Jemma answered.

He slammed down again. "I'm telling you, it won't fucking move!" He hadn't parked anywhere the tires could get stuck in the mud. Something else was keeping it in place. By the sound the tires were making, Jemma could tell roots had wound around the truck. Vesna's power. She could see them in the road, coiling toward the truck like dozens of snakes.

"Shit," she muttered. She knew what she had to do. She just wasn't sure if she could do it in time. She leaned out the window, muttering a new string of words. The roots slackened around the tires. Still, more were coming. "Now, Val!" Easter cried, aware of what Jemma was doing.

When Val hit the accelerator again, the truck jerked forward and tore free of the roots Vesna had sent toward it. Val clenched his jaw and sped down the gravel road away from the bridge and the roots coming after them. Jemma looked out the back window one more time.

AJ stood in the middle of the road, growing smaller. His body was stiff and seemed to belong to someone else, not him. The eerie form of Vesna coiled back into her usual shape. She had turned herself into the roots coming after them.

Jemma dreaded what they would have to do next since she knew AJ would not stay there. He and Vesna were sure to follow.

Jemma was pressed between a crying Dougy and the door as Val took the truck down the gravel road at an alarming speed. Sharp turns appeared, and his driving was not helped by the growing darkness or the injury in his right hand. He used it to move the wheel, but it was evident on his face that he was still in much pain.

Easter remained silent, staring out the window with a shocked look on her face. Jemma also remained quiet. Dougy continued whimpering in pain. Phil and Clide sat in horrified silence with the occasional spasm or shudder. Jemma hoped they had drunk enough that they wouldn't remember what had happened the following morning. Whatever story they told would be linked back with witchcraft, which, while true, would only lead to more speculation about Mama B and her three young employees.

We're trying to save this town, and they're going to turn on us instead, Jemma thought. She had to put such thoughts aside for the time being. She looked down at her phone and found it dead. Her father could be calling and texting, and she wouldn't know it. The thought of getting into big trouble also came to her mind. *It won't matter if AJ comes back and tries to kill us,* she thought.

Easter cried out, interrupting her thoughts, as Val took a sharp turn a little too fast. The tires screeched as he hit the brakes, and the end of the truck went off the road toward a ditch just. Val was able to right the vehicle in just enough time to get back on the road. Another truck, coming in the opposite direction, passed them a moment later. With Val's speedy, precarious driving, they almost side-swiped one another. The other driver blared his horn. This seemed to jolt the other two boys from their stupor.

"Wh-where are we going?" Clide demanded. "Where are you taking us?"

Jemma ignored him. "Phil, give me your shirt so I can bind up Dougy's wound."

Phil scowled. "You give him your shirt!"

"I'm a girl!"

Their shouting only distracted Val more. "Would all of you shut the hell up?"

Groaning, Phil removed his still wet, mud-plastered shirt. Jemma tore it into strips and dug around in her satchel until she found herbs she could apply to the wound. Dougy cried as she touched the gash. "Hold still," she ordered. "If you do, it won't be hurting anymore in about five minutes." The jolting of the truck over potholes and loose stones didn't help matters.

Dougy continued whimpering as she tied the strips of Phil's shirt around his thigh. The herbs and shirt would do enough until they reached Gran's Rest. Fortunately, Mama B had closed the bed and breakfast for the weekend, citing repairs so they could have the grounds to themselves for whatever healing and cleansing became necessary.

When they arrived, the bed and breakfast was dark. Had Mama B gone to bed? Jemma sensed she hadn't. "Around back," Easter suggested.

They found the old holler witch on the back slope of her property, assembling what would be necessary for the cleansing ritual. Old oil lanterns glowed along the path, lighting where she had set up several jars and bottles of herbs and liquids. She had basins full of ingredients, and the whole area smelled like an exotic garden. The moon was almost full and cast a silvery glow over the land.

Everything around them teemed with magic, but it felt different from what Vesna had created with her vines. Mama B's face looked both relieved and concerned when she saw the teens. Easter and Jemma each had one of Dougy's arms around them. Phil and Clide had to be yelled at before they agreed to come with them.

"By all that is holy on this mountain—" Mama B murmured. "Come with me, children. Come with me." They followed her inside. The girls lowered Dougy onto a chair in the kitchen for Mama B's ministrations. Val stood nearby, still in pain from his hand but no longer moaning. Jemma set aside her satchel and Easter her bat.

Hurriedly, they told the old woman what had happened at Gallagher's Gallows. Mama B's eyes went wide when she heard where they had been. "Place was cursed 'fore Vesna went there. Ain't no surprise she could work magic there so well."

"What do you mean?" Easter asked.

"Well, you know how there's good, healthy magic on this mountain?" Mama B explained as she prepared remedies for the boys.

"And bad on Kalhoun's Crest," Jemma added.

Mama B nodded. "Now, magic is a neutral thing. It becomes good or bad based on how it's used. For centuries, the magic on this mountain has been used to heal." She pointed at what she was putting together for the boys. "Whereas what's been used on the devil's mountain," here she referred to Kalhoun's Crest, "has been used for all manners of disorder and chaos. Gallagher's Gallows was once a neutral place, but after that man hung himself or was killed, whatever the case may be, dark spirits took to roamin' there. It's just the place an old witch deep in the dark Art would look to cause harm."

She lowered her voice so the boys could not hear her. "Which leads me to our possible solution to this whole damn ordeal."

Jemma and Easter leaned closer.

"If we can get AJ here, we can break Vesna's hold on him."

"Because the magic here is good. Vesna can't taint it unless she's been here a long time," Easter added.

Jemma finished. "And the magic here might be stronger."

"It just might," Mama B said. "My guess is Vesna can't work magic except through AJ. You think he'll follow us here?"

Jemma remembered seeing him on the road and the look of desperation and fury on his face. She nodded. "I have no doubt."

Easter's voice was calm when she added, "He's probably on his way here right now." There was apprehension in her eyes, but perhaps she had accepted what deep shit they were in. All it took now was working together.

And making sure we don't kill anyone but Vesna in the process, Jemma thought. But would it really be killing? Was she alive?

Mama B seemed to read her thoughts. "It's possible Vesna

faked her death. I saw the body, but I never made sure it was hers."

Jemma's heart skipped a beat as the horrifying thought settled in. "You mean it could have been someone else, and she made it look like her?"

Mama B's face and voice were grave. "The Art, when used wrongly, can give one all sorts of diverse abilities."

Jemma remembered her mother saying something similar but in a positive way. She shoved any thought of her mother away, not wanting to consider the implications of her words.

Mama B went on. "I'm now sure that she has been lurking these hills, waiting for the right opportunity to get revenge. She found it in the form of a vulnerable person who has a connection to the Art but is untrained."

"AJ," Easter breathed.

Mama B nodded. "His weakness in the Art isn't just his ignorance. He is weak mentally, emotionally, and spiritually. He will need more than a magical cleansing. He will need the truth and the strength to deal with it."

This sounded like a problem for later. If AJ ended up dead or killed the rest of them, it wouldn't matter.

"She is just a living woman underneath it all, though," Mama B lamented. "More or less, anyway. She is sustained by exposure to the deep well of life that is part of these mountains."

"And she knows how to use it since she was once in a coven in these parts," Easter added.

Mama B gave her a nod. "Do you girls know what this means?"

Jemma ventured, "I think so. If she's driven out of Solomon's Cross, she won't survive."

"Precisely," Mama B answered. "She is still sealed off from her power, and she probably doesn't even know why she wants vengeance. The magic she is working on and through AJ, however, is still cruel, instinctual, and violent. Such magic eats away at a person."

Jemma thought of how gaunt AJ had grown. When she'd met him, he had been lean but muscular. In a matter of nine months, he had transformed. She imagined he was even more eaten away on the inside.

"Weren't her memories erased too?" Easter recalled.

"Yes," Mama B told them, "but her hatred of Kalhoun County might be deep enough that it has gone beyond the mind and has settled in her heart."

"Can we use beast-tongue to stop her? I know it's risky, but shouldn't we be using anything we know?" Easter ventured.

Mama B shook her head. "She cannot be manipulated. Beast-tongue affects the heart. It can make an animal or a person *act* as though they love something, but it can't make them actually love it. By extension, using it to remove memories could remove the reason for hating someone or something."

"But if the hate is strong enough," Jemma interjected, "reason has nothing to do with it."

"Yes," Mama B answered. "We must hope now that AJ has enough heart and reason left behind all the dark magic worked over him. If he does, the beast-tongue and cleansing can be used to help him." She finished preparing the herbal remedies for Val and Dougy. "Let's help these boys, and then we will make our plan."

CHAPTER TWENTY-TWO

The witches at Gran's Rest were lucky enough to have bait in the form of three distressed, drunk teenage boys. What they were not lucky in was everything else. They were tired, hungry, wet from the stream, and only had a certain amount of time before a possessed boy and his witch momma came after them. Further, they didn't know how much time they had. It could be minutes or hours.

Jemma had never imagined she was a witch, much less tried to stop a boy from sacrificing his friends. Easter had never imagined she was either, but she was a little better at remaining level-headed when she was put in charge of attending to Val's and Dougy's wounds by applying Mama B's herbal remedies.

The poultice would make Dougy's leg as good as new, assuming he lived through the night. Val had a lesser injury and would be fine without a poultice, but he was grateful that Mama B made him one anyway. It would help him heal faster, though he wouldn't be swinging a bat anytime soon without pain.

He took the bat anyway. Without magical herbs to throw at his attackers or the ability to turn into an animal, he needed *something*.

Mama B took Jemma to the cellar to make another "special brew." Jemma could tell Mama B didn't want the boys to know what it was from her vague description. Once they were in the cellar, out of earshot from the boys, she began gathering new jars of herbs.

"What are you making?" Jemma asked, but Mama B did not explain for several minutes.

"A sleeping draught, of course," Mama B replied as if it were obvious.

"Oh, of course." Jemma paused. "Why?"

"If we put those boys to sleep, they won't resist being bait. We'll tell 'em it'll help 'em sleep," Mama B explained. This was truthful enough. If they were able to save the boys, they would never have to know how they had been a part of it.

"How long will the draught work?" Jemma asked.

"Long enough to get done what we need to get done, I hope."

Mama B also mentioned that Vesna and AJ would not be able to get up to Gran's Rest unless her wards were taken down. Any human could walk onto the property if she allowed them, but a magic person would be thrown back like a dog running into an electric fence. "Once the wards are down, girls, anything can happen. We will need to be ready," Mama B told Jemma and Easter once they were back in the kitchen.

This whole time, Dougy, Clide, and Phil had been staring at the three women, clearly confused by what was going on. Jemma wondered what kind of thoughts were running through their moonshine-fogged heads. No doubt, they were seeing the rumors from town come true. "What in all the witchy shit—" Clide murmured, but Easter shoved a cup in his hand.

"Drink."

"What the fuck is this—" Phil started as Easter handed him one too.

"Don't smell like moonshine," Dougy complained.

"Tea. Drink it," Easter commanded again. The tea contained

Mama B's sleeping draught. The boys sniffed and scowled, not liking how it looked or smelled. "If you don't drink it," Easter told them, "all your scratches and sores won't heal." Dougy drank right away, and the other two boys followed reluctantly.

Val also drank some tea, but his did not have a draught in it.

Moments later, all three boys were slumped over the table, snoozing loudly. If AJ's sense of where they were didn't alert him enough, their sleeping sounds would. "Do we leave them here?" Val asked, looking ruefully into his cup as if, at any moment, he might fall asleep too.

Mama B shook her head. "We'll take them to the Twilight Grove."

Val turned. "The what?"

Outside, to the left of the property, was the shed Jemma had recently painted. It backed up against a low, stone wall. Over this wall was a grove of trees Mama B referred to as the Twilight Grove. The way the trees stood in a circle allowed for moonlight to filter down, filling the grove in a silvery glow. Here, Mama B and Jemma had conducted some night training, for there were creatures to work magic through at night that they could not find during the day.

"I'd like to not have my home destroyed in the process," Mama B muttered. "AJ will sense where they are on his own. Or Vesna. Whoever it is that's really in charge." On the one hand, it was Vesna's power driving the whole thing. On the other, it was AJ's vengeance toward the three boys that drove him on. Vesna and AJ needed one another's power.

So, we need to sever them from one another, Jemma realized. It wasn't going to be simple, though.

"We should hide somewhere they don't see us right away," Val suggested. Even though he didn't have the power the other three did, he wanted to feel just as included. He held the bat in his left hand, determined to use it even with his injured one.

"We could separate, two of us going on either side of the

grounds," Jemma stated. "We close in on them and unleash our power."

Mama B nodded. "Might be just the thing we can do, but remember, no plan will go according to how we want it. We will have to rely on instinct and prowess."

"Right," Val said, "instinct and prowess." He seemed unconvinced.

Val and Jemma worked together to haul Dougy outside and to the left toward the Twilight Grove. Mama B and Easter took Phil, and Val and Jemma returned to Clide. They placed the boys in the center of the grove, and it was then that Jemma saw Mama B's reasoning for putting them there. All around them, vines snaked across the ground and through the trees. With their power, they could use the vines to trap anyone who might come into this area.

Mama B and the three young people returned to the front yard. Straight ahead was the road and a line of trees forming the larger portion of the forest on the mountain. To their right, the slope dipped downward into another part of the forest. In front of the building itself, however, the land was flat and cleared.

Mama B walked to one end and then the other before going straight ahead. At each spot, she lifted her hands into the air, closed her eyes, and murmured words to herself. The wards came down. Val couldn't see anything but Mama B standing there. Easter and Jemma, however, sensed something had dropped like a sheet dropped off a clothesline.

"Do you see that?" Jemma murmured to Easter, for she had seen a thin shimmer in the air as the wards dropped. It was gone almost as soon as she had seen it.

Easter shook her head. "See what?"

"Never mind." Easter hadn't been training as long as Jemma, so it made sense that she had not yet been taught about wards.

Once the wards were down. Mama B and Val stood at the end of the grounds closer to the Twilight Grove, while Jemma and

Easter stood on the other side of Mama B's home, pressed against the stone wall. They waited. "Not long now," Jemma murmured.

The first sign of the arrival was not what any of them had expected. A buzzing sound filled the air. At first, it sounded far away, but as it grew closer, a tremor in the ground told Jemma what was about to happen. The ground began to writhe. *Vines!* she realized. Vesna had sent her vines forth first. And...something else.

Jemma squinted in the darkness. The sound of insects buzzing grew louder. Joining it was the sound of flapping wings and the haunting note of an owl's hoot. An instant later, a screen of flying nighttime creatures erupted at the edge of the grounds. The air was thick with them and almost looked like smoke in the dark.

Insects, owls, and bats. They careened forth as one wall of controlled beasts. Jemma gasped. She did not know beast-tongue could be used to such magnitude, to control so many creatures at once. She supposed, though, that the many years Vesna had practiced the Art in malevolent ways had given her this level of power.

From behind this wall of creatures, AJ and the ghostly woman appeared. Jemma was not able to get a good look at them before the screen split in two, half of it soaring toward where Mama B and Val were concealed and the other half to where Jemma and Easter were hiding.

"Jemma!" Easter cried, but she had already moved. She stepped in front of Easter, throwing a concoction of herbs into the air that cast a net over them. It was like a bug screen with a thin net so insects could not get through, but because it was magic, the owls and bats could not tear it off of them. The animals plummeted down and collided with the net, unable to reach the girls. Jemma hoped Mama B had saved herself and Val using a similar defense. Not only did the net keep the creatures from attacking her and Easter, but it also stung them like hundreds of little bees.

The bats, owls, and insects flew away, their noise filling the air as they changed direction. Jemma let down their shield and stepped out from behind the house. They had to work quickly. She spied AJ stomping toward the house. When he stopped still and sniffed the air, he realized his old friends were not inside. Jemma looked at Vesna, who was floating up to him, her feet above the ground. She jerked her head and AJ did the same, making it clear to any onlooker that she still had control over him.

He looked at the Twilight Grove, then, emitting a low snarl, he stomped toward it. "Yes, step right into the trap," Jemma urged quietly.

From the other side of the yard, she had a clear view of the stone wall. The moon was above the trees by this point. Mama B's head appeared, having sensed Vesna's arrival. Her face turned ashen, and she froze. *No, Mama B, this is not the time.*

Jemma had no doubt that seeing her old coven sister turned mad was having an unpleasant effect on Mama B, allowing old memories and wounds to resurface. *She's gone now, Mama B. Vesna is gone.* She hoped Mama B's regrets about Vesna would not come back and make her unwise. As soon as the fear appeared on Mama B's face, it was gone, replaced by stoic determination.

"Ready?" Easter asked from beside Jemma.

"Ready as I'll ever be." It could be simple. Control the vines crawling across the grounds. Trap AJ. Bind Vesna. Jemma made to leap forward, but before she could, a scream escaped her throat. It was cut off as the hand that had just jerked her back, slapped over her mouth. She writhed and thrashed, but the grip upon her was hard and tight. The hands were slimy, the fingers abnormally long. A hiss filled her ear. A haint! A haint had her!

She thrashed with enough strength to break free from its grip. Whirling, she caught sight of the haint before it launched at her again. She threw the creature back against the stone wall of Mama B's house, and something cracked as if bones had broken, but the haint snarled in her face again, its long teeth covered in the same slime that was now on Jemma's clothes.

She grabbed the creature around the neck and threw it to the ground. She wasted no time pulling up some of her magic and sending a ball of golden light into the creature. The light spread like rope over the haint, binding it to the ground.

Where the hell had it come from? Had Vesna's power been strong and dark enough for the haints hiding in these hills to dare come crawling up to Gran's Rest? It was possible. In fact, it was the *only* possibility. Otherwise, why would they bother? The wards were down for the first time in decades. This was their chance to strike.

A spike of panic went through Jemma's chest as she remembered Easter. She spun to find that Easter had been jerked back by another haint. Jemma bolted toward them, but as she did, Easter scrambled out of its hold, and transformation took hold of her. A red wolf stood where Easter had just been, fur bristling and fangs bared.

She looked more fearsome now than she had the first time Jemma had seen her in this form. This wasn't like the fight Easter had had with Annie. Growling, she pounced on the haint. The night creature's shriek rang out as Easter's wolf teeth plunged into her neck.

Jemma skidded to a halt, mud spraying up all around her. It was what she had to do to avoid tripping over the roots and vines writhing on the ground. "Easter! Hurry!" she cried out. "We have to—" Her words were cut off at another sight. "Oh, fucking shit." Clamoring up the side of the darkened slope were more haints. At least a dozen of them.

Jemma's heart pounded so fast she thought it might tear from her chest. "E-easter!" Easter was there a second later, still in wolf form. "Run!"

They bounded across the yard toward the stone wall. If they got there in time and Vesna and AJ were already within the Twilight Grove, they could put up another ward and keep the haints out. But would they have the time? It took everything within them not to trip over the vines and roots. Cool night air tore at them as they ran.

"I can feel more of them!" Easter shouted. She had turned back into her human form, but only long enough to tell Jemma was she knew. "They're fighting each other in the aether. I can feel them!"

The aether? So, there was some parallel realm where the creatures roamed. Easter's sense of it confirmed Jemma's earlier suspicions. *And this is why we work together.* The thought was barely in her mind as Easter turned back into a wolf and they cleared the last of the vine-infested ground.

A gleaming blue light lifted above the stone wall. With a cry, Val leapt over the stones just as Jemma and Easter vaulted over the wall. The haints were not far behind. Jemma whirled, throwing herbs at one. It shrieked as it became weighed down by a stinging net of nettle. Val swung his bat, battering one in the side of the head. He swung it again, taking out another at the shins. A third. The blue light was an arc in the air.

Easter only took a moment to gather herself before she leapt back into the fray, growling, dodging, and running. She collided with the creatures as they came for her. Jemma spun, searching for Mama B, AJ, and Vesna. She saw them in the Twilight Grove as she had both expected—and dreaded.

AJ was within yards of the boys, Vesna close behind them. Mama B stood between AJ and the boys. Jemma sprang after AJ. There was no time to put up the wards as she wanted to do. Val and Easter would have to hold their ground for as long as it took.

The vines crawling along the ground were Vesna's doing, but the magic here was good. It was under Jemma's control if she wanted it to be. Sensing Jemma coming, Vesna turned, snapping her head in Jemma's direction. A vine lashed out, tripping the girl. She fell, the world spinning as she hit the ground with a heavy thud. She groaned as pain filled every part of her body.

She crawled across the ground, clawing at the mud, which was churned up from recent rain. She pulled herself to her feet, gritting her teeth.

"This mountain is mine, not yours." She ground the words out. AJ heard her and turned. The surprise in his eyes turned to molten fury. She cried out, and as the vines broke away from Vesna's grasp, they came into her control. She imagined her magic flowing through the vines instead of Vesna's, and that let her push her power forward. It felt like something snapped into place within her body. She sent the vines forward, knocking AJ off his feet and then binding him to the ground.

He couldn't go near the boys as long as he was pinned down.

This gave Mama B enough time to go after Vesna. She blasted the woman with golden light. It got Vesna off-kilter enough for the vines to stop snaking across the grove. The ones holding AJ down, since they were in Jemma's control, held.

All she had to do was keep AJ where he was. She turned as Vesna straightened. A cracking sound followed as she snapped her head toward Mama B. "Vesna, it's me," the old holler witch began, but whatever parts of Vesna Mama B had once known were gone, leaving behind a skeleton blazing with vengeance and fury.

Her hissing voice filled the air. AJ struggled on the ground. Jemma held the vines fast, knowing Vesna was giving him instructions again. If Jemma's power didn't hold, he could snap the binds. It would only take him two more steps with his knife in hand to slash Clide, Dougy, or Phil's throats.

Focus, Jemma, she told herself. *Hold him down.* She turned her head again. *Come on, Mama B. You can do it.* Cries from beyond the stone wall could still be heard as Val and Easter battled the haints.

Mama B summoned her power, and once again, tendrils of golden light drifted from her fingers. They wound around Vesna, wrapping her tightly like cords. Bound, but not yet sealed. Jemma could feel Mama B's magic wavering. It felt like it would break at any moment. Jemma's heart hammered on. She hadn't thought about it until now. If Mama B ended Vesna, her power would be depleted. It could break. Killing a coven sister could do this.

Mama B cried out, and with it, Jemma felt the breaking of her power connected to the Art. Vesna also screamed. It cut through the air, and the trees responded, shaking violently in a wind that had just now risen up.

Mama B reached behind her. Jemma hadn't realized she had the McCarthy's hunting rifle until this moment. She pointed it toward Vesna. A pained "Sorry" fell from her lips. Half a second later, she pulled the trigger. The bullet punched forward. The shot rang in the air. Vesna fell with a groan, the bullet in her heart. Screeching sounded out all around them. With Vesna's power gone, the haints retreated back over the mountain. The owls, bats, and insects, which had been flying all around them this entire time, also retreated.

Mama B stumbled to the edge of the grove and lifted her hands. With the last of her power, she put the wards back up. She was barely able to do this. Her power was depleting rapidly. Easter and Val appeared just as she finished. Both were covered in dirt and their own blood. Val breathed heavily, the bat hanging from his right hand. It was lathered in black ooze. Easter returned to her human form and stumbled toward Mama B. She had also sensed the old holler's witch breaking off from the Art.

Mama B slumped to the ground, too weary to stand any longer. "Come on, let's go inside," Easter urged her. A revitalizing tea would help her. She needed to stay awake lest the Art take her body too. Val stared, wide-eyed at AJ on the ground. The boy's eyes were fixed on the fallen Vesna. Horror filled his face, and his scream rang out. "Noooo!"

Despair and rage filled his voice. He was seeing his mother die again. *Even if it is not the same one,* Jemma thought as she crawled over to him. Her power was weak after fighting so hard. She searched for what she had left, a small light deep inside her. She pulled it up and reached out, searching for a connection between her and AJ.

She knew she shouldn't use beast-tongue on humans, but it was all she could do. *I won't control him. I will just show him I am trying to help.* Some small part of him still had to be untouched by all the manipulation and sorcery. At least, that was her hope.

Tears sprang into her eyes. She didn't know why she felt so emotional. Perhaps it was the sorrow on AJ's face. Perhaps it was having felt Mama B's connection to the Art severed. Perhaps it was all the gravity and surprise of the night hitting her at once. She reached for AJ, grabbing his hand as the vines fell away from him. "I'm sorry. I'm sorry for everything I did." She choked the words out. "I am sorry for my part in all this, for what I did in the cave, and—"

She couldn't finish. AJ scanned his surroundings wildly. Finally, his eyes met hers. He seemed shocked by her tears. "Please," she begged him, "work with me. Find some part in yourself to help me make things right."

As she spoke, she felt it might be too little, too late.

AJ's hand tightened around her own. Her labored breathing caught as she felt something else as well. It was like a weak grip reaching to take her offered hand, but inside her, connected to her power, like a circuit being completed. She looked up, seeing Easter had returned from helping Mama B to see if she could assist Jemma. She stood above them, breathing hard. The look on her face told Jemma she felt it too. A connection sealed not just between her and Easter but also with AJ.

She gasped. This was it. AJ was the third to create their coven. He had reached out with what little, untrained power he had and connected it with theirs. A grave thought came to her. If they were connected, the magical manipulation that had been worked over him could extend into their power. *And ours into his,* she thought. She looked at Easter. "We can cleanse him with our power, but we have to do it together."

Easter sank to her knees and took AJ's other hand. His eyes rolled back, but he gripped their hands. "Go on, Jemma. You can do it. Complete it," Easter told her in a trembling voice.

"I'm scared," Jemma confessed, her voice almost gone. She was terrified she would mess it up and the new rush of power into AJ's body might kill him instead of heal him. She had hoped Mama B would be the one doing this. *But it is me or nothing.* She knew this deep in herself. There was no other way.

She closed her eyes and visualized her power going into AJ and driving out the darkness still lingering there from Vesna's torment. *Will I see his memories again?* This felt like an invasion, but if it saved his life, it would be enough. She pictured her magic trickling into him instead of rushing. As his body gradually filled with light, the magic within her dimmed. *Hold out. Hold strong.* She thought the words, but they were in Mama B's voice, spoken time and time again during her training. She gasped out loud, "Hold on."

AJ's hold on her hand grew stronger. Finally, as she felt the last of her energy deplete, he raised his head. At first, his expression was blank, then he began to cry. "Wh-what happened?"

Had the cleansing rid him of memories too? He glanced in the direction of Vesna's fallen body. "Sh-she was in me. Her...her voice—" He could remember. That was a relief. His awareness did not last for long. His eyes rolled back, and he sank to the ground once more, exhausted.

Easter looked at Jemma. "He needs food."

Jemma nodded. She looked at the gray light peeking over the mountains in the east. Dawn was encroaching. In a couple of hours, it would be light out.

"Wow." They turned at the sound of Val's voice. He had stood there, watching with his mouth hanging open. "Does that mean AJ's a witch too?"

Easter chuckled in disbelief. "Maybe not a witch, but he's got magic for sure."

Val scratched his head. "I can't figure if that was something really fucking cool you two just did there, or if I'm really fucking glad I don't know shit about magic."

"It was all Jemma," Easter said, looking once more at her friend with a slight smile. "You did it, Jem."

Val walked over and helped them carry AJ inside Gran's Rest. There, they found Mama B sitting at the back door, staring out over the grounds as the first light of dawn touched her sacred grounds. Easter and Val went back for the boys, who had just begun stirring and demanding to know where the hell they were and what the hell had happened to them. Jemma stood and watched Mama B.

A single tear rolled down her cheek. She brushed it away as soon as she noticed Jemma standing there. "I'm relieved, is all."

Jemma knew there was more. Relief that Vesna's spirit had been dealt with. Returning regret for how much Vesna had suffered years ago. Remorse, perhaps, that her connection to the Art was broken. Relief that she was done after such a long time. A small smile formed on the old woman's lips. "I was glad to do it while I could. I am going to miss this place."

An ache built in Jemma's chest. What did Mama B mean? Was she planning on leaving? She did not ask. She didn't have time to. Easter and Val entered with the boys, trying to explain what had happened without revealing they had been used as human bait for a sacrifice which, thank God, hadn't happened.

There was some back and forth about how, if the boys kept their mouths shut about AJ and the creepy bitch, Mama B wouldn't be callin' up their parents to report their drinking. These threats seemed to work, and Easter and Val had escorted the boys upstairs so they could sleep off their moonshine. Easter prepared something for AJ to eat. The boy was slumped on the couch in the living room, sound asleep.

Jemma heard truck tires crunching on the drive, then headlights appeared. She reached the front door in time to see her father climb out onto the gravel, his face filled with worry. He saw her standing there, covered in black ooze, dirt, and her own blood. Or maybe it was AJ's. She wasn't sure. They were all pretty banged up.

Relief filled his face as he rushed forward and crushed her against his chest. Oh, what a story she had for him.

CHAPTER TWENTY-THREE

Tad and Jemma went back to Gran's Rest the next day at around dusk.

No guests were there, and Easter and Val were still at home, recovering. They had not told their parents the full truth of the events, only that they had gotten caught up in an altercation involving AJ and three teenage boys drunk on moonshine.

Their parents had been concerned but, trusting their children, did not ask any more questions. Easter and Val were on thin ice, though, since less than two months ago, they had been arrested for trespassing. Though not charged, the whole town had talked about it for a couple of weeks.

"Best we lay low for a while," Val told Jemma over the phone as she and her father drove to Gran's Rest.

"If we can. Magic and trouble brew whether we want it to or not," Jemma answered. She had a feeling that with Vesna gone, they would not face a new threat for some time. They all needed a break, and she hoped the mountains would give them one.

Val chuckled. "Well, now I have three Artsy people to watch after me. See what I did there? Like, the Art? Aye?"

Jemma rolled her eyes. "Talk to you later, Val. Tell Easter I said hello."

Easter had slept for the entire day. "I will." He hung up.

They reached Gran's Rest and found the Kilmers were there. AJ looked better already. He was still not back to his old self, but some color had returned to his complexion, and he didn't give anyone a smoldering glare. Still, Jemma avoided his gaze. Ever since the connection had been made between them, she had felt strange around him. He had started out as her least favorite person in town, and now he was in her coven?

Coven-mate? she wondered. *He's certainly not my sister.* She still hadn't discussed the new change with Easter, who she *could* consider a sister. Nine months ago, the last thing she would have imagined in her life was being a part of a witch's coven. Now here she was, about to perform a ritual only she could enact.

RJ stood beside his son, leaning on his truck with his arms folded across his chest. He also appeared to be doing better, though he was not fully recovered. That was what the cleansing ritual was for—full recovery for all of them. Jemma glanced at her father. She was doing this for him, for the years of control he had been under without knowing it, and for herself. After all the shit she had been through, including her mother's return, she deserved a fresh beginning.

"Mr. Kilmer," Tad greeted, nodding at him.

RJ grunted in response and shifted his weight. "AJ tells me we're gonna talk first. 'Bout what, I dunno. I'm not sure why we had to meet here of all places." He cast hard eyes toward Mama B's house.

Tad smiled and patted his shoulder. "Mama B will explain everything."

They rounded the building and found her. She had also changed. She appeared thinner. More bent. Her hair had turned from gray to silver. Since the magic had left her, Mama B looked much older. Jemma helped her to her feet. The old holler witch leaned on her cane and on Jemma.

"Shall we begin?" She grinned at the Kilmers. "We have quite the story to share with you."

They sat in the back gardens on newly purchased chairs. Mama B began by telling the Kilmers the story without her full history in Solomon's Cross and everything having to do with Vesna. She was uninhibited by any perceptions RJ might have had about her. As she had stated to Jemma, "It don't matter anymore what he or anybody else thinks of me. I'm gonna be gone soon anyhow." Again, she mentioned leaving, and Jemma wasn't sure why. She didn't ask. She was afraid to.

As expected, RJ was taken aback by her story. He even went so far as to leap to his feet. "And you've got my son believing all this witchy bullshit! I'm going to call the police now and get rid of this crazy witch. You call yourself the last witch of Kalhoun County, and let's make it stay that way!"

Except she isn't the last, Jemma thought as she glanced at AJ. For the first time since they had arrived, she looked into his eyes. He glanced away, moving his attention to the ground.

"RJ, please sit." It was Tad's firm voice this time.

"You believe this too?"

Tad produced a knowing smile. "As a matter of fact, I do. Look, I know it sounds crazy. Insane, really." He leaned forward, folding his hands together. Slowly, RJ lowered himself back into the chair beside his son. "But you see, I owe my life to Mama B and my daughter. They saved me twice. First from a boo hag, and then from…" he laughed and scratched his head, "my ex-wife."

RJ's eyes narrowed. "What's she got to do with this?"

"A whole lot," Jemma cut in, knowing the next part was going to shock Mr. Kilmer even more. She slid over a photograph of her mother. "Do you know this woman?"

RJ's eyes went wide as he picked it up.

"Delilah Anne Nox, my former wife, and Jemma's mother,"

Tad explained. "She's also the woman who got you into this shit. Not that she had anything to do with your son going, well…"

"Crazy," AJ offered. "I went crazy."

Jemma felt for him and wanted to reassure him it wasn't his fault. Some of it was hers, and the rest was Vesna's.

"She had everything to do with how you were acting," Tad explained. "Annie's a tricky one, and we all hope she won't wiggle her way back into Kalhoun County."

Jemma's expression hardened. "If she does, she'll find three people who know the Art waiting to drive her out."

Tad turned toward her. "Three? I thought you said Mama B…"

Mama B and Jemma inclined their heads toward AJ. The young man shifted, uncomfortable under Tad's and RJ's surprised stares. "Yeah, it's me." He sounded unconvinced.

"So, we've come here to have this bad magic, you call it, wiped off?" RJ asked, seeming a little more open to the plan.

Mama B and Jemma nodded, and the latter said, "Except it's not quite as easy as that."

"A cleansing ritual," Mama B stated, "which Jemma will do since I am no longer able to do it myself." She had been drained by sitting there and telling the story.

RJ thought it over for a long time. AJ's eagerness to have it done and Tad's belief in Mama B finally convinced him. Grumbling, he rose to his feet. "All right, let's get this shit over with."

They went to a cleared part of the slope. The sun was almost down, leaving pink rays peeking through the mountains. Jemma took her father's hand and AJ's. Tad looked down at his daughter with a smile. "I am afraid of what is going to happen, but I trust you." Jemma, who had been apprehensive about the ritual, felt a little better. His words gave her faith in herself.

AJ reached out for his father. RJ was more reluctant. Finally, he clasped hands with his son and Tad. "What now? We gonna sing *Kumbaya?*"

Jemma smiled. The old RJ was coming back. "Not quite."

She closed her eyes and imagined the good magic within her flowing into her father. AJ did the same for his parent. There was more to it as well. They used an herbal concoction of Mama B's strongest, finest gatherings and sprinkled it over their hands, then clasped hands again. When they finished and withdrew, the herbs were gone. Erased from their skin.

"That it?" RJ asked.

"How do you feel?" Jemma asked.

He thought about it and nodded with a small smile on his lips. "Better. A whole lot better." They turned back to Mama B, who had looked on with pride in her eyes.

"Well done, Jemma. Now, if you don't mind, I'd like some help inside. It's bedtime for me."

For the next couple of weeks, everyone went back to pretending everything was normal. Business picked up at Gran's Rest. The place was booked for the next several weekends, so Jemma, Easter, and Val were busy. They had to take on more responsibilities now that Mama B did not have much energy. They took to running the place while Mama B remained the old, wizened face of the property. She told stories in the evenings by the fire. Instead of gathering and combining herbs, she made jams and marmalades that she gave to guests on arrival.

This left very little time for Jemma and Easter to discuss AJ and that Mama B was leaving, whatever that meant. Tad continued to work and was happier and lighter now that Annie's control over him was gone. He spent a lot more time with Linnea, and things seemed to be going well with them.

Jemma finished school for the semester. They had not seen AJ since the cleansing ritual, but RJ had returned to work and seemed to be his normal self. That gave the town room to act normal again, too. No one had noticed that Clide, Dougy, and Phil had disappeared for the night since that was a normal occurrence for them, but Dougy's cousin Ray-Ray Butcher was puzzled that the three boys wanted nothing to do with his moonshine anymore. "Made us see crazy things," they told them.

The town still had questions about the fire at the Kilmers' and the woman RJ had taken up with for a couple of weeks. They also wanted to know why, all of a sudden, RJ and AJ liked being up at Gran's Rest. This produced all kinds of rumors, but RJ, since he was a longtime resident of the town, put them to rest.

The fire had been an accident. He took full responsibility.

The woman was an out-of-town specialist who'd helped him see that AJ could use some time in natural surroundings. That was his roundabout way of stating that Annie Nox had helped him realize that magic was real and could be used in bad ways, and he didn't want his son doing that. He did not tell anyone her name, of course. After a few days, the town stopped asking questions, satisfied with RJ's answers or the narratives they had devised on their own.

AJ was still on the outs, but Clide, Dougy, and Phil treated him a little better. People at school didn't make fun of him or whisper about him as much. That was the report from Easter and Val. AJ had been to school once and then disappeared. They had been concerned at first but quickly found out he was at home, repairing the destruction caused by the fire with his father.

As for the Kilmers' sudden fascination with Gran's Rest, the town was told the place did AJ good. It was helping him recover better than the mental institute had. And so it had, but he hadn't been back since the cleansing. Not until Jemma was pulling weeds in a flowerbed with Val and Easter one sunny day. They heard a truck come up the drive and turned, expecting Tad, but it was RJ's truck. AJ climbed out.

He approached them, a hesitant expression on his face. He looked as he always did—wearing jeans, boots, and an oil-stained white tank top. His expression, however, was less hard. Still wary but sheepish. "Jemma, could I talk to you? Alone?"

Jemma did not hide her surprise, but she stood, wiped her dirt-covered hands on her pants, and said, "Sure."

Easter gave her a concerned look and Val a wary one as she went off with AJ. She led him around back to the stone bench against the back of the house. There they sat and overlooked the cleared slope. "You might be wonderin' where I've been the past few days," AJ started, staring at the ground instead of looking at her.

In truth, Jemma had only wondered once or twice since she had been busy with work around Gran's Rest.

"Well, I was here at night, talkin' with Mama B and helpin' my dad during the day," he told her.

"What did you and Mama B talk about?" Jemma asked.

He shrugged and looked up, though not at her. His light-blue eyes traveled across the grounds. "Everything. Magic. What's going to happen to me." He glanced at her sideways. "She says I'll need training, but she can't do it. She says you and Easter know what to do. I've come to ask you if…if you'll do it. If you'll help me." The expression on his face was so open and so unlike anything Jemma had seen in him before that she couldn't help nodding.

"Of course, we'll help you." She wasn't sure what that would entail or if she was up for the task, but it would have to start with a semblance of friendship. She extended her hand, grinning.

AJ looked down at it, unsure.

"I'm not going to cast a spell on you just by touching you," Jemma told him. Her grin grew. "Though I could."

He took her hand, and though the shake was brief, it was firm.

"What does your father think of all this?" she asked.

AJ did not answer, and it wasn't until he sniffed that Jemma realized he had tears in his eyes. "He says he's never been prouder." AJ paused before adding, "We're both unsure about what all this means, especially him. The town, too. They still think I'm insane and my dad had a full mental breakdown. Us hanging around here won't help perceptions." He gestured at their surroundings.

"No, it won't," Jemma admitted. "But screw them. We just saved their asses."

A slight grin appeared on AJ's face. "Yeah, I didn't get it until I realized that."

"Realized what?"

"I didn't get your whole magic thing until I realized you were trying to save the town. At first, I thought you were just bein' selfish. You see, I knew about you and Easter because she told me." By she, Jemma knew he was referring to Vesna. She wondered what other wounds had reopened for him. Ones concerning his mother, perhaps? He still had a long way to go in his healing. Jemma did too.

She pulled her knees to her chest and perched her chin on them. "Folks are going to talk, but you have me, Easter, and even Val, though it's going to take him more time."

AJ nodded as if he had already thought of this.

"I'm here for you. To talk about anything. Magic or whatever else." She paused. "And I'm sorry again for what I did. I had no business messing with your mind like I did."

The slight smile AJ had worn earlier returned. He finally looked her in the eyes. "It saved my ass, so don't be sorry. Besides, I thought of a way you can make it up to me."

Jemma's brows rose. "What's that?"

He grinned. "I'm not too keen on working in a hardware store. My father thinks I should be in natural surroundings more anyway."

Jemma smiled, knowing what he was about to ask.

"I was wonderin' if you could get me a job here? I'll do anything except cooking. I'm a terrible cook."

"Good thing we already have one." Jemma chortled. "I'll see to it. A lot is changing for you, AJ Kilmer, and—" She paused, thinking about the first time they'd met and how she had punched him in the face. Besides her own mother, he had been her least favorite person in the world. "Well, I'm glad I met you."

Surprise sprang into his face, but he recovered a second late. "Me too, Nox." He paused. "I'm sorry, for what it's worth, for all I put you through. And that your mom came back and messed shit up for you." He shrugged. "Guess you could call it a stroke of homespun fate."

Jemma's brows furrowed. "Never heard that one."

"It's a saying in my family. Like when someone from your blood or your home comes along and decides the course of your life. For good or for worse. I think things will get better, though." Jemma thought the same. At least, she hoped they would. AJ's grin returned as two figures appeared around the corner. He nudged her in the ribs with his elbow. "Looks like change is on the horizon for you too."

Jemma looked up to see her father walking toward her with Linnea on his arm. Both wore broad smiles. A ring glittered on Linnea's left hand.

CHAPTER TWENTY-FOUR

Tad and Linnea's wedding was thrown together over the course of a few weeks. All things considered, it was an easy affair to assemble. For one, Linnea already had her grandmother's old dress, which she tailored and customized to her liking. Jemma discovered many things about Linnea during that time, like she was good at sewing and she didn't like cake. It was decided that cake wouldn't be served at the wedding. Mama B was put in charge of all the food, including alternative deserts.

The venue was easy to secure, and Mama B wouldn't accept a nickel for allowing the happy couple to use her property. "The fine folks who come here to visit will need something to celebrate anyway!" she had declared.

Ever since Gran's Rest's Grand Opening, no big celebrations had been held. Easter put herself in charge of decorations, and Val was appointed by Jemma to help Tad with anything he needed, like finding a suit and good shoes to wear.

Val was also in charge of finishing the repairs around the property leading up to the event. His favorite task, though, was painting Just Married on the back window of Tad's truck and attaching cans to the bumper with string.

On top of all the wedding preparations, Gran's Rest was abuzz with normal activity. Due to the arrival of consistently warm weather, guests had booked in droves. For the next month, no rooms were available. This meant Jemma and Easter, who ran things at Gran's Rest more than Mama B did, had plenty on their plate.

They took care of everything from making sure the linens and towels were washed after guests used them and replenishing them to making sure the cook had all the food she needed. Then there were Jemma's tasks as head groundskeeper. "If this keeps up," she told Easter one day, "I'm either going to have to promote someone to groundskeeper or hire someone else."

As Jemma promised, AJ was the newest employee. He was their delivery and errand person and took on inventory responsibilities too. He kept to himself most of the time, but when he interacted with other staff, he was friendly enough. There wasn't a soul on the grounds who disliked him. Even Val, who was taking his time warming back up to his old friend turned enemy, didn't hesitate to work alongside AJ anymore.

When it came time to put the guest list together, Jemma was in a quandary. All the guests at Gran's Rest would be welcome to watch the ceremony and join the reception. Val wanted some of the kids and their parents from Cider Creek to be invited, and Tad and Linnea consented. Some folks from town were invited, but since the wedding was to take place at Gran's Rest, they expected many would decline. RJ and AJ readily gave their RSVPs, saying they would attend. Jemma had a feeling RJ had put in AJ's RSVP. AJ, however, did not seem upset about going.

The other guests consisted of Mama B, Jemma, and the McCarthys, as well as a couple of Tad's close work friends. Linnea, they discovered, didn't have much family in the area anymore. She had a sister in a neighboring county who would come and an aunt and uncle in Kentucky who were willing to drive down for the wedding. Other than Jemma, Tad would have no family present. He said that was just as well since many of his family had taken Annie's side in the divorce.

They would think his marriage to Linnea was "too much, too soon." That made Jemma wonder if Annie had ever controlled Tad's relatives, but she decided it didn't matter. Annie wasn't here, and she was too busy to give her mother any thought. There were more important matters to attend to.

The last of the preparations were complete in mid-May. The spring flowers bloomed, and they put together bouquets for Linnea and the outdoor tables. The bride came up to assist Jemma and Easter. While Easter was attending to a guest's request in another room, Linnea took the opportunity to tell Jemma, "I'm so happy your father proposed. You know that, of course, but I want you to know it means the world that you're happy for us."

Jemma smiled back, sensing there was more.

"Would you be my bridesmaid?" Linnea asked at last.

"Nothing would make me happier," Jemma assured her.

Life was changing again, this time in a way Jemma welcomed. It would be an adjustment when Linnea moved in with them. She had her senior year ahead of her and much work to do around Gran's Rest. In addition, she had this whole magic-coven thing to work out with AJ. In the past few weeks, she, Easter, and AJ had been too busy to talk about training. It would have to come sooner rather than later, though.

Tad and Linnea wanted to get married close to sunset when the colors in the mountains were at their most beautiful. The tiered slope was staged for both the ceremony and reception. With the guests occupying blankets and chairs on the slope, the happy couple was married in front of everyone. Jemma stood to Linnea's right in a lilac dress Linnea had bought just for her. She held a bouquet of Mama B's favorite flowers from the property: azalea and mountain laurel.

This was a different sort of ritual, and although it was not magical, it felt like it could be. The vows and "I do's" were finished when Jemma looked out over the crowd. She saw Easter and Val beaming from the front row. Mama B sat beside them and was dozing off. AJ was with his father on the other side of the aisle, and although he didn't smile, he was here, and he didn't look like he would blow up at any second. That was enough to make Jemma happy.

"You may kiss the bride!" the minister announced. Cheers and applause rose up as Tad dipped Linnea close to the ground and gave her a long, dramatic kiss. Laughter ensued, and as the couple walked back down the aisle, more of the mountain flowers were thrown over them.

With the couple inside, everyone moved to clear the space for the reception. AJ helped Mama B relocate to a spot on the back porch from which she could watch the frivolity without being in the middle of it.

"She's fading," Easter told Jemma in a solemn tone as they watched AJ help Mama B sit on the stone bench. AJ looked wholly different as he helped her than he had before. He was gentle and wore a kind smile. What a transformation they had seen in him.

Jemma nodded. Mama B's magic was broken, and the last of her coven was gone. Nothing bound her to this life anymore. It wouldn't be long before...

Jemma didn't want to think about it. An ache welled up in her chest. Mama B had been the best thing about coming to Solomon's Cross. Easter squeezed Jemma's hand as if to tell her that, even if Mama B moved on, she would not.

"I'm going to go talk to her," Jemma told her friend.

Easter moved off to help Val and the others finish preparing for the reception. Jemma approached Mama B and was given a kind but tired smile as she sat on the bench beside her. She remembered how, several months ago, she had sat here with the old witch for the first time. Then, she had been uncertain about many things—Mama B most of all.

"Do not be sad, my dear," Mama B told her, sensing her thoughts. "I am glad. I am tired and eager for rest." A small smile parted her lips. "I can take that rest, knowing the new coven will watch over these mountains."

She patted Jemma's hand. "You, Easter, and AJ, with help from Val, of course." She chuckled. "That young man should play in the major leagues. He sure knows how to swing a bat." She looked around at the grounds, where lights twinkled in the trees, put there for the wedding.

Chatter filled the slope, and music drifted from one side of the grounds where a stringed quartet had assembled. Moments later, Tad and Linnea remerged, and at the behest of all the guests, they began their first dance. Everyone gathered around them—everyone except Mama B and Jemma, who remained on the stone bench. "How lovely it all is," Mama B mused. Her hand remained on Jemma's. "I hope the three of you can make it even lovelier when you take over."

Questions and doubts filed Jemma's mind. How were three teenagers supposed to run the bed and breakfast and have magical control over Solomon's Cross and its surrounding hills? How on earth was Jemma to do all that without the wise advice of Kalhoun County's oldest holler witch? Mama B had become more than an employer or a mentor; she was family. As much of a family as Jemma had besides her father, anyway.

She looked at the lawn once more and caught sight of Easter and Val, whom she considered to be the siblings she'd never had. Even AJ might feel like family one day.

Last, her eyes went to her father and Linnea. Although Jemma didn't see herself calling Linnea "Mom" anytime soon, it was a much better situation than having Annie back.

Soon there would be new challenges to overcome, perhaps ones harder than what they had already faced. "I know the three of you will be okay," Mama B stated, her voice sounding far away, "but I am happy to leave this place in your hands."

Jemma had a hard time wrapping her mind around that. For decades, Mama B had lived on this mountain, a wise, gentle woman whom those in Solomon's Cross came to for healing and wisdom. Though her reputation had declined in recent years, her memory was still good. Jemma didn't know how she was to carry it on and do so in a way that honored Mama B the way she deserved to be honored.

She met the old woman's eyes. She wanted to voice her doubts and fears, but she knew it would work itself out. Mama B had trained her for this day. She had done the same for Easter. All that was left was to help AJ find his way, and they had made a good start on that.

Mama B sensed the things that weighed on the young witch's mind. "Don't worry, my dear. I won't leave quite yet, though you won't need me for much longer."

Jemma felt warm inside.

Mama B winked and smiled. "Just a little more."

AUTHOR NOTES - MICHAEL ANDERLE

JUNE 22, 2022

Thank you for not only reading this book but these author notes as well!

So, I am heading to Paris because my wife *loves* Paris. Since all (men who want to stay happily married) like to do things for their wives, I suggested Paris needed to be one of the stops during our month in Europe.

We are here for business purposes, but we had a few days to kill between an event in Holland and an event in London. Paris is an easy train ride from Holland (a little under three hours) and an easy train ride from Paris to London under the water.

Well, except that "fearing for my death while drowning" issue my imagination brings up. I used the fear that the train tunnel under the water would somehow get flooded by cracks in the wall in a book series (*The Unplanned Princess*).

At least my fear pays for something, right?

It's hotter on this train than it is outside during June!

Excluding the trip on the Orient Express out of Beijing a few years ago, every train trip I have taken overseas has been very comfortable.

Until this trip.

I suspect it is somewhere in the high seventies or low eighties Fahrenheit right now in this coach. I have a tepid breeze coming out of the A/C unit under the window roughly eight inches below my head next to my left arm. I'm tempted to just lay my head on the vent (suffer the lines it will make across my forehead) and try to fall asleep.

OMG, THE BUGS!

I had a chance to stay in a cute villa in Tuscany for a few days of downtime last week. I spent three exquisite days reading on the front lawn in the morning and evening (after the hot part of the day. On Friday (my last day there), it was a bit cloudy, so the daytime temperature never got that hot.

I decided to play hooky from work and read in one of the most wonderful locations I have been blessed to "work."

Reading is part of my work! Yes, it does feel like cheating sometimes.

Judith couldn't come outside because her blood is a fine wine to any bugs that bite humans. I rarely have issues, so I ignored her warnings about using bug repellent.

Well, we leave at 8:30 AM Saturday morning and arrive at the hotel in Rotterdam at 3:45 PM. We go out and enjoy the local stores Saturday night and chill on Sunday.

Roughly 3:30 PM Sunday, my back is itching, and I start to scratch it on the edge of an open door.

Out of the blue (!), I realize I have a wife who would probably help me with the scratching issue, so I ask Judith to help me. She takes one look at my back and says I have bites ALL OVER. I ended up with a minimum of ten big red bumps on my back and realized that while Tuscany was beautiful…

You have to be careful of bugs when reading in a lawn chair on a grass lawn. Perhaps next year, I'll use some Off or similar. I might not smell nice, but I won't have dime-sized red bug-hickies bothering me at night, either.

Enjoy your day, and talk to you in the next book!

Ad Aeternitatem,

Michael Anderle

> MORE STORIES with Michael newsletter HERE:
> https://michael.beehiiv.com/

BOOKS BY MICHAEL ANDERLE

Sign up for the LMBPN email list to be notified of new releases and special deals!

https://lmbpn.com/email/

For a complete list of books by Michael Anderle, please visit:

www.lmbpn.com/ma-books/

CONNECT WITH THE AUTHOR

Michael Anderle Social

Website: http://lmbpn.com

Email List: http://lmbpn.com/email/

https://www.facebook.com/LMBPNPublishing

https://twitter.com/MichaelAnderle

https://www.instagram.com/lmbpn_publishing/

https://www.bookbub.com/authors/michael-anderle

www.ingramcontent.com/pod-product-compliance
Lightning Source LLC
LaVergne TN
LVHW041800060526
838201LV00046B/1068